WICKED BETRAYAL

Darkwater Reformatory, Book One

MARTY MAYBERRY

WICKED BETRAYAL
Darkwater Reformatory
Book One

ASIN: B083HNKZLG

Hummingbird Press

Cover art by *Black Bird Book Covers*
Find them on Facebook **here**

 Created with Vellum

For Mom.

You'll never have the chance to read my books,
but I know you would've been proud.

Miss you.

Acknowledgments

Jes, Lee, Lana, Stephanie,
Laura, & Katrina
Awesome critique partners.
This book is infinitely better
because of you.

And for my husband
and children.
Thanks for sticking with
me through this journey!

Nothing beats being locked up in supernatural juvie. If only committing murder wasn't my only way out.

Framed by the head of the Seeker's Guild and sent to Darkwater to serve a life sentence, I'm doomed. The prison is located in the fae world, on an island in the middle of a forbidding sea. Wizards sent there never return.

The moment I arrive, I'm forced to take a series of initiation tests with a snarky, too-hot fellow inmate. If the creatures trying to kill us don't do him in, I just might. Yet my birth father's at Darkwater, and while he could be the warden, a guard, or a fellow inmate, I'm determined to track him down. He stole something from me when I was a baby, and I want it back.

Once I get what I came for, there are two ways out. Survive the Challenge—another series of trials that take place in the ever-changing, magical catacombs beneath the prison, and they'll send me to pre-release at Darkwater Reformatory. Or I can fulfill the secret blood bond I made with the Master Seeker. Eliminate a fellow inmate and the Master Seeker will transport me home.

…Except the inmate I must kill is the wizard I'm falling for.

Chapter 1

The beady glass eyes of the stone wexal cat statue watched me as I fidgeted in the front lobby of the Seeker's Guild Headquarters.

At least, I thought it was a wexal cat, with its large, pointed ears, sleek face with luxurious silver whiskers, and a long, bushy tail. Three-feet tall and about the size of a bobcat, wexals had been extinct for over a thousand years. I'd only seen images of them in books. This one had an inky-ebony coat, as richly black as the magical threads my sister, Fleur, used to create power.

The cat sat on its haunches and whenever I glanced away from it, I swore it inched closer. But I didn't catch it moving. Except for those damn glowing green eyes. They tracked my every movement. If I'd come across it in the wild, I would've turned and bolted in the opposite direction.

For now, I couldn't run.

Almost an hour ago, an assistant had admitted me into the fortress and agreed—after some persuasion—to notify the Master Seeker I was here. I'd blurted out why I'd come, spilling my guts onto the floor like my boots shucked mud with every shift of my feet.

Would the Seeker agree to see me?

A clang drew my attention to the back of the room where the assistant wheeled a small serving cart into the foyer from a door to the left of the enormous staircase. Steam wafted from the pot, and the pungent, spicy aroma of hornwit tea scented the air.

Bringing the cart to a halt in the middle of the two-story room, he studied me with one eyebrow lifted.

My stomach rumbled. Only the fae knew when I'd last eaten.

His eyebrow rose higher, and his gaze dipped to my belly. Fingers tightening on the cart's handle as if he thought I'd wrench it from his grip, his lips thinned even further. If he kept at it, they'd disappear.

Hornwit tasted nasty even if you dumped in a bunch of sweetener, so I'd beg water instead if I was offered a drink. But the cardamom pinta cookies arranged neatly on the pretty plate looked as yummy as the ones my stepdad made. Those, I'd happily devour, and then lick the crumbs off the plate.

"When can I see the Master Seeker?" I asked. No cringing in the corner for me. I needed the information, and I'd been told only the Master could deliver. I'd paid a stiff price for this location but coming here had put me one step closer to my goal.

It hadn't been easy to track down the Guild's hidden stone fortress high in the Icean Mountains. With only one known flit transport center in the area, I'd had to walk here from the center. I'd hiked for nearly two days, only crashing in the small tent I'd carried on my back when I couldn't make my feet take another step farther. I'd carried water but nowhere near enough food.

"Ramseff will give you ten minutes," the assistant intoned. Tall and skinny enough you might miss him if he stood sideways, he strode behind the cart toward the parlor on my right, his long robe brushing the floor. The solitary cup and porcelain teapot on the top of the cart clinked with the movement. Without saying anything else, he entered the parlor.

An expanse of polished tenet wood floor stretched between me and the parlor. My boots, coated with muck, would leave a mess, something my mom would've scowled at me for doing. It was one thing to hang out on the rug with clods of mud falling off my feet but another to mess with that pristine surface.

The weight of the cat's gaze cut through me as I shucked my boots and, on stockinged feet, scurried after the assistant. I paused in the arched entry. The room was made up of one wall with a bank of curtained windows, another with a huge granite fireplace, and the final two with floor-to-ceiling bookshelves.

An older guy sat on a green sofa, squishing back on the cushions. Like the cat, he watched me; a common theme in this place.

The assistant settled the teapot, cookies, and single mug onto the low table in front of the man I assumed must be the Master Seeker—the most powerful Seeker of us all.

What to do? Should I stride into the room or hover here and tell the assistant I'd made a mistake and I'd come back later?

No. The assistant had said I had ten minutes. I'd be a fool to waste them.

My shoulders collapsed when I contemplated how challenging it had been to get here only to be told I had mere minutes to plea my case. Weeks searching for any scrap of a clue had been followed by my deal with Katya then flitting to the base and hiking through dense woods to get to this location. In minutes, I'd be standing outside, dreading the long walk back to the flit center. Worrying about the eyes that had tracked me as I hurried up the forest path.

Need made my back stiffen. With a lift of my chin, I walked as calmly as possible over to a high-back wooden chair that had been placed opposite the sofa. I dropped down onto the hard surface and met the intense, milky blue gaze of the Master Seeker.

The assistant wheeled the cart from the room, leaving us alone in ticking silence.

"My assistant filled me in on why you're here." Ramseff scratched the side of his neck and then tugged on the hem of the black tunic down over his matching pants. The dark, seamless material was broken only by the white embroidered heron on his left pocket. "What can you—a lowly apprentice Seeker—offer me in exchange for this information?"

So much for the social niceties like, *how are you*, let alone, *would you like a cookie*? The glare he shot me twisted his elderly face.

It looked like my odds of convincing him to help me were dropping by the second.

My body twitched, but I kept my face neutral. Yes, I needed the information. And yes, I'd pay almost any price to obtain it. But the last thing I needed was for him to catch a whiff of my desperation.

"I'm a Level Five Seeker, now," I said, hoping only I heard the shake in my voice. "No longer an apprentice."

"Tria, Tria, Tria." His snort cut through my confidence, and he lowered his head and slowly shook it. "At best, you're a Level Three, child." Leaning forward, he poured hornwit tea into the mug and lifted it. His long gray hair brushed his shoulders as he pressed back into the sofa. Examining me over the mug's rim, he sipped his drink. "Toying with a Level Five does not make you a full Seeker." He lowered his cup back onto the table with a dull thud.

Dragging my gaze from the cookies and hoping I wasn't drooling, I steadied my feet on the hardwood floor. "I'm *close* to a Level Five," I offered reluctantly. Levels were fluid, meaning on one day I might generate a Level Five spell only to find it impossible to go higher than a Level Three after that. But I studied all the time and was determined to solidify the highest Level as soon as possible. Only with endless practice would I be able to consistently create a Level Five spell and be able to say I'd mastered the Level.

Movement out of the corner of my eye drew my attention. I jolted and couldn't hold in my gasp.

The wexal cat sat on the granite slab in front of the fireplace, its green eyes trained on me.

I turned back to Ramseff to comment, and he stared past my shoulder blankly, as if his mind had left the room already. Another peek toward the fireplace showed the cat was gone. Had I imagined it being there?

"What are you looking at?" the Master Seeker growled. "You seem distracted. Is our conversation too boring for you?"

"No! It's just…"

Ramseff brushed my sputtering aside like a pesky nat. "Spit it out, girl. Just what?" His chest rose and fell as he heaved out a sigh.

"I need to find my birth father, Bastian Spires." It felt odd to speak his name out loud, as if I revealed something I shouldn't. For my entire life, I'd kept my true parentage a secret, claiming the sketar witch who'd raised me was my blood father. When I'd transferred to Crystal Wing Academy and met my grandfather and half-sister, I'd hoped my grandfather could tell me where Bastian might be hiding, but most believed he was dead.

I'd been unconvinced. If he was dead, I'd...know.

In exchange for a few rare trinkets, Katya had verified Bastian *was* alive. But the sorceress had been unable to reveal anything else, stating only the Master Seeker could pinpoint my birth father's exact location.

"I must say, I admire your ingenuity," Ramseff said. "Few are capable of locating our headquarters. Of those who find their way here, only one or two are able to get past my assistant's wards. But you're the first who dares come to beg a favor. Because you've impressed me with your efforts, and to prove how kindhearted I am, I'll give you the information you seek at no cost."

My spine perked up. "You will?" I'd thought I'd search for years before I got the chance to confront my father.

"He's at Darkwater Prison."

"My father's in jail?" Darkwater had been built on a remote island in the middle of a fathomless sea. In the fae kingdom. I stifled my groan. Only those with authorization or special magic were allowed to part the veil separating Earth from the fae kingdom. Ages ago, the fae had split rather than go to war, and many of them had come here to settle. They'd created the veil to keep the two groups from crossing over and killing each other. Sure, some Sídhe were allowed to travel to the fae kingdom— mostly for diplomatic missions—but the opportunity was rare.

I did not possess special magic. I was no diplomat. And it was doubtful anyone would authorize my passage.

"Your father is in the youth section of the prison, known as the Reformatory," Ramseff said.

"Youth?" I wasn't sure why I focused on that word alone.

"Eighteen to twenty-year-olds are permitted to apply for admittance."

"I see." From what I'd heard, the Reformatory and main prison were located side-by-side on the island. The Reformatory was believed to be a school, though I didn't know what they taught. Maybe the usual subjects like at the Academy.

It couldn't be for rehabilitation purposes. Criminals arrived to serve their sentences, but from what I'd heard, the only way off the island was in a coffin.

"He's a teacher in the Reformatory?" I said. "Or is he the warden, the janitor, or a guard?" Maybe he worked in the kitchens. A prison would employ a large support staff like the Academy.

"I'm afraid I'm not feeling generous enough to share further information with you." Ramseff lifted his mug and calmly drank. "You asked for your father's location, and I've given it to you." His gaze flicked to the foyer. "You may leave now."

"But, but," I spat out. "How will I get there?" It was vital I talk with my dad.

He smirked. "Surely a Level Five Seeker such as you can arrange this on your own."

It was impossible. I'd never get through the veil, let alone to the island.

Anger and frustration dueled inside me. My hands clenched at my sides, and I gnawed on my tongue to keep from hurling the wrong words out. That would get me nowhere.

Hold on a sec.

I pulled my cointage from my pocket and dropped it onto the table with a clang. The disc didn't grant unlimited spending, but I should have enough credit, courtesy of my generous parents, to satisfy Ramseff.

His low growl rumbled through the room, and florid color rose in his cheeks. He slammed his mug on the table and hornwit tea slopped over the sides. It sizzled when it hit the surface. "You hope to bribe me?" Clouds of rage arcing with lightning stormed around his head. Did he possess a weather skapti in addition to a Seeker's? Skaptis were inherent skills we used magic to enhance. Few had more than one ability to develop.

"How else can I pay?" I asked with a shrug I hoped came out casual. Inside, I alternated between quivering and fuming.

His head tilted as if he was unsure what to make of my response. Or maybe he was evaluating my worth. Would I come up lacking? "In order to reach the Reformatory, you'll need to explore different options."

In other words, there was no monetary price I could pay for transport. Despair rose inside me. I'd come so close. I'd found my birth father's location but he was no closer to me than he'd been the moment I verified he was alive. Yet I'd come all this way…

My spine stiffened. "Isn't there anything I can—?"

"Leave!"

I suppressed a growl. Snapping and snarling would get me nowhere. What could I do to convince him to—

He flicked his hand in the air and bellowed. "Seredon."

The assistant stepped into the room. "Sir?"

Ramseff's hand flicked to me. "Show her out."

"Of course, Sir."

"Okay, then." Standing, I swiped my palms on my thighs. "Thanks." Not really, but I'd remain civil. He had shared where my dad was and that detail was important. I swallowed past the lump in anger my throat and strode toward the foyer, my stockinged feet swishing on the polished surface. My head remained high. I'd ask my grandfather. He might be able to—

"Perhaps we needn't be hasty," Ramseff said. "There might be a way. If…"

I turned and supported myself with my hand on the terat wood trim outlining the archway, to keep my shaky body from giving me away. "If what?"

"I need a small favor. In exchange I'll arrange for your transportation to Darkwater."

I could finally confront my father.

My legs trembled, threatening to dump me on the floor. I returned to the chair and sank onto the hardwood surface. "What kind of favor are we talking about?"

In my experience, favors came at stiff prices.

His fingers tapped steadily on his leg, and he wouldn't meet my eyes. "I have a minor problem. It's almost not worth mentioning. But someone with your unique set of skills might be able to help me bring about a solution."

"What would I have to do?" There was no hiding the eagerness in my voice. Despite my reservations, excitement burst through me. Close. I was so close!

"You may leave, Seredon," Ramseff told his assistant.

"Very well, Sir." Seredon backed from the room.

Ramseff stared at me while a clock somewhere nearby ticked an entire minute.

Despite my urge to push him to tell me what he needed, I remained patient.

Ramseff cleared his throat. "Before we proceed further, I'll need your bound promise you'll do as I ask and not speak of this to anyone else."

I reeled back, banging my shoulder on the upper edge of the chair hard enough I winced. "You need a bound promise before you'll tell me what I need to do?" A bonded promise required blood. My blood. It could only be broken when the promise was fulfilled. Or the person making the promise died. It might be best not to think about that part of the clause.

"A favor for a favor, shall we say? Do this one little thing for me, and I'll send you to your father." His voice deepened. "I believe you need something from him."

How had he found out? I'd told no one.

I *was* desperate to talk to my dad, but how high a price was I willing to pay?

"Decide," he said, his fingers tightening on his legs. "A chance like this won't come again. My offer will be gone in three, two, o—"

"I'll do it." Whatever he asked. I *had* to. Otherwise…I shook my head. *Do not think about it here.* He might some-how…know.

A conniving smile flittered across his face before it smoothed, making me wonder if I was already too late.

"Hold out your hand," he said.

I extended it forward, palm exposed. He mumbled a string of fae words too quickly for me to translate, and my blood pooled, forming a small circle in the depression of my hand. Ramseff suspended a triangular, silver pendant over the blood and it disappeared, sucked up by the cloudy stone in the center of the pendant.

"Lovely," he said as he hung the pendant on a chain around his neck. "Your promise to complete this task is now unbreakable." The slick satisfaction blooming on his wrinkly face sent fear bolting through me. I wanted to run but there would be nowhere to hide from a bond made with a Master Seeker. He'd be able to track me beyond death.

He'd own me until I'd fulfilled my part of the bargain.

A wave of his hand, and a large gold ball with a glossy, opaque surface appeared to hover between us.

"I'd like you to eliminate someone for me," he said as if discussing the pinta cookies he'd consume with his mug of hornwit tea.

I blinked. "You said a small favor. You can't mean murder." I couldn't do it!

"This person is essentially a criminal already. He'll soon be slated for death."

"Then why do I need to hasten that along?" This didn't make sense. What wasn't I seeing here? "He'll die anyway."

"I want it done as soon as possible, not after his relatives host multiple appeals."

I held up my hand that still stung from the bloodletting. "Hold on. You're saying he hasn't committed a crime yet?"

"No more than you."

The Master Seeker *knew* the crime this person would soon commit. Did he also possess a divination skapti? Only rare Sídhe could harness more than one ability. But this man was the leader of all the Seekers. No one rose to this high a position without considerable power and cunning.

If he could do divination—although no one could see everything—I didn't stand a chance of outwitting him.

Unease prickled along my spine, making me itch, and a bitter flavor pooled in my mouth.

"Come," he said, waving toward the ball. "See."

A dark gray mist swirled inside the ball. The fog slowly cleared, and a picture formed of the Academy's eastern pasture, with the forest behind. Someone walked there. Oh. Professor Trarion. My sister, Fleur, had taken *Magical Creatures and How to Tame Them* with the fae teacher. She was sweet and kind and a lot of fun. I liked her.

I leaned forward, watching as another person slunk behind the Professor, picking up speed. They…My breathing shuddered to a halt.

It wasn't just any person—it was *me*. She'd removed the jacket I still wore and had knotted the sleeves around her waist, but otherwise, she was even dressed the same, right down to my *Seekers do it better* t-shirt.

My jaw dropped, and I turned to Ramseff. "How…?"

"Careful," he said in a cheery voice, but his eyes… They were sharp enough to slice open a vein. "Watch or you'll miss the best part. It's about to happen."

The person following Professor Trarion—no, *I*—pulled a knife from a sheath on her calf. She rushed toward the Professor and sunk the knife deeply into the Professor's back. No sound was released into this room, but I felt the Professor's death shriek as if I stood right behind her. In some ways I *did* stand behind her.

Dread splintered my bones, and I moaned.

Professor Trarion collapsed onto the ground, and the person—me—fled toward the woods.

"No," I wailed, my fingers knotted together on my lap. "What have you done?"

"Me?" Ramseff asked with a low chuckle. "I haven't done anything. *You* have."

"But I didn't." I cupped my cheeks as pain rushed through me. "It's not me. I'd never… Who is that?"

"A wizard who needed a favor. Much like you."

He couldn't have known I was coming here, yet he seemed to have arranged for this…assassination while I sat across from him, salivating about cookies. Forget hunger. I wanted to throw up.

"This wizard's payment came due," he said casually. "And now they've fulfilled their side of our blood bargain."

Waves of horror roared over me, drowning me. "I...I..."

"The favor I need?" His words pierced the flit-space yanking me away from the Guild's headquarters. "I'd like you to kill a young man. His name is Brodin. Complete this task and I'll arrange for your extraction from the Reformatory." He stood. "It's time for you to leave, child. Darkwater waits."

I gaped up at him, barely hearing his words. Professor Trarion! She needed help.

Who was this man, this Master of all Seekers? Seekers were cops, always the good guys. They delivered justice.

Not murder.

Yet...I'd promised—blood promised—to commit the same crime.

"Monster!" Jumping up from the chair, I ran at him, my hands lifting.

Ramseff flicked his fingers toward me, and I froze.

The room compressed. Wavered.

I landed with a jarring thud, my knees biting into the ground on the edge of the eastern pasture of Crystal Wing Academy. My gaze blurred as I rose and spun around.

The Professor lay unmoving, the blade still sticking up from her back. Slick blood pooled around her, glossy and dark. Lifeblood.

The person warded to look like me was nowhere to be seen. I stood in their place after what must've been a seamless switch.

"Her!" someone shouted. "She did it. Tria stabbed Professor Trarion!"

Run.

I raced into the forest, my stockinged feet pounding the path, and my heart slamming against my rib cage. Darting around bushes and trees, I leaped over logs and aimed for the mountains. If I was lucky, I could—

They were on me in a flash.

Whimpering, my breathing grew ragged. I was shoved from behind, and I tumbled forward. The earth slammed up to meet me.

Stupid to think I'd never outdistance centaur Seekers. Their hooves ground into the soil as they surrounded me and, when I peered up, fury blazed on their faces.

"Gotcha," Roark said. "Caught in the act. Your Council trial will be swift."

One of the other Seekers—Harline and a former mentor—laughed. The harsh sound grated across my skin. "Darkwater's the only place that'll claim you now."

Of course. Ramseff's *favor*. I'd committed a crime and would now be sent to the Prison. Once I found a way to the Reformatory, I'd be able to confront my birth father. But in exchange for my freedom, I had to kill Brodin.

Hauling me to my feet, Roark and Harline secured my wrists and ankles with unbreakable, magical binds. Tenna devices. I'd learned about the fiery, magic-suppression bands in my Seeker's classes.

The bindings tightened as the embedded spells bit deeply, severing through my flesh and drawing blood.

It dripped on the white snow like a massacre in progress.

Chapter 2

"We condemn you to life in Darkwater Prison," the nasally-sounding council member intoned. One of his six arms pounded the gavel as he stared down his furry snout at me. "No chance of parole."

"Here, here," another council member said, leaning forward in her chair. Her wizened face tightened and her hair—a nest of wiggling worms—flicked forward, across her shoulders. "A worthy sentence for a murderer."

While friends and spectators gasped in the seating area behind me, my legs quivered and the world spun. I would've fallen on the floor if the two burly guards flanking me hadn't latched onto my arms and held me upright.

Throughout the trial, I'd denied killing Professor Trarion, but no one believed me. They called witness after witness who testified about my actions.

Fingers raised and, *That… That girl did it!*
I saw her, I did. With that very knife in her hand.
She stabbed the Professor!

Dirty wizard, she is. She ran away whilst the poor woman lay on the ground, drowning in her own blood.

My defense kept rushing up my throat, eager to burst free, but it was crushed by my blood bond promise. I couldn't tell them about the arrangement with Ramseff. Assuming they'd believe me if I could spit out the words.

My sister, Fleur, sat bravely in the room throughout it all, tears she couldn't contain trickling down her cheeks. Creases heavy in his elderly face, Cloven, my grandfather, couldn't hide his trembling shoulders.

"Take her to Darkwater," the elderly council member shouted, shaking her fist at me.

Cloven and Fleur sprang to their feet and rushed from the courtroom.

Mom, sitting beside my stepdad in the front row, flinched. Dad released a pain-filled sigh. As wizards rose and shuffled through the door in the back of the courtroom, Mom and Dad got up and came forward to join me.

"Don't ye be thinking of runnin'," one of the guards said to me. He tapped one of the tenna devices strapped around my wrists and the band flickered red, orange, and yellow, lit by inner, magical fire that suppressed the wearer's power.

They'd be removed upon my death.

Was there no other way out of this horror than by killing Brodin?

My stepdad rubbed my shoulder, his face suddenly appearing at least ten years older.

Mom pulled me into her arms. "Honey. My baby." Her chest lifted and fell with a shudder. "I bet this has something to do with your father," she said quietly, for my ears alone. "Nothing you can say will convince me otherwise. Why didn't you give it up years ago? You don't need—"

"I do." All my life, a part of me had been missing. He'd

stolen it from me when I was a vulnerable baby, and I was determined to take it back. "You know I have to find him."

"How in the world will passing through the veil and going to Darkwater..." She stepped back, and her bunched-up knuckles lurched up to press against her mouth before her hands splayed out at her sides. Her eyes widened. "I get it. He's *there*."

"You have one minute," one of my guards said in warning.

A minute would never be enough, but convicted criminals had no right to ask for more.

"I'm going after him," I said. "He needs to—"

The door in the back of the room slammed open, and our heads jerked in that direction.

A tall guy about my age with rangy brown hair and feral eyes rushed into the room. He didn't stop to look around, but scrambled up over the back row of seats, edged down to the center aisle, and then bolted our way.

Four guards carrying tenna devices slammed into the room behind him. As the tennas smacked against their legs, they shot slender, blue lightning bolts in the guy's direction. Bellowing, the guards split and ran toward the front of the room. Magic hit a wall and it smoldered and fractured. Bits of cinderblock shot through the air. I ducked, even though it was doubtful the missiles would reach this far.

The guy, gaping at the guards, smacked into me. I woofed as we tumbled backward, onto the hardwood floor. With my hands pinned behind my back by steel bands, I couldn't break my fall. He was big and made up of solid muscle, and he weighed a ton.

My right hip and shoulder took the brunt of the fall, and I yelped in pain.

Snarling, the guy braced my shoulders, his thighs

spreading around my legs. His lips peeled back to reveal razor-sharp fangs, and he lunged for my neck.

A slake? No, they didn't have fangs. They sucked power from others with their ether.

"Ah!" I bucked and kicked, but he had me pinned and I couldn't break free.

His hands tightened on my shoulders, and he snarled, his breath hot on my skin.

At this rate, I'd be ripped apart before I reached Darkwater. And to think my biggest fear had been the other inmates discovering I was a Seeker.

While my shrieks echoed around us, one of the guards snatched the back of the guy's shirt and hauled him off me. Spiked claws erupted from the guy's fingertips, and he lashed out at the guard, who yelped and stumbled backward. Tipping his head back, the guy howled like a beast at the moon.

I never thought I'd be grateful to see a bunch of guards gathering around me. They leaped onto the guy and dragged him to the ground while he emitted guttural barks and did his best to slice and dice their flesh. Maybe he was a shifter and not a slake? That would explain why he hadn't sucked my power. Not that the guards had given him a chance.

I had to admire his effort. Unrestrained by tennas, I would've run, too. And if I had claws and fangs, I would've used them to my advantage. He might've escaped if he hadn't come after me.

Mom and Dad stood silent with raised eyebrows before Dad helped me onto my feet and pulled me away from the feral guy who nipped and snarled, his limbs thrashing against his bindings. There was something slightly appealing about his raging fury. In a situation like this, I shouldn't find him cute, but I did.

My mom brushed off the back of my long-sleeved prison outfit, cooing. "My gosh, Tria. You're dirty!"

As if I cared about that?

I wigged my shoulders and crushed fingers and was relieved to find everything still functioned as it should.

The guards hauled him to his feet, tenna'd and somewhat subdued. From his feverish gaze, I wasn't sure anything would truly subdue this guy. They hustled him across the room and out the door on the left wall.

"Well," Mom said. She slid her arms around her waist and shivered. "That was…" Her long dark hair—like mine—shifted across her shoulders as she shook her head.

"I've been doing the calculations," my dad said, continuing where we'd left off as if I hadn't been attacked and almost bitten by a feral guy. He rocked back on his heels and wedged his lower lip between his teeth. Only the slight waver in his words let on that he was scared about what would come next. "We'll get a second mortgage on the house, which should be enough for an appeal. Then we'll—"

"No," I half-shouted. My heart ached at the thought they'd do this for me. I couldn't let them.

One of my guards growled and stepped closer. Back off buddy. Promise not to run.

For now.

I brushed him off with, "Sorry," and turned back to my dad. "Please. Don't." My belly twisted into a knot. I couldn't leave them destitute when any appeal was futile. The evidence had been overwhelming. Everyone believed I'd killed Professor Trarion and nothing anyone did would sway them to believe otherwise. "It won't do any good. They won't change their minds, and you'll be stuck with a big bill."

"But—"

I leaned into his side like I'd done as a kid. Though I'd grown almost as tall as him through the years, I still looked up to him in more ways than one. "I'll…find a way out of this." Somehow.

He wrapped his arm around my shoulders and squeezed. Kissed the top of my head. Shifting me around so his back faced the guards, his steady gaze met mine while he carefully slipped something into my prison uniform pocket. "I snuck it past security," he whispered with a sly smile. His voice then lifted, as if nothing had just happened. "Take care, kiddo. Be safe."

"I will." As if that was possible. We were talking about a fae prison filled with supernatural beings who'd also been sentenced to life for crimes as bad as mine, if not worse. This was the magical super-max of the fae and Sídhe worlds, one of the few times the two factions combined.

A guard grabbed my arm. "Time to go." At least he didn't fling me to the floor or gag me. But I hadn't (yet) tried to bite anyone.

My dad stepped backward and gave me a curt nod. The second my hands were free, I'd find out what he'd dropped into my pocket.

"Can't we have another moment with her?" Mom asked, her words shaking. Her hand reached out as if she'd latch on to me and hold me tight. Then they'd never be able to take me away.

With a grunt, the guards dragged me toward the same door the others had taken the shifter guy.

"Don't forget all I taught you!" my dad called out as they hustled me through the open doorway.

Part sketar witch, my stepdad was descended from trolls, though scales only coated his shoulders and lower legs. Because of how sketar witches were treated by Sídhe society and Elites in general, he'd kept that part of himself hidden. Mom didn't care and neither did I. His scales were awesome. Dark brown and rippled, they gleamed like tiny opaque pools filled with secrets. My biggest dream as a kid had been someday growing my own. Dad had laughed when I told him, and I could tell he was pleased I wasn't repelled like so many others.

Sketar witches don't just use herbs to craft spells, as I'd been taught at the Academy. They could secretly twist elemental magic in ways never imagined by the Sídhe. My stepdad had taught me all his sketar tricks, some of which I'd used at Crystal Wing. I'd planned to share everything I knew with Fleur…

Fleur. My belly ached like it had been punched. She'd rushed from the courtroom without saying goodbye. I mean, I got it. She was upset. She couldn't bear to watch them haul me away. But it hurt that I wouldn't see her one last time.

As the door slammed shut, I gave my dad what I hoped wasn't a panicked look. Because I was scared shitless, and I didn't want anyone to know. My mouth had gone dry, my heart had decided rioting was the best option, and sweat slithered down my spine, making my prison tunic cling to my back.

With the tennas on, I couldn't host a single spell against the guards. Believe me, I wanted to. But with the tennas encircling my wrists, my suggestion they release me would be met with blank stares.

I peered over my shoulder as I stumbled along a down-sloping hallway beside the guards, hoping I'd see Fleur and my grandfather. My belly squirmed and my heart shrank when they didn't appear.

While I sniffed and told myself…Well, I didn't know what I tried to tell myself, because there was nothing that fit, the guards took me to the building's basement and hustled me down the hall to the transport hub. I'd arrived here three weeks ago after I'd been captured by the centaur Seekers. Until my trial, I'd been housed in a cell a floor up from this one.

I assumed they'd flit me from this building to the veil between our two worlds.

The scuffed floor in the oval room they pushed me into showed plenty of use. Multiple lifetimes' worth of convicts had passed this way before me.

Pulling me to a stop, the guards spoke together in hushed whispers.

I stared at the round transfer disc embedded in the floor on the other side of the room. Fear told me to bolt, to run until I was ragged, but it was useless. Even if I wrenched free from the guards, I wouldn't get more than a few steps before they tackled me.

Tennas kept a wizard placid.

No rabid shifter guy waited in the room with his fangs bared. I wasn't sure if that disappointed or relieved me.

The moment I'd been waiting for since I was flitted from the Academy by the Seekers had arrived, and I couldn't hold in my shakes. Soon, I'd be transported to the fae world, where I'd begin my new future at Darkwater.

With a sharp poof, a circle of fiery orange and red flames emerged from the disc, lighting up in the room.

The guards dragged me closer. I'd be burned! While I sputtered and fought them, they pushed me over the knee-high wall of fire and forced me to stand in the middle of the circle. The flames licked up my calves, not burning but *tasting* my skin. They nipped me as I passed, sharply in warning. *Remain inside. Or else.*

A rumble in the floor shook the building.

"He's hungry," one of the guards said casually.

"Who?" I shot out.

"The beast is the flame, and the flame is the power," the other guard said.

Like that made sense.

"Something touched me in the flames." I swallowed, but the lump of dread in my throat wouldn't go down.

"Just taking a nibble," the first guard said with a snicker. "Bigger bite comes next."

The second guard grinned. His elbow hit my side. "Wouldn't want to be in your place right now."

While I'd been determined to stay strong throughout this and I'd mostly been successful, I couldn't contain my shivers any longer. Terror about what would come next wracked my frame. Once I left here, I'd never see my friends and family again.

Unless I committed murder.

Tears I couldn't contain trickled from my eyes but, with my hands bound behind my back, I couldn't swipe them away.

"What happens now?" I asked one of the guards in a croaky voice, praying he wouldn't notice my sniffles. "Will you flit me from here to Darkwater?" Sometimes, just knowing what would happen next made it bearable.

He chuckled as if he enjoyed my fear. "Not quite, sweetheart."

The snide nickname dried my tears in a flash, replacing my fear with anger. My hands clenched into fists behind my back. "Don't call me sweetheart."

His low, slimy laughter rang out, and he shouldered the guard standing beside him. "This one has spunk."

The other guard studied his nails and frowned. "Darkwater will knock that out of her."

"To make things clear," a third guard said. "Your flit power and ability to ping were stripped from you by the Council the moment you arrived."

I'd tried both and suspected something like this already. Without these abilities, I was helpless. Hopeless. My eyes stung, and I blinked fast.

"You'll learn everything you need to know at the Prison," the guard added.

No holding back my shudder.

When I was little, my grandma on my dad's side would tell me bedtime stories. To her, scary stories were fun. Whenever she visited, she'd spin tales that couldn't be true. Now, I wondered. She'd once told me about Darkwater.

"The fae, they built a stone fortress," she'd whispered in her high-pitched, scratchy voice. "High it be." Her gnarled hands—like the tiny branches on an ancient tree—wove smoky pictures in the air that were swept from the room before I could blink. "They placed it on a craggy island. Far away. Hidden from everyone, in the Sea of Despair."

Staring at her with fawn-wide eyes, I'd huddled beneath my blankets, afraid if I breathed, I'd miss her next words.

"No bars be needed." Leaning forward, she'd tapped my nose. "You want to be knowin' why, lieblie?" Her pet name for me.

She'd died too soon.

With a gulp of fear, I'd nodded.

"Whoever escapes the building…?" She'd smacked her thigh with her palm like she was killing a nip. "Becomes the hunted. Not by the guards. Not many of them be needed, like with the bars. It's what waits for the poor soul outside they need to be fearin'. Creatures." Her voice hissed, weaving more beastly pictures in the air. "And beings older than the fae."

How was that possible? There had been no one before the fae. They'd started us all. After a war, the fae split.

Some of them had come here, to the parallel universe. They'd called themselves the Sídhe and now, Elites. I was one of them. I'd *been* one of them. Now, I was nothing.

"They be eager for fresh meat." My grandma's voice echoed in my mind as the guards grinned together and repeated *sweetheart* over and over, rising in volume in a torturous chant. "If the things on the island didn't get 'em," Grandma had said. "When they reach the water, what hides in the deep will finish 'em off."

Wizards didn't die from old age at Darkwater Prison.

The door burst open, yanking me back to the present.

Yelling, the guards rushed toward the opening.

Chapter 3

Cloven and Fleur rushed into the room like sunlight chasing away shadows.

A flick of Fleur's hand and the guards came to a shuddering stop.

My cheekbones ached from smiling; it hurt to see her. I'd just started to get to know my little sister.

I was going to miss her.

A year ago, my Seeker skills had lit up during a class. A spark deep inside me had suggested someone was waiting for me. Someone important. The thought had haunted me until I let my power range free. It found her. I'd known immediately she was my sister. Not sure how, but the thought had blazed in my mind like a beacon that would never snuff out. My mom had already told me about my grandfather, Cloven, but she hadn't been aware my birth father had been with someone after he left her.

Cloven's snarl cut off the guards' taunting, their words fizzling like a vrilla being told she could no longer dance. The beautiful mountain nymphs were perpetually in motion. Cloven lifted his hands, his long, deep blue robe swaying, and the guards cowered and slunk away from the fire circle, moving over to the opposite wall, where they slouched and scowled at Cloven.

Go, Grandpa! If my hands were free, I would've clapped.

Fleur stood at his side, her hands also lifted, fireballs flicking across her fingertips, ready to be hurled. *These* flames would bite, not take a taste like the fiery circle had done with me.

The guards must've remembered they were the ones in charge here, because they booted off the wall and stomped around the circle, aiming at Cloven and Fleur. Brave on their part, but they didn't—yet—know my sister, let alone my grandfather. Cloven was now Headmaster of Crystal Wing Academy and he wielded magic like a sword. Fleur was not only an Unraveler—the sole person in our universe capable of negating any bespelling known to wizardkind—she could generate fireballs and throw them with increasing precision. And those weren't her only skaptis. She'd yet to tap them all, and I imagined she'd go down in history as one of our greatest wizards.

As the guards stomped closer, Cloven drew himself up, stiff and imposing. His demeanor rivaled King Niles, who I'd only met once. "We have permission from the council to be here," he said in a lofty tone.

Good move on his part. Was this where they'd gone when they ran from the courtroom? The guards wouldn't challenge the king.

They melted against the walls again, where they stood grumbling. Bet they weren't used to being thwarted. Power corrupted everyone and here, they ruled.

Cloven approached me first while Fleur pinned the guards in place with her glare. With a flick of Cloven's hand, the flaming circle retreated. It whimpered like a chastised pup before it curled beneath the floor.

"Tria. I…" Cloven blinked before thinning his lips, fighting for control. "So many things I've wanted to say to you, but we no longer have time." His fingers cupped my shoulders, and he stared into my eyes. "Be brave," he said in his deep, burly voice. With a heavy sigh, he drew me close for one last, final, warm hug. I drank it in, hoping to store the feeling deep inside. Then I could remember it later.

"There *is* a way out," he whispered, before stepping backward. I frowned and started to speak, but he tapped his lips and gave me a sad smile. "Don't forget."

A way out, huh? Once I had what I needed, I would find it. I refused to spend the rest of my life in prison for a crime I didn't commit.

As for Brodin? Killing him wasn't a true option. I wouldn't add another death to Professor Trarion's.

Who was he, and what had he done to draw the interest of the Master of all Seekers? I'd know once I figured out how my blood bound promise played into the plan.

After Cloven backed away, Fleur tiptoed closer. Her fireballs licked up her arms then dissipated. She paused outside the scorched circular mark on the floor. While her tears had stopped falling, from the way her red-rimmed eyes swam, I knew it was only a matter of time before more spilled over.

We'd barely had the chance to get to know each other and now…

I tried to swallow back my pain but it wasn't going anywhere. It would remain lodged in my chest like a spear for the rest of my days.

As she stepped forward boldly, she stomped on the

emerging flames that teased her legs. Pausing over them, she fisted her hands and growled. A snuff, and the fire disappeared.

Yeah. Don't mess with my sister.

Releasing a soft cry, she bounded onto me and wrapped me in a big hug. My hands, secured behind my back, kept me from touching her. Reassuring her. Which was a stupid wish on my part. Since I'd met her, I'd tried to be the best big sister possible, to make her believe she was cherished and protected. I'd done everything I could to keep her safe. Now I was the one in need of protection.

If only we'd met years ago. If only we'd had more time.

"Quite the outfit, sis." She tugged on the long sleeve of my prison uniform and pressed for a smile that didn't make it to her eyes. "I know you didn't do it." Only fierceness and complete conviction came through in her words.

"There were witnesses," I said. "They saw me kill Professor Trarion." So scared about what might happen next, I couldn't stop shaking.

Fleur braced my forearms and stared into my eyes. "It'll be okay."

How could it be? Professor Trarion. Her blood… Her still face. I didn't do it but I felt guilty. Why had she been on Ramseff's hit list?

Bile rose in my throat, choking me, but I forced it down.

"Donovan's asking the king to intervene," Fleur said. "He'll do something."

Funny how she had confidence in him. Why would King Niles care about me? He barely tolerated Fleur, and that was only for his brother Donovan, her boyfriend's sake. Her new Elite status helped when it shouldn't matter. She was a good person, fun and kind, and beyond selfless.

Her Unraveler skills could be the main reason he listened to her at all. He could be scared she'd unravel all his court Bespeller's magic.

"It was murder," I hissed out. I wanted to tell her I'd gone to the Master Seeker to find our father's location. What would she think if she knew? "The king isn't going to grant me a pardon." Special dispensations like that were saved for upper-class Elites, not the daughter of a sketar witch and a middle-class wizard, both Level Four accountants working at a small firm in the city of Grathe.

"Grandfather is doing all he can," Fleur said, pushing to keep the conversation positive. "We'll find a way."

Cloven nodded as if he understood everything Fleur said, though he was some distance away and we spoke in whispers. But then, he was my grandfather, as well as the Headmaster of a school full of teenagers too determined to get themselves into trouble. He'd need to overhear things from miles away.

"Time to go," one of the guards said. Leaving his hiding spot near the wall, he cautiously approached, moving sideways as if he thought that made him a smaller target. If I wasn't so sad, I'd laugh. He carefully placed his hand on Fleur's shoulder then hissed like touching her burned. "Time for you to leave. The girl's about to depart for Darkwater."

"I'm going to stay with her until she leaves," Fleur said in a voice that came out firm but shook as much as my fingers pinned behind my back. She drew in threads, franticly, and fireballs formed in her hands again. She'd defend me to the death, but I couldn't let her.

A second guard, who seemed to have lost his mind, strode across the room. He latched onto Fleur's arm and hauled her backward. "Sorry, Miss, but you must leave the circle."

She snarled and he retreated, his gaze darting to me. Did he hope I'd defend him?

If she fought them, they'd try to hurt her. Maybe even press charges if she got in a few blows. I couldn't let that happen.

"Go," I said, my voice croaking. "I'm okay. We'll…see each other again." Even I couldn't hear the promise in the words. We both knew it wouldn't happen. This was the last time we'd be together. The misery sinking through me was mirrored in her lavender eyes.

Her fireballs disappeared and she keened, her knees trembling. Cloven rushed forward and led her from the circle. The moment they'd moved past the scorch marks, the flames erupted with a harsh woof.

And something breathed roughly behind me.

My skin rippled as if a sharp-limbed creature was hitching itself up my spine, and I spun to face the danger.

An ogre stood inside the flames with me, his sullen gaze drifting down my body. He must've flitted here from… somewhere. Was he part of the beast below the floor?

Tall, wide, and bald, he loomed as he strolled around me, grunting while checking me out from all angles. A band of leather tied around his waist cinched in the brown, stained fabric that reached to the middle of his hairy thighs. His burlap tunic had been left open at the top, revealing tufts of gray hair. I couldn't stop staring at the wort-abscesses peppering his face like rotted sausage chunks on a three-week-old pizza. The abscesses wiggled as if something festered beneath the surface. Fearing they'd burst and goo would splatter everywhere, I reeled backward, but his hand snaked out and latched onto my arm.

"This da last of 'em?" he rasped to the guards.

"For now." The guard's dark gaze drifted to the scuffed

boards beneath my feet. "The other one has already departed."

Was he talking about rabid-guy? The guard had hesitated before saying *departed*. They hadn't killed him, had they? Sure, he'd run. He'd acted aggressively. But he hadn't bitten anyone from what I'd seen.

"Come along, then, gil," the ogre said, his thick fingers digging into my flesh. "No time to be awastin'. The veil parts for only a tad." He cackled, revealing crooked teeth shaped like arthritic thumbs. A wort-abscess burst on his cheek, and he swiped the green gook away with the back of his hand. He stared at the slime before wiping it across the front of his tunic.

The floor shook as if the hidden beast was eager to consume me. Blue mixed in with the red and orange flames. They swayed like zombies with arms linked, dancing around a bonfire.

Fleur broke away from Cloven and rushed toward me. When she reached the fiery wall, it grew to waist-height, eager to keep her out and keep me trapped within with the ogre.

She beat at it with her fists then flung fireballs that connected but fizzled, like ice cubes tossed into an inferno.

Cupping her mouth, she shouted. "Be careful." Her voice broke, and she sagged. "Love you."

Tears smarted behind my eyes and I damned them, because they revealed what I'd been trying to hide. Fleur sobbed big fat droplets that rained down onto the fire circle. The moisture was sucked up and the beast beneath the floor grew bigger, darker.

"Love you too, sis," I gulped out. "I'm sorry."

"Don't say that!"

The wall of fire thickened and arched up over me and the ogre, encasing us in flames.

"This isn't the end. Please." Fleur lifted her arms and called threads. Every color imaginable flowed toward her. Bespellings in the vicinity better beware. My sister was on a rampage.

My heart split in two. I'd miss her. It wasn't fair. But, then, none of this was fair. Mom was right. I should've let it go. My birth father could've kept…

Fleur frowned, and the moonstone set in the blade strapped to her thigh pulsed with growing magic. Power. Her arms lifted, and she closed her eyes. Back ramrodding, she thrust her hands out and a sonic wave shook the room. But amazement filled her face when she opened her eyes, because her power hadn't penetrated the wall of flames. The magic ricocheted back at her, and she was flung backward, into Cloven's arms. Eyes wide, she strained to break free.

At least he'd be there for her, now that I no longer could provide the protection she needed. While she was strong, she was also vulnerable. Wizards were eager to take advantage of her. At least she had Cloven and her boyfriend Donovan standing at her sides.

"We'll free you," she shouted. "I promise."

Cloven gave me a firm nod, confirming her statement. How could they? It was hopeless.

"Don't risk yourselves," I shouted.

"I'll do whatever I—"

"No," I said, pushing the word past the ache in my throat. "Please." I'd never forgive myself if she was hurt while trying to help me.

Like a doomed house succumbing to the inferno engulfing it, the fiery walls and ceiling wavered. The creature beneath the floor—the fire an extension of its body— wound rippling red and orange hands closer, until the heat scorched my skin. It burned.

Jerky laughter erupted from the ogre, and his hand gripped my arm tighter. I couldn't escape. I couldn't move.

As the fiery beast ripped through me, I closed my eyes and bit my lips together, drawing blood.

Pain dug its claws into me, and I couldn't hold back my scream.

Chapter 4

Kicking and grunting, I tried to break free from the ogre's grip but he didn't let go. Colorful fire surrounded me as the beast beneath the courthouse tried to cremate me alive.

I shrieked as panic roared through me in a blinding wave.

But as fast as the flames had engulfed me, they receded, until nothing remained but another scorched circle ringing me on the rough-cut wooden boards underneath my feet.

The room, Cloven, and Fleur were gone.

As the smoke drifted away on the crisp, salty breeze, the ogre hauled on my arm. "Dun be dawdlin', gil." He waved toward…water.

We'd landed on a dock. Decent-sized waves smacked against the pilings beneath us, and the swish and gurgle of the ocean echoed in the nearly-black night.

Two moons—one large and round and creamy yellow, the other pale blue—huddled close together, halfway up the sky. Their opalescent, greenish light wavered across the endless sea.

Despair sunk into me. There was no going back now.

"Where did the fire go?" I asked. It seemed like a stupid question when every bit of the world around me had completely changed.

"Where it always goes," the ogre growled, and I assumed he'd heard the question a billion times before. "Done eating."

What, exactly, had it eaten?

"Wait." I peered around, unable to fully absorb my surroundings. "This…" I'd expected an island with a fortress. And *creatures*. "Where are we?"

He nudged his chin to a wavering circle behind me. "Veil." His burly arm swept out, toward the sea. "Fae kingdom."

My great-great-great a billion times great-grandmother had come from this world after the fae argued and half left for the parallel universe. They'd settled and built the Academy and many other schools like it on Earth.

The people my family had come from had originally lived *here*.

Magic had been born in this world.

"I meant, where's Darkwater Prison?" I asked. "I thought we were going directly there."

"Can't flit."

"Can't flit here, as in the fae world?" Fae wizards couldn't flit? How did they—

"Dun be stupid, gil." He yanked on my arm, and I bit back a cry of pain. I stumbled after him as he dragged me along the dock extending out into the ocean, our feet making dull thuds on the wood. A large, shadowy structure loomed in the distance. "No flitting in or out of Darkwater."

"Oh." It made sense. If incarcerated wizards could flit, they could escape.

"No talking," the ogre snarled. He sniffed the air. "Things…lurk. Dun wait for sluggish wizards."

Who wouldn't wait? I dug in my heels, as much as I could while I was bound with magical ties and being dragged by a seven-foot-tall ogre. "No."

His thick lips twisted, and he leaned away from me, though he maintained a pinching grip on my upper arm. "Dun have time for this. Need to be paid for delivery."

I was a delivery.

My chin rose. "I'm not going anywhere with you until you tell me where we're going." Hopefully, he didn't hear the shake in my voice. I might be bringing on my own death with my defiance, but my choices were either to fight him or give into despair. I preferred to go down kicking and screaming.

"Told you. Darkwater."

"Which is in the middle of the sea. Last I knew, they hadn't built the prison near a beach." Waves crashed against a rocky shore behind us. "That's how I heard it. Murder. Veil. Prison." I hauled on my arm, determined to break free and run toward the shore. Not that I'd get far with my hands pinned behind my back and while wearing tennas, but it was worth a try.

He snapped his teeth, and his grip bit deeper into my arm, hard enough I winced.

I scrambled along beside him, my breathing coming fast already. Fear bounced inside me, a ball with sharp edges eager to slice free. "Were the, um…" Damn cracking voice was giving me away. I swallowed back my tears. "Were the flames part of the veil?"

"Flames, smames." He shot me a scowl. "It digested us."

I grimaced. "Something ate us?" My belly rolled.

"That." He pointed in the direction we'd come from.

"Veil digestive tract." The deep, harsh laugh he released shot hot air across my face and made gooseflesh pepper on my skin.

When I tripped over a knot in the wood, he hauled me up off my feet and close to his face. "Yer stallin' and there'll be nun of that. I think ya need a lesson." His lips peeled back in a saw-toothed smile. He tossed me forward.

As I tumbled forward, I groaned. With my hands secured behind my back, I couldn't break my fall. But I didn't land on the boards; I dissolved into nothing and was dragged down, down…

My lungs choked off as if a hand had slapped over my face. Terrified, I thrashed, while the fingers tightened. The tiny bit of air I sucked in was thick, dark, and consuming. The thunder of my heart drowned out my scream.

I landed on the boards. With the wind knocked from me, I could only lay there, groaning. My eyes leaked, and I couldn't hold back my sobs.

The ogre hauled me up and held me dangling in front of his face again while he sneered. "Now ya behave?"

Razing my lower lip with my teeth, I gave him a jerky nod. I sniffed and rubbed my tears off my face on my shoulder.

After tossing me onto my feet, he latched onto my arm and dragged me down the dock. I stumbled behind him, my feet slipping on greenish slime coating the surface, making it more challenging than walking on thin ice. A flock of dim lights drifting overhead snagged my attention and I peered up at the warped version of the cute wilty-sparks I'd always enjoyed. As I stumbled behind the ogre into the gloom, I tipped my head back to watch them.

A wilty dove toward me.

The ogre ducked. Why? Wiltys were friendly. Sure, this group was made up of colors I'd never seen before, steel gray, inky blue, and a darker red that resembled congealed blood, not hearts and roses. But wiltys wouldn't harm a nat. They thrived on light touch and affection.

The wilty plunged into my head with enough force to drive me to my knees. I curled into a ball on the slimy dock, trying to shrink into myself. The creature dug in, snarling through my hair, ripping at my scalp, seeking…

With a grunt of disgust, the ogre wrenched it from my scalp, taking half my hair along with the pest. Gasping and swallowing back fresh tears, I scrambled to my knees as the ogre tossed the wilty into the murky water beside us. It floundered for only a second before something roared up from beneath the water and gulped it down. The other wiltys shrieked and attacked us.

The ogre scowled. Bellowing and swinging his hefty arms, he snatched them from the air while I cowered beneath him. A few slipped past him and latched on my exposed skin, biting deep. I rolled on the dock to dislodge them and would've fallen over the side and become fae bait if the ogre hadn't snagged the back of my tunic and hauled me back beside him.

When the barrage ended and the wiltys had either fled or been sent to their death in the water, the ogre yanked me to my feet. "Now you've done it."

Me? I'd been walking. Watching what I'd thought were cute little wiltys floating above me. I couldn't take this. I—

"Can ya run?" he asked, cocking one thick eyebrow.

Snarled hair in my eyes, I reeled back to stare up him. "Why?"

"Them things hunt in big packs. We pissed 'em off."

A whirring rush built around us, as if a billion mosquitos had scented blood and were moving in for the kill.

"Go!" He shoved me, urging me farther down the

dock. I staggered forward. The ogre stuck to my heels, grabbing wiltys out of the sky and throwing them sideways.

How far did the dock go? Were we running all the way to Darkwater?

Crunches, grunts, and muted shrieks echoed behind me as the ogre wrangled with the flock of wiltys. They plunged into the water and were gulped down by greedy creatures that scrambled for dinner, gnashing their long, sharp teeth.

My heart hammered against my ribcage as fear took hold of me and shouted *run!*

A few wiltys landed on the dock ahead of me. In the past, I would've fallen rather than harm them, but these babies were out to get me. I stomped on them, popping them beneath my sneakers. Membranous, wiltys had no bones, and I cringed as I crushed them.

Ahead, the end of the dock approached. A low wooden boat with a solitary mast bobbed in the water. Two ogres bailed over the side and lumbered our way. Would they help with the wiltys or rip me to shreds?

My grandma's stories hadn't prepared me for killer wiltys or ogres, let alone what might come next.

Thighs overrun with spasms and my arms cramping from their position behind my back, I decided the ogres were safer than the wiltys and raced in that direction.

One of the ogres swept past me to join the first in battling the wiltys. The second lifted and tossed me over his shoulder, compressing the wind from my lungs. He stomped back down the dock, heading for the boat. As we approached, he gathered himself and leaped, spanning the stretch of churning ocean between the dock and boat in one stride. He landed on the deck with a huff then dumped me forward, off his shoulder.

My butt bit the wooden surface and pain spiked up my spine. My hands were crushed between me and the unforgiving wood.

I snapped backward, and my head hit the deck.

The world cut out.

Chapter 5

My right shoulder slammed against something solid, and pain shot into my head. I bit back a moan.

The world swayed and rocked and tipped me in all directions.

I was gonna hurl.

As my belly cramped, my eyes snapped open. A black, web-like mesh covered my face and for a second I thought Katya had trapped me for her children's next meal. Squeals erupted from deep inside me. But when I jerked my head back in panic, the web slid sideways.

Great. I was freaking out about my damn hair.

At least I no longer felt like vomiting. My stomach might host a rebellion in the future, but it had retreated for now.

My gaze wavered as I stared around.

If I didn't know better, I'd think I'd drained an entire bottle of verdeen all by myself.

This is what happens when your brains smacked against wooden decking. Which, I guessed, was better than being shredded by feral wiltys. Or eaten alive by spiders.

But if I had a concussion, I was out of luck, because there didn't seem to be any healers rushing toward me, offering their services.

I sat on a curved wooden bench spanning the back of the boat. Eight or ten other, shorter benches snaked ahead of me on either side of the ship. A narrow aisle fed down the center, toward a platform that had been built across the pointed front.

Multiple paddles fed through holes on the side of the ship, to aid in propulsion. The right one swung up, out of the water, and my jaw unhinged. A mouth on one of the wide, flat heads opened, revealing sharp teeth, before it descended, back into the water. When it rhythmically appeared again, a fish flapped in its mouth. It gulped it down and burped before it dropped back into the water.

An ogre strolled over to the rail and, when a paddle appeared with a fish, the ogre grabbed it before it could be eaten. He tossed it over his shoulder and it dropped into a hole in the decking. Dinner?

Other than me, there appeared to be only one other prisoner on board, slumped against the railing on my left.

Four ogres labored on the boat. One tugged on a rope that looped around the mainmast, while a second steered the ship. The third continued "fishing," while the fourth stood at the point, his meaty paws clutching the rail as he stared down at the water.

Two moons fought to shine through murky clouds overhead, and a few unfamiliar constellations winked in clusters on the horizon.

A broad white sail fluttered from the mast in the center of the ship, bowing out as it caught the wind to drive us forward. We'd sail to Darkwater, then, or was this just another part of a lengthy journey?

At least this part didn't involve digestion. So far.

A burst of wind charged over me, flinging my hair forward.

Wiggling my head, I shifted the strands out of the way and peered over my shoulder.

An enormous round creature about ten feet tall and equally as wide perched on the back of the ship, its four clawed feet digging into the railing. Its beaked mouth opened, and another gust of wind roared across me. The sails weren't being filled by ordinary wind but by this…thing.

Spittle peppered my face, and I cringed. Whirling around to face the front, I hunched forward, trying to avoid being coated. It was a lost cause; I sat directly in front of the creature.

While I'd been knocked out, someone had moved my hands from behind my back to my front. I stretched my fingers and wiggled them, grateful they still worked. My tenna wristlets had been attached to a gleaming green chain secured to a ring driven into the railing on my right. Either the ogres were trying to keep me from diving overboard or they expected me to go down with the ship if it sank.

After peering around to make sure I wasn't being watched, I slid my linked hands over to the side of my thigh. Dad had given me something in the courthouse, and I needed to find out what it was. I couldn't dig into my pocket and pull it out, but I could feel it through the prison uniform.

About four inches long and tube-like. Hmm. I traced my fingers along the length and identified my knife. Cool. It could save my life.

Cricking my neck to loosen it, my gaze caught movement on my left. My lips flatlined when I saw who was sitting on the opposite end of the bench.

Rabid shifter dude from the courthouse scowled my way.

"You," I croaked. A desert had set up business in my throat, shriveling my vocal cords. I'd just about kill for a drink of water and a hair elastic, neither of which would be coming my way anytime soon.

"Me," he grunted, mocking me. His hands shifted and the gleaming green chain connecting his tenna wristlets to the decking clinked.

"At least they have you restrained," I said. No trying to gnaw on my neck this time.

"Afraid I might do something to you if I was free?" His voice came out deep and husky. Was the tone natural or was he as equally thirsty as me?

I huffed. "I'm not worried in the least."

He wiggled his broad shoulders and pulled the chain tight, testing the bolt driven into the floor. While his arm muscles strained against his shirt, the chain remained secure.

"If I was you," he said in a snarly way that could only be taken as a threat. "I'd be very scared."

My sigh bled out of my lungs, but really, what did he think he could do to me trussed up like he was? "If you can't behave, I'll ask the ogres to give you different accommodations." Like the ocean. The thought might be snarky, but I wasn't having my best day. And he was…well, irritating.

"Thought you were dead," he grumbled.

"You sound disappointed." I fed him a sweet smile, hoping to irk him as much as he was irking me. I was rewarded with a subtle downward turn of his lips. His irritation was tasty; it was all I could do to hold back my grin. "Were you worried I'd die and rot beside you?"

"Kinda hoped it would happen, actually." His nostrils

flared, and grim humor shone in his deep brown eyes. "Rotting's too good for you, though."

"Don't hold anything back there, dude." What was with him, anyway? Yes, we were in a tenuous situation but you'd think he'd be looking for an ally, not trying to antagonize the only available option.

"While I'd love to see it happen, there won't be enough time for you to rot." His gaze drifted forward before returning to me. "We'll arrive at Darkwater within the hour."

"You know this because…" I squinted but saw nothing ahead of us but water.

"Been here before." His brows drew in sharply. "If you slump against the railing again, they might decide you're done for and toss you overboard." His offer came across with heavy sarcasm.

My brain wouldn't stop pounding, and he was only making it worse. "You always behave like this or is it just a phase?" First, he'd tried to bite me and now he was trying to get me tossed into the sea for a date with those things with long teeth. "I'll pass on the swim." Although, it would be nice to wash off the wind creature's spit.

"Could be your last opportunity," he said. "After we arrive, who knows what might happen to you."

This guy was something else. "I'll take my chances at the prison."

Another blast of wind roared around me. It hit the sail and the fabric strained forward. I shuddered. I'd be coated in slime by the time we arrived.

Rabid guy chuckled, happy to see me squirm. "Just so you know. Death might be easier now than later."

I could understand self-preservation. To survive in a supernatural supermax, I'd have to remain hyper-alert, but his crankiness couldn't be explained away that simply. Something else was going on here.

"You deserve to die," he shot out. "For the crime you committed."

"Bites to be incarcerated, doesn't it?" My gaze took in his chains. "Don't see you walking around free or working with the ogres."

He snapped his wrists up, hauling on the chain, but it remained secure. "These are temporary."

My lips twisted. "I don't plan to keep the fancy jewelry for long, either."

"Most wizards die within their first week at Darkwater. You'll be among them."

It was a good thing my grandma's stories had not contained stats. "Doubt it." A fierce need to survive burned inside me like a torch. I'd confront my birth father once I located him, and then find a way free. As for the murder I'd been directed to carry out, that item was still on the menu but I wasn't sure I wanted to take a bite.

"You being cocky will just make it happen faster," he said. "Which isn't necessarily a bad thing."

"Wanting to make it through this isn't being cocky. It's about keeping a positive attitude." Something Fleur said kept her going all the months her boyfriend had been bespelled to forget her. She'd suffered. They both had.

"What makes your odds any better than everyone else's?" he asked with a sneer.

Pivoting, I faced him but bit back a groan when my head screamed about the rapid movement.

He fed me a grin that made it clear he enjoyed seeing me suffer.

Some of my brain matter must be lying face-down on the deck. "Why are you acting so nasty?" I asked. As far as

I knew, I'd done nothing to deserve it. But, hell, maybe I'd snored while I was out and disturbed him. Somehow.

"You expect sweetness and flowers?"

Talk about a useless conversation. Heaving a sigh, I turned away from him and stared forward.

One of the ogres had stretched out on a bench three slabs away from mine. His snores rang out louder than a herd of hibernating aldakors.

"Don't count me out yet," I said, nudging the support post of the bench ahead of mine with the tip of my sneaker. "I have a few things left I'm determined to do before I depart this world."

"Like what?"

I tilted my head and analyzed his face, unsure if I heard scorn or interest in his tone. His sullen expression hadn't changed, making it difficult to tell. "I'm going to take back something that's mine. And then I have to kill someone." Or find a way out of my blood bond promise, assuming a way existed. I was still working on that part of the equation.

The guy directed his gaze toward his booted feet. "Guess we share both tasks."

"Oh, yeah?" He had to be humoring me. "You and I have something in common?" I released a chuckle but winced when the left side of my chest spasmed. Had I cracked a rib when I'd been thrown on the deck?

"My life was stolen from me," he growled.

"Mine, too, but that's not what I'm after."

"You don't want to live?"

"Sure I do, but these things," I lifted my wrists, "Everything that comes with prison bindings is controlling my future at the moment."

"Same."

"You said we share both tasks. Living, I get. You planning on killing someone, too?"

"Soon." No denying the vehemence in his voice. "Once it's done, I'll have my life back."

"A two for one deal, then. You do realize that committing murder will keep you at Darkwater forever, right?" If anyone knew about that fact, it was me. I nudged my head toward his tenna devices. "Kill someone at Darkwater, and you'll never get those things off."

"Tennas are the least of my worries."

"If you say so." I couldn't imagine how he thought his freedom would be restored if he murdered someone but look at me. I was supposed to kill someone for the very same reason. "You didn't happen to make a deal with a Seeker, did you?"

"A cop?" Horror lifted his gruff tone to mid-range.

I shrugged. "Some would call Seekers cops."

His gaze narrowed. "I bet you would."

"Why me?" Anxiety leaked into my words. Was there any way to keep my Seeker abilities secret? From everything I'd heard about the Prison, it was going to be a huge challenge just to survive. The last thing I needed was for anyone to find out I was a Seeker.

Had been a Seeker. I doubted they'd let me back into the Guild now.

"Seekers are chopped meat at Darkwater," he said with grim satisfaction.

Call that a no. "I'm not a Seeker." Not any longer. What would I do with my skapti now?

"Stop lying." He smirked. "Your Seeker skills and experience will be useless at the Prison."

So, he knew. How did he find out?

"I used to find lost wizards," I said sadly. Friends and sisters, mostly. "Doubt there's a need for that at a prison."

The right paddle emerged from the water, this time clutching a squirming eel-like thing in its mouth. I expected the paddle to chow through it but the eel wrapped itself around the paddle's neck and squeezed tight. With a pop, the paddle's head was severed from its wooden body. While I blinked, the eel jumped into the water. A new head wiggled out from the paddle's neck.

"Things lost at the prison are never found," the guy said, returning my brain to the conversation.

"You sound like you know a lot about the place."

"Enough."

An answer that shared nothing. It was clear this guy wasn't being completely honest with me. No matter. It wasn't like I'd spend time with him in the future. If his stats were accurate, he might be fodder within the week. Not me. I was determined not to die before I'd pinned down my father.

A long, low roar skimmed through the air. Unfortunately, we seemed to be heading in the direction it had come from.

Beastly or from the spirit realm? It was hard to know in the fae world. The Academy hadn't offered many classes about fae life. Even if they had, they wouldn't have included details about the prison.

"What did you do to be sent to Darkwater?" I asked, making conversation.

"Sought revenge," he said.

Interesting way to phrase it. "Sought, you say. I take it you didn't see success?"

His palms ground together. "It's still in the works."

Wiggling my shoulders, I shifted on the hard wooden bench, trying to find a more comfortable position. Wasn't happening.

The intermittent roars ahead of us grew louder, punctuated with gut-wrenching shrieks.

The sly grin on Rabid Guy's face grew bigger.

Maybe, when we got off the ship, I'd suggest he go ahead of me.

"It would've been better for you if you hadn't woken up," he said.

I sighed. "Back to that, are we?"

"Always."

"Well, thanks. It's kind of you to think of my wellbeing." Sure. "I'm not dying yet, and I don't plan to anytime soon." I tried to sense his mood but I was no empath. He sounded angry. I wasn't thrilled with the situation, either. "I get it. Darkwater is a prison. There's no escape and no leaving outside of death."

"Not only that."

This useless conversation was making my temples pound. It hurt to breathe. To move. To think. "What's the point of all this?"

"Just sayin'."

"Just sayin' nothing. I've heard enough about Darkwater already to know my odds are better there than by bailing into the sea."

"You don't know the most important part."

"You mean the Reformatory?"

He cricked his head, peering at me through the gloom.

Ahead of us, the sleeping ogre groaned and rolled over to face us. How he could rest on the bench was beyond me.

"Heard about the Reformatory, have you?" Rabid dude said.

"My grandmother told me lots of stories about Darkwater."

He snorted and stretched out his long legs. His booted feet bumped the bench post ahead of him. "Kiddie tales?"

"She was a sketar witch. It wasn't just tales. She *knew*."

His gaze flicked down my front. "You don't look like a troll."

I rolled my eyes. "Because I'm not. I'm Elite." I wasn't saying it to claim bragging rights, just stating a fact.

"Good for you." He snorted. "Your Elite status means nothing now. Not in the fae kingdom."

"Can't see how you know anything more about this than me."

"I'm fae."

"We're all fae."

"You came from the other universe. You're part human. Sídhe. I'm from here."

I studied him with new interest. Not *that* kind of interest. *Curiosity*. That's all my feeling was. "You don't look fae to me."

"Because I don't have clichéd pointy ears, long white hair, and I'm not super-tall?"

"You're tall enough." From what I could tell, he'd stand at least a head over me and I was a decent height myself.

"Tall enough for what?"

"I don't know. Reaching for a can on the top shelf?"

"Why would I want to do that? And what's a can?"

"You're tall enough, okay?" I growled.

His gaze was drawn to the horizon. "Told you. I grew up here."

"I doubt at Darkwater." My turn to inject some sarcasm into the conversation. In our own, personal dialogue competition, he was winning all the events. I needed to increase my comebacks or get out of the game. "Or do you mean you grew up in the sea?" Ha-ha. The hit on my head was bringing out my snarky side.

"In the air. It's a part of me. It's in my skin, my blood, and my soul."

"Sounds whimsical."

"Factual."

"No one grows up in the air."

"I did."

He'd taken the conversation off the deep end again, but chatting with him had made what would've been a scary time go faster. Even with his obvious disdain, he wasn't as horrible as I'd thought when he leaped on me. When he tried to bite me. Or even when he'd wished me dead.

An ogre stomped down the aisle between the benches, kicking the sleeping ogre's legs out of the way as he passed. He carried a jug.

"Drink," he said, tilting it my way.

Thank the fae. The brackish water tasted better than Donovan's best verdeen. That was saying something since his older brother, the king, made his own brew with specialty fruits grown at his orchards. I guzzled until my belly ached to explode.

The ogre offered the water to the guy beside me but he turned his head and stared out at the sea. With a huff, the ogre returned to the front of the ship.

"I'm Tria," I said. "You're weird, but it's nice to meet 'cha."

He scooted around to face me. "I already know who you are." His gaze darted to my right arm, which I rubbed through the sleeve, because I'd fallen on it and it ached. "Don't pretend. You know who I am."

"Can't say that I do."

He grinned sickly, and a worm of unease burrowed deep into my belly.

"I'm going to kill you," he said. "Once you're dead I can take back my life."

"What the fae are you talking about?" I growled out. The sleeping ogre slanted his eyes my way before growling and rolling onto his other side.

"You act as if you don't know," he said. "Which tells me even more about who you are as a person."

How was I supposed to know who he was? The ogres hadn't exactly introduced us.

"Tell me!" It wasn't every day someone threatened my life so casually. I had to know why.

"You truly want to know?"

"Yes!"

His flinty gaze narrowed on my face. "Ordellia Trarion was my mother, and I saw you murder her."

Chapter 6

Rabid guy was Professor Trarion's son.

Some would call this too great a coincidence, but fate was eager to snag me in her net and leave me with no hope for escape.

Why had the Master Seeker paired me up with the Professor's son? This had to be his intervention. *His* net.

"You were there?" I hadn't seen him, but I hadn't exactly been taking in the wizards in the area before I fled.

"Not in the field, or I would've tackled you," Professor Trarion's son said. His voice grated higher. "I would've strangled you until your tongue popped from your mouth and your eyes bulged and your head—"

Squeamish, I held up my hand. "I get it."

Eyebrows narrowed, he studied my every move. "We ran into each other inside the Academy right before you did it."

No, I hadn't been inside.

"I was talking with someone inside when you drove your knife into her back."

"It—" *Was someone bespelled to look like me* froze on my

tongue. Damn blood bond. It kept me saying anything that would clear my name.

"I heard the shouts and went outside…" Exquisite pain filled his face, and he gulped. "I saw you running toward the woods. There was no one else around her."

I lifted my chin, but my voice shook. "I didn't do it."

"I love this," he said with a slick grin.

I fed him a sour look. "You love what?"

"Seeing you unsettled."

"This isn't me unsettled." Sure. I couldn't even convince myself. "I'm just thinking."

"Better think fast." He yanked on his cuffed hands, and I swore the chain groaned. "If I don't get you, the other inmates will, *Seeker*."

It would be useless to ask him not to tell. Better to let him think I didn't care. "Go right ahead and shout it out to the world. I can protect myself."

"Not from what's coming."

My hands clenched but the gesture lost its impact because they were linked with gleaming green restraints. "From anything."

He grinned.

"What's your skapti, anyway?"

"I'm an Influencer."

From what I remember from my *Skills For the Ages* Class, an Influencer could sometimes manipulate outcomes, not just wizards. They were stronger than Persuaders, who could only make suggestions and hope they were carried through.

I scrunched my nose at him. "How does your skapti go with your rabid buck teeth?"

He stiffened. "I don't have buck teeth."

"Fangs. Whatever."

Blinking, he drove his gaze from mine. "I don't have

fangs, either."

Not at the moment but…I'd seen them. "When you were trying to gnaw on my neck, I pegged you as either a slake or a shifter. Maybe you're both."

"I don't need to drink power. It finds me all on its own."

Which didn't answer the shifter part of my comment, but whatever. It hardly mattered if he could turn into something else. "I can't see how being able to influence me is going to get me killed." A brave statement. My knees shook because I *could* see how an Influencer could present trouble. Some suggested Seekers could resist the pull, but since Influencers were rare, the theory hadn't been adequately tested. "Besides. Remember? We're wearing tennas. You won't be able to use your magic."

"I'll find a way around them."

"Good luck with that."

"When I do, I'll convince you to jump off the prison roof."

I rolled my eyes. "Like I'll do something like that?"

"Or suggest you slit your wrists."

"Studies show that wrist-slitting is an ineffective way to take a life. Arteries are deep and hard to hit. Veins might be closer to the surface, but they'll clot off too fast to kill a person."

He scowled. "Then I'll influence someone at the prison into tying you down and torturing you."

"Go for it, dude. Like I said, I can protect myself." When Dad married Mom, I'd joined a long line of sketar witches. I knew all their tricks. Since Seeker skills would be nearly useless at the prison, I might be able to fall back on Dad's training. If sketar magic worked, I could create unusual spells that would—

"Watch me," he said.

"Not worried, rabid boy."

"I'm nineteen. Not a boy."

Definitely not a boy, but how could I let my mind go there? This guy was much too threatening to be considered love interest material.

He fumed. "And I'm not rabid."

"Feral then."

The brief, upward curve of his lips suggested being called feral pleased him. Weird.

"For what it's worth," I said. "I didn't kill your mom." That, I was allowed to say.

"Witnesses saw you stab her in the back with a knife," he snarled. "She collapsed on the ground and bled to death while you ran away."

"It wasn't me."

"She died before I could save her!"

The pain in his voice made my heart seize. I couldn't bear it. I'd liked the Professor, though I'd never thought to ask if she had a family. And I knew how I'd feel if someone murdered my mom or dad. I'd want to kill the person who'd done it, too.

"I was framed," I said, the bitter taste of it rising into the back of my mouth. While I hadn't killed her, I'd taken off, bolting into the woods. Like a coward. If I'd stopped to help her, would she be alive now? I should've stayed and called for a healer. Maybe then, I wouldn't be in this situation.

Although, that was unlikely. The Master Seeker had a plan he'd put into place, and I was one piece of his intricate puzzle. I needed to step back and look at the entire picture to find a way out.

"Framed," he said. "Like I believe that?"

Unsettled and feeling guilty—which was somewhat justified—I slumped against the rail.

A shadow passed across his face. "You sound so convinced. If I didn't know better—"

"It's true."

"Prove it to me, then."

"Thought you were going to kill me to get your revenge and regain your life?"

"Let's just say I'm willing to humor you for a short time. I'll give you a chance to convince me you didn't kill my mother."

"Why?"

He shrugged.

"Nice of you to make the offer." I scoffed. "But it's kinda hard to prove I didn't do it when the witnesses are beyond the veil."

"If that truth lives within you, it'll shine through."

"Sounds fancy."

"Magical."

My huff was followed by a big gust of wind from the spitty beast riding the rail. I hunkered forward, wincing until the slimy rain halted. Then I turned and faced him again. "Magic sounds lovely but unless you're an empath or you can touch me and somehow see if I'm telling the truth, there isn't much chance of anything shining anywhere."

"Not if you don't believe."

I tilted my head. "Is this a fae thing?" Despite my reluctance, I was intrigued.

By this situation.

By him.

"What do you mean by a fae thing?" he growled.

"I wasn't trying to be insulting." Odd that I was carrying on a perfectly normal—mostly—conversation with a guy who believed I'd killed his mother and wanted to end my life for the crime.

Fortunately, we were both restrained. So far.

He'd tried to harm me back at the courthouse. If the guards hadn't hauled him off, would he have ripped through my throat and ended my life?

"We're here," he said.

Bolting upright, I stared around, but I couldn't see anything in the fog that had crept in when I wasn't looking. "Here, as in Darkwater, here?"

"Soon."

Stretching my neck, I tried to see ahead but between the sail billowing about, thanks to the gusting creature behind me, plus the formerly sleeping ogre rising and scurrying forward to get ready for our arrival, even my Seeker skills wouldn't be able to part the mist.

"Just so you know," he said.

I tipped my head his way. "What?"

"I'm giving you a chance you don't deserve."

One side of my lips curled up, the only evidence of enthusiasm I could generate. "Thanks?"

"I don't like you. I'll never like you."

"Ditto, Feral Boy."

"Don't call me that," he snapped.

So much for being happy about the nickname.

"Don't try to bite me again," I said. "And I'll try my best to forget to call you *feral*."

Like I'd gouged him in the side, he scowled and his cheeks went ruddy. "Don't even dream I'll ever be friendly to you."

"Duly noted." I'd feel the same if our positions were reversed.

How he must hate me.

I'd stolen his mother.

But he was wrong about one thing. I hadn't stolen his life.

Chapter 7

Fed by the rank gusts from the being behind us, the boat surged forward, slicing into the fog like a well-honed blade. As if we were squeezed through a clenched fist, we popped through to the other side.

I'd expected sunshine by now. Muted daylight, at least. But the night still dominated, without a hint of dawn in sight.

I frowned as a cloud-like substance drifted through the sky, approaching us. After the attack-wiltys, I hunkered low, cautious. The cloud descended and buzzed around my head before landing on my face, hair, and shoulders. While I squirmed and shrieked, they stung worse than wasps.

An ogre turned and scowled, as if I'd ruined his day by crying out.

Standing, I waived my bound arms in the air, driving them away. They retreated, en masse, then turned and dove toward feral guy.

His chain didn't allow him to lift his hands higher than chin-level, but he gave it a valiant effort. Grunting, he dropped to his knees to extend his reach.

I grumbled, but rose and, with my arms stretched toward my seat because I couldn't reach any other way, I added my feet to his defense, striking a few blows of my own.

Like chastised pups, the tiny beings whimpered and fled back into the darkness.

After watching until I was confident they wouldn't loop around and attack again, I turned to Feral.

His brow had twisted itself into a knot.

"I take it you're not thrilled I helped." I wasn't sure why I'd done it. Maybe because I'd run when his mom needed help… Guilt.

"You don't know what I think."

"Fair enough." Up close, he was… His messy hair and deep brown eyes held too much appeal. That chiseled chin…

Before I burned up, I backed away. "Even murderers can do good things for others," I huffed as I returned to my bench.

"Thought you said you weren't a murderer."

Leave it to him to latch onto that part of my statement. "I was speaking in general."

"Why did you help me?" He almost sounded bewildered.

"I'm a kind person. Sometimes."

His intent gaze remained on my face. Was he waiting for me to reveal a murderous side so he could shout, *got ya*?

"It's almost as if you don't realize people are multifaceted."

"Murderer."

"Here we go again." I slumped against the rail. "And you're welcome."

"I didn't thank you."

"I noticed." I peered around, hoping more wasp clouds

weren't heading my way, but I couldn't see more than twenty or thirty feet ahead. "Is it dark here all the time?" Frustration about this situation was digging a hole through my stomach. The spitty gusts bursting past me didn't help much, either.

"Why would you think that?" he said. *Are you stupid?* was heavily implied.

"How am I supposed to know? You're the one who grew up here." I held up my hand. "Oh, wait. No. You didn't grow up *here*. You grew up *in the air*."

"No need to be sarcastic."

"You plan to kill me. Why should I be anything else?"

His nose lifted. "I granted you a reprieve to convince me otherwise."

I dipped my upper body forward in an exaggerated bow. "Greatly appreciated, kind feral boy."

He snarled, proving my point.

"Why?" I asked.

"Why the reprieve?"

"You didn't say."

His gaze drifted toward the island rising through the mist ahead of us. "I don't know why."

"Vague."

"Honest."

This time, anyway.

"Let's call it a game," he finally said.

"In what way?"

"I'll give you the single chance I imagine anyone would…" His lips flattened. "*Kill* for. After that, when you least expect it, I'll move in and it'll be over in seconds."

"So much for granting me a reprieve." Despite my bravado, I couldn't hold back the goosebumps rippling across my skin. Intriguing appearance aside, he appeared physically stronger than me, and he had a never-ending urge to see me dead.

Tugging on his tennas, he strained to break the chain, blanching his hands with his efforts. Fire lit inside the bands and arced around his wrists, but the flames didn't seem to cause him pain. "The best part about it is you'll have to watch your back all the time."

So, he wanted to torture me in a subtle way. Stress me out, knowing I'd be scared, worried he'd attack the moment I turned away.

"I planned to watch my back already. It's a prison, remember? Everyone has to be careful there. Otherwise, those stats about one-week newbie survival rates wouldn't exist."

"You mentioned the Reformatory," he said. "If you take the Challenge, I will, too."

"What Challenge?"

"I don't know a lot, but I've heard to get to the Reformatory, you have to pass a series of tests."

"Like pen and paper tests?" Even as I said it, the heavy feeling in my gut told me I was wrong.

"Like something-trying-to-eat-you tests."

"I'm savvy. I'll survive." I might sound confident, but my pulse had picked up. What was I getting into here?

"Things might get interesting during the Challenge," he said.

"You're suggesting you'll play a cat and mouse game with me. I'll be taking tests while you'll be testing me."

"Exactly." If he wasn't in profile, I *might* be able to read his face. It was wise of him to turn away.

I'd never enjoyed tests, but what could I do? I had to reach the Reformatory. If that took a Challenge, I'd lift my hand and volunteer. "What do you know about the Challenge?" When he said nothing, I huffed. "You're just a bunch of empty threats."

"You'll see."

"As I said. An empty rabid dude."

He growled.

"What happens if I don't make it past the Challenge?"

"If you're lucky, you remain in prison."

Somehow, remaining in the prison didn't sound lucky. My nerves twitched, making me jumpy.

The back of the ship jolted upward. A quick glance behind told me the wind creature had jumped off. A solid splash followed. Was the beast part fish? I'd met and worked with all kinds of magical creatures during my lifetime, but I'd never seen anything like this one.

The boat drifted toward the island, helped along by the current. Two ogres drew down the sail and tied it neatly while a third stood at the front, straining forward like a mounted figurine on the hull. The fourth steered.

We floated up to a dock like the one we'd left behind, and the boat came to a halt. Two ogres bailed over the side, their feet thunking heavily on the wooden surface below. They scrambled around securing ropes to posts that would hold the ship in place. The remaining two ogres stomped over to us and unclipped our tennas from the chains, then hauled us over to the dockside of the ship.

"Go," one of them said to me.

"Get lost," the other told Feral. Since he hadn't told me his name, I'd picked one for him.

"This is it?" I said. "We make our way to the prison on our own? Where are the guards? Shouldn't we be escorted there? Someone needs to give us directions."

The one who'd steered the boat grinned, revealing teeth like big pieces of corn. "Demandin' gil, aren't you?" His gaze swept down to my feet then returned to my face. "Need an orientation, do ya?" Wiggling his eyebrows, his mocking glance swept to the other ogre, who chuckled, urging him on.

I nodded as unease wiggled through me. Me and my mouth. I wasn't going to like what came next. I dropped my voice and tried to come across placating. "Can you at least tell us where we need to go?"

"You're a prisoner, gil. You're not entitled to any more than all them others. But I do like grit, gil, so I'll give ya a tip."

My spine tightened because…this didn't sound good. "Lay it out for me."

"Want to live? Get to that building." His arm swept out, toward the hill where a craggy black stone fortress stood, spires and turrets reaching toward the sky. "There's yer tip. No guards. No escorts. You're on yer own."

"If that's the case, what keeps prisoners from running free?" I had a solid idea from my grandma's stories, but if he gave confirmation, he might spill a clue I could use to my advantage.

Feral's gaze darted from me to the ogre, to the shore, then back again. His muscles tightened like a runner crouched at the starting line of a big race.

I felt as if I needed to warm up. Stretch.

Shaking my head, I turned back to the ogre. "I walk up the path to the front door and tell them I've arrived?" Should I feel insulted that I—a prisoner—wasn't being treated like crap? "I thought I'd be dragged through the main entrance in chains, made to walk the gauntlet past seedy guys calling me sweetheart and sugar butt—"

Feral snorted. "Sugar butt?" His gaze drifted down my body, and the gesture didn't make me feel warm and fuzzy. "Hardly."

Someone needed to kick him.

I huffed at his comment. "Then I'd pass a bunch of prisoners running metal cups along steel bars. I also expected sadistic guards." Clichéd stuff, but I had a healthy imagination.

"Expect the last, gil," the ogre said. "Git through this test first. There be plenty more like it in your future."

"She doesn't have a future," Feral said.

Really wanted to kick him.

"Okay." I wasn't enjoying this situation in the least. I thought I'd be taken to the prison, where someone would explain each step before it arrived.

"Only one way to pass this test." The ogre's grin widened, revealing hunks of something that looked like meat wedged between his teeth. "Survive long enough to get to prison."

Feral inched toward the rail.

"*If* you get there, you'll get yer orientation." The other ogre said with a smirk.

Below, the two who'd jumped off to secure the boat were climbing a rope ladder dangling over the side. One gaped over his shoulder then climbed faster, panic suffusing his face. The other flung himself up the ladder behind the first as if he worried something would eat his feet if he lingered.

One thing Grandma said about Darkwater had stuck in my mind. *It's what waits for the poor soul outside, they need to be fearin'. Creatures. And beings older than the Fae.*

The low howl we'd heard as we came closer to the island erupted from the woods. It morphed into an ear-splitting roar, like a giant beast had awakened. But it had already been awake. It had known we were coming. And now it knew we had arrived.

My heartbeat ground to a halt.

The climbing ogres hitched their legs over the rail and

tumbled onto the decking. One glanced to us while he rose to his feet. "You kids better grow wings."

"Why?" Feral asked, his hand snagging the top of the rope ladder.

Good idea. I hurried to the rail and peered over the side, assessing the twenty foot drop. I'd taken on worse during the physical parts of Seeker training. This wasn't a jump I'd want to make without practice. The question was: did I dare wait for Feral to make his way to the bottom before using the ladder?

When the howl erupted again—closer and moving through the woods encroaching either side of the path leading toward the fortress prison, the ogres jostled each other and laughed.

Sunlight peeked over the horizon and then bolted up into the sky. I might've been happier if I'd been kept in the dark.

"If you don't git going on yer own," one of the ogres said, stomping forward with his arms outstretched. "I'll be happy to help yer along."

There were a few keys to surviving a drop like this and none of them involved being flung over the side by an ogre.

"What about these?" I asked, holding up my bound wrists. "How are we supposed to defend ourselves without magic?"

"No power for the tests, gil," the ogre who'd steered the boat said. "But since I like ya, I'll give ya better odds." He unlinked our wrists. While our magic was still suspended by the tennas, at least we had our hands free.

A few other things about falls had been drilled into me during Seeker class. Locate a stable landing target. Keep your legs together while maintaining your form. Relax and let your body go limp as you drop. Land on both feet and roll.

Feral had climbed over the rail and appeared to be frozen at the top of the rope ladder. My chances of getting to the ground in time to avoid whatever was coming dropped by the second. I couldn't wait for him to take his time reaching the bottom.

Another roar, more a mangled shriek, was followed by heavy thuds of giant footsteps. As far as I could see, nothing moved, but that meant zilch. We were about to be hunted.

The dock ended at a rocky shore and a cliff stretched above it. A field full of grass in need of a good cutting continued from the top of the cliff to the woods. A path snaked through the woods all the way to the prison.

Simple first test, right?

Not if I was bait.

Deep in the forest, something big moved. The treetops swayed and bent, shoved aside by a giant hand. Whatever it was, it was coming this way.

Sweat trickled down my back to pool at my spine, and my mouth went dry.

Time was up. It was Feral or me, and I wasn't going to sacrifice myself for a guy who got excited about torturing me.

I scrambled over the side, dangled my legs, and sited where I needed to land.

An ogre pushed me off the ship, and I tumbled toward the dock.

Chapter 8

The ground came up too fast.

My feet smacked onto wooden planks, and the impact speared up my spine. Diving forward, into a roll, I tumbled then came to my feet in a crouch. Not stopping, I kept going, bolting down the dock and onto the beach. My sneakers bucked and slid in the sand, making the first part of this test rough going.

Behind me, the ogres hooted and called out bets, but I didn't turn. They were the past, and my future lay ahead.

Directly in front of me, something long, milky green, and centipede-like erupted from the sand. Gulping, I leaped over it and ran, but another popped up farther ahead. A third beside it. More, until I lost count. A bug army!

My brow narrowed, and I stiffened as I took in the foot-long creatures. Coating the ground in a squirming mass, they wiggled, flinging sand every which way to expose their bodies. One must've seen me slowing, my brain frozen in shock, because it scrambled toward me on millions of feet with its front crab claws snapping.

Go! As I race forward and jumped over it, the insect's limbs stretched up and scraped along the bottom of my feet. I prayed my sneakers would hold together until I reached the prison.

Sweat trickled down my brow, and I kept going. Only about forty feet of beach left to cross. A squirming nest of centipedes between me and the cliffs, but I could make it.

More of the insects burst from beneath the sand, coating the beach around me. A lethal bug SWAT team, they attacked, their claws snagging my pants and threatening to pull me down.

Steady thuds from behind me told me Feral wasn't far behind.

His hoarse grunt rang out, signaling they were attacking him, too.

I pumped for speed. Finally, my Seeker training was paying off. I'd…

Tripping over a cluster of centipedes, my feet went out from beneath me. I groaned as I was tossed forward, the sand not as forgiving as it should be considering how squishy it felt under my sneakers.

Bugs clawed my limbs, while others jumped onto my back. Snipping and cutting, they'd make quick work of my clothing.

As I sprang to my feet and ripped bugs off my body, others sliced through my prison outfit and dug into my skin. Snarling, I failed backward, onto my butt as more centipedes burst up from below ground. They scurried across my thighs and belly as I jumped to my feet.

"Problems?" Feral shouted as he flung himself past me.

Damn long legs. Damn male muscles. He'd use them to his advantage.

As I took off after him, centipedes scrambled up my body, aiming for tender flesh, their claws scratching and digging. With a guttural shriek, I twisted and swiped them off then kicked them away. Spinning, I took off after Feral, who'd made too much progress already.

Adrenalin poured through my veins, giving my heart the strength to pump faster. My lungs heaved as I sucked in great gulps of air.

As he ran, Feral flipped bugs off in all directions. His arms flailed, and his legs churned up sand. He tripped and slammed face-first on the ground. In seconds, he was covered in centipedes.

If I was wise, I'd pass him and keep going. He'd become part of the newbie stats, and I'd no longer need to worry about when he'd decide to kill me.

But I'd only run about five feet before my footsteps slowed. The bugs took advantage of my pause and clambered up me. Plucking them off, I tossed them aside and turned.

Feral lay on the sand, roaring while struggling to get to his feet, but the weight of a zillion bugs pinned him down.

Dizzy, I stumbled over to him. As more centipedes squirmed up out of the sand, I grabbed fistfuls of them off Feral, flinging them as far as I could before grabbing more.

Our combined efforts freed him, and he thrust himself off the ground and onto his feet.

He earned his name when he turned his gaze my way. Wild and untamed, he appeared savage, ready to rip someone to shreds. His lips parted, revealing the razor-sharp fangs I'd seen at the courthouse. Before I could blink, they'd retracted, making me doubt they'd existed at all.

"Come on!" he shouted, rushing toward the cliffs. He darted a look over his shoulder as if to make sure I followed.

I caught up to him by the time we hit the base of the

cliffs. A glance in either direction told me there was no other way off the beach than up. I could barely see ten feet above us with the newly formed, greenish mist floating around.

"We've got to go up!" Feral said. "It's the only way to the prison."

"After you, then." With a smirk, I waved to the wall. "You can take on whatever challenge waits for us at the top. Let me know what to expect, would ya?"

"Sure. I'll leave you for the creatures creeping up behind you. I think they plan to make a go for it all at once."

My flesh crawled, and a quick look showed thousands of bugs marching toward us.

"Outta my way." I squiggled between him and the wall and, jumping, tried to grab a bush, hoping it would hold my weight long enough for me to find footholds. I couldn't reach.

I raced to the right, looking for a better place to climb.

Steeper than they'd appeared from the ship, when we'd been level with the top, the cliffs appeared insurmountable, especially enshrouded with the misty fog. But there was no going backward. Even as we paused, the army of centipedes rushed toward us. They'd be on us in seconds. Dragging us down. Shredding our skin to reach vital organs. We'd be dead before the sun hit the middle of the sky.

My breathing ragged, I told my muscles to conserve energy for the climb, but it was a challenge when I wanted to scream and rip out my hair. The bugs hadn't reached me yet, but I still felt them crawling across my skin.

I leaped up and grabbed onto a stubby bush growing out of the sixty-degree cliff incline. My feet dangled as I struggled for purchase on the wall, and my treads scraped the coarse surface. Dirt rained down on the centipedes scurrying below. A few bold ones started climbing the wall, their feet sticking like suction cups to glass. I needed to go faster!

Other than the bushes, roots, and a few random rocks, the cliff face was smooth, making it difficult to climb. I stabbed my feet forward, creating grooves my toes could use to cling to the wall. Moving higher, I inched over and around stubby brushes and used thick clumps of grass to yank myself toward the top.

A few brave centipedes came after me, though most had fallen. Wounded, they became prey, the others attacking, snipping them to pieces with their claws and eating them alive.

Bile rose in the back of my throat, and I shoved it down with a heavy swallow. No time to puke. *Keep going!*

Feral and I were neck-and-neck, and I was psyched to see I was about halfway to the top. Pushing myself, I passed him. I was determined he'd be the straggler, pickings for the thing in the woods, not me.

A centipede sunk its claws into my heel, and I grunted and stomped down, sending it flying. It bounced off the wall and slammed onto the ground. I watched in horrified fascination as its buddies descended. The remaining centipedes on the wall stopped and stared up at me. As if they'd received a signal audible only to them, they turned and started making their way back down the wall.

Were they giving up or had I somehow passed the test? If so, yay for me. It hadn't been easy crossing the beach, but I'd done it.

I tamped down my excitement, because I hadn't reached the top of the cliff, let alone the prison, yet.

Turning, I continued climbing, aiming for speed. A squirming feeling told me this challenge wasn't over yet.

Feral inched his way across the wall until he was beside me. He paused. It could be the moonlight playing tricks with my vision, but I swore something I hadn't seen before gleamed in his eyes. It couldn't be admiration. The dude wanted to kill me for murdering his mother.

"You…" he said.

"Me…"

He shook his head. "Back there on the beach…"

Awkward and uncomfortable about where this seemed to be going, I brushed him aside. "It was nothing." Why had I done it? If I'd left him, I would've been safer at the prison.

"It *was* something."

"Don't go soft on me, now," I puffed as I hauled myself up a few more feet. Sweat trickled down my temples and dirt coated my forearms to my elbows. My toes screamed from slamming them into an unforgiving cliff face, and my leg muscles spasmed from supporting my weight.

"Wouldn't think of it." He caught up and leaned in so close, we bumped shoulders. "I still hate you."

"Just keep that in mind," I said as I flung myself upward. About twenty feet left to go. My body protested already.

"Not a problem." Derision came through in his voice, and I was grateful to hear it. I couldn't let him close. No, I didn't dare let him close. He'd finish me off if I let down my guard.

I'd latched onto a bush sticking out of the cliff when it came alive, morphing into thin, bark-like bands that snaked around my right wrist, hissing.

Feral's yelp told me stubbly shrubs around him were coming alive, too.

With nothing to hold onto, I slid down the incline. Another bush shifted and a snaky branch wrapped around my neck.

My cry burst past my clenched lips.

Scraping across roots and bushes, I tumbled downward, toward the sand.

Crap! In seconds, I'd be centipede fodder unless I was hung partway down the cliff by the band around my neck.

My fingers clawed at the wall, trying to find purchase, but my nails tore and each bush turned into more viney bands that hissed and snapped and reached for me.

My knife! Reaching into my pocket, I yanked it out.

The blade slicked free as I fell toward the beach. Centipedes erupted from the sand and strained upward, hoping to pin me down for a feast.

I hacked at the vine wrapped around my throat. My lungs wheezed as I strained to drag air through the narrowing space. With a snap, the vine around my neck severed. I dragged in briny air as I continued to fall.

Before I could attack the one around my wrist, I jolted to a stop too far down from where I'd been. The sinewy plant creature squeezed my wrist tighter than my tenna.

I wheeled to my right and couldn't hold back my horrified shriek.

A girl about my age hung from a vine, her tongue dry and blue. Her protruding brown eyes stood out starkly against her face that was paler than snow on a cold winter's day.

Grunting, I wrangled myself away from her and slammed my toes into a crack in the wall, finding purchase. I had to get out of here, away from her body. Away from the same fate hovering so close I could taste it on the bitter wind.

Blubbering, I hauled on my arm, but the vines bit deeper. Blood trickled toward my elbow, turning into burgundy sludge on my sleeve when it mixed with the mud. My fingers had gone numb, and I was afraid they'd fall off.

Eyes narrowed, Feral stopped above and glared down at me. What was he doing? This was his chance to get ahead, to beat me to the prison, though I wasn't sure this was a race for anything except our individual survival.

A hoarse cry rose from deep inside me as I inched upward. I had to make it; no giving up now. I couldn't let go and join the girl dangling dead on the cliff. With my knife, I slashed at the hissing vine wrapped around my wrist. My heart beat double time as panic took hold.

My feet gave way, and I tumbled down a few more feet, snapping to a halt when my toes hit a narrow rock protruding from the wall. Spinning, I attacked the plant around my wrist.

Feral growled then started making his way back to where I sawed at the band. It wouldn't give way.

"There's a…" I shot out, terror lifting my voice.

"What?" He smacked a snake-vine wavering toward him, and it flipped in the other direction.

I nudged my head at the girl, unable to look. "She died here, on the cliff. Not long ago."

"Fuck," he said, staring past me. He held out his hand. "Let me have the knife."

Did I dare?

"I'll help you, and then I'll…" His gaze drifted her way.

"Cut her free?" I said. She deserved that, rather than be left staring blankly toward the sea.

My hand ached and my fingers had lost all feeling. Anxiety sliced through my belly. I was gonna die here like the girl, and there wasn't anything I could do about it. I hated feeling helpless.

"Why not leave me here?" I gasped out as I clung to the wall. "This thing will tighten and my hand will fall off. You can watch me drop to the beach and be eaten by killer centipedes. Mission accomplished. I'll be dead, and you'll be able to get on with your life." Prison life, but he'd have his vengeance.

"Told you I'd give you a chance." His face stilled. "One she didn't get."

Handing over the knife, I braced myself on the tiny rock ledge as he sawed on the vine, his face containing an intensity I hadn't seen in him before. This couldn't be a concern for my wellbeing. If I knew Feral, he wanted to ensure *he* was the one who eliminated me, not random plants on the side of a cliff.

Leaning closer, he continued to attack the vine. Others snapped out, trying to gain purchase on his arms and legs, but he gouged them with the knife, and they reeled backward.

"It's not loosening," I said, trying not to let defeat leak into my voice. I'd barely started this test and it looked like I was failing already. Would sunset—assuming I lasted that long—find me dangling here, a tasty niblet for the centipedes or the shady creature hiding in the woods?

"Don't give up yet," he said.

"I'm not," I snapped, but my voice held no kick. "Sorry. I'm just…scared."

"Who isn't?"

"Not you."

"You don't know me." Steel grated in his voice.

"Thank you for helping me." I couldn't hold back the words. While I didn't like leaning on him even for this, I was grateful he was here. Whatever happened, I wouldn't face it alone, like she had.

"Don't go soft on me now," he said, sounding too close to kind.

"Only in your dreams, feral *boy*."

His fingers stilled. "You don't know a damn thing about my dreams." He attacked the vine with renewed vigor, as if he was eager to get this over with and flee.

"I imagine you dream about my death," I said, a snide edge coming through in my words. It was a protective mechanism or a wall I needed to put up to protect myself from him. "One that's as painful as possible. Am I right?"

Ignoring my comment, he hacked at the vine. It snapped as the hissing strand severed, and my hand jerked free. The cut vegetation loosened from around my wrist and dropped, tumbling down the hillside like a dead garden snake.

"Thanks," I said.

"Take a second to catch your breath," he said, his attention focused on nearby plants weaving in the air. For now, they were far enough away they couldn't grab onto us. A quick look up told me we could work our way around them to reach the top. "I'll go…" His gaze had fallen on my right upper arm, where my sleeve had slipped partway toward the shoulder. He frowned as I twisted my hand to make the material slide back to my wrist. "No."

"No, you won't cut her free?"

"It's not that. It's…" His face solidifying to stone again, and his attention dropped toward the girl. "Nothing. I'm mistaken."

Okay.

Confused, I clung to the cliffside while he made his way across the wall.

I'd expected him to sever her tie and let her finish her

fall, but, while new vines attacked him, he climbed down the side of the cliff, taking her to the sand, where he kicked centipedes out of the way and buried her.

This feral boy made me question every decision I'd made in life.

Chapter 9

Returning to where I waited, he solemnly handed over my knife. I pocketed it and then turned to face the sea. As waves lapped on the shore, I wished the girl well.

But we couldn't stay here. I pivoted and attacked the cliff, climbing higher. Not because I didn't need a longer break, but because being close to him unsettled me. I'd come here with one purpose. Two purposes, if I fulfilled my side of the Seeker's bargain. Neither of them included odd feelings for someone eager to kill me.

As I climbed, I watched for plants that looked like the snake bush. A plant-army, they kept attacking, but I was able to dodge out of their reach.

Feral turned them into punching bags, smacking them away when they dared to draw near.

Thirty feet left to go, but I had to move to my left to avoid a cluster of hissing vines straining to reach me.

Fifteen feet. Move to the right then left again.

Feral stuck with me, just below as if covering the rear. He'd only watch out for me until it was his turn to slit my throat.

Five feet. Only a tiny bit more to go.

Hauling on a clump of grass, I yanked myself over the edge and flopped on my belly on the top. While I caught my breath and my muscles screamed, Feral dropped onto the ground beside me. He rolled onto his back and stared at the sky.

I'd helped him on the beach, and he'd helped me here on the wall. We were even.

I jumped to my feet, prepared to burst into a flee. I'd cross the field and hit the wood path at a dead run and... Not sure why, I paused before I'd gone a few feet. I couldn't resist turning and reaching out, offering him a hand up off the ground. Talk about aiding and abetting the enemy.

As if it sensed my floundering weakness, my manacle shot fire along the surface, an overcharged glow worm secured around my wrist. Gold and red sparks flickered onto the ground by my sneakers.

"Thanks, but no thanks." Pushing my hand aside, Feral rose to his feet and looked around.

I liked that he hadn't taken me up on my offer because it suggested we were back where we'd started, with him eager to deliver death and me trying to evade it. Not a cloudy scenario where we needed each other.

He squinted toward the prison and, when his hands landed on his hips, he posed with his shoulders stiffening into military precision.

By the fae. Was I about to be exposed to mansplaining? Or, in his case, faesplaining?

"From now on, we should—" he began in a superior tone.

While we'd been climbing, the sun had moved across the sky.

It winked out of existence.

"Isn't that convenient," I said. "Are we supposed to take the rest of the tests in the dark?"

"I don't think so." Feral snarled and paced back and forth in front of me. "This… It could be a trap or the next challenge. One thing is sure. Without light, we can't see what's coming at us. If we're wise, we'll stay here and start out again when it's light."

"But we have to reach the prison."

"We won't make it there at all if something grabs us in the dark."

"You're right." I frowned as I glanced around. "So, we wait *here* until morning?"

"That's what I'm going to do." He scuffed his sneaker across the dirt, revealing ledge beneath. "You're welcome to do what you want."

Take on the next test by myself? After what happened on the beach and then the cliffs, I might do better with Feral at my side, as weird as that sounded.

"I imagine it's as safe here as anywhere else," he said, squinting toward the woods which had gone eerily silent. No insects and no night bird calls broke the stillness. My skin crawled as if something watched.

"I guess it's better here than on the beach." Probably. "Will the vines reach up this far?"

"They didn't follow us over the edge, which leads me to believe we've completed that part of the test."

"Stopping here could be part of the next challenge. What if you're wrong about waiting until morning?"

"I'm never wrong." He said it without a hint of conceit in his voice.

What would it be like to have that amount of confidence in myself? While I was happy to jump into anything, especially if it helped someone else, I second-guessed my actions all the time.

"If it makes you feel better," he said with a hint of a sneer. So much for us having a reasonable conversation. "We can take turns sleeping. Then we won't miss anything sneaking up on us."

"You'll trust me to watch while you sleep?"

"No more than you'll trust me." His lips squished together. "One wrong move on your part and it's over."

"Threats, threats, threats. Just so you know, it's getting tiring."

"Never let down your guard."

I snorted and propped my knuckles on my hip. "No chance of that around you."

His mouth curled up, but his gaze remained sly. "Except when you sleep."

"As if I'll be able to do that now?"

"Tell you what; we can call a temporary truce." He extended his hand. "We'll watch out for each other tonight and return to being sworn enemies in the morning."

"Why would you do that?"

"I need to sleep as much as you."

"You also need me to finish the tests."

"I can do this on my own."

"Like you handled the bugs on the beach? You weren't doing so well then."

"We've…" He growled. "Okay, so we *do* need each other."

I chuckled. "Don't like the idea much, do you?"

"Would you?"

"Nope. But I'm tired, and I smacked my head on the deck. My brains must be scrambled. Otherwise, I'd never consider something like this."

His hand nudged forward. "So, a truce until morning?"

I'd be stupid to fully trust him. However, I could

remain half-awake. If he made a move toward me, I'd butt my head into him and run.

Reaching out, I tapped his fingers, the closest I wanted to get to him.

I dropped onto the ground.

Overhead, the moons rose, and a scattering of stars twinkled in the indigo sky. My belly growled but it would have to gnaw on itself. Short of eating dirt or grass, there wasn't anything around worth sampling.

He sat as well, facing me, keeping his distance.

"Sleep," he said. "I'll take first watch. Nights are short here."

"How short?"

In the forest, a muffled yip was followed by stomping and a piercing shriek of something brought down by a hunter. Tucking my legs up, I wrapped my arms around them and shivered.

"About six hours."

"Three for each of us, then."

"Less than that the longer you keep talking."

I huffed and dropped down onto my side and tried to find a comfortable spot on the ground, but there was no hope for that. More yips in the forest didn't encourage rest, either. I kept waiting for the next shriek.

And Feral. He stared with a puzzled expression on his face. How could he watch for threats if he spent all his time looking at me?

I thought I'd lay there forever, my eyes trained on him while he remained focused on me, but a wave of exhaustion washed over me and dragged me under…

I startled awake to a hand landing on my shoulder.

"Your turn," Feral said softly.

"You see anything?"

"Nothing. It's…" He gazed toward the woods. "There's something there. It's watching. But it didn't come near."

The tiny hairs on my neck lifted. "Creepy."

"Yeah. But I…"

"What?"

"I watched out for you so you could sleep in peace."

"Careful or I'll start expecting sweetness and flowers."

He snorted but he didn't turn snarky, proving I was seeing a side of Feral that would disappear come morning and the end of our truce.

Sitting up, I stretched my ice-cold body, hoping to drive enough blood through my veins to thaw myself out. He watched me, the weight of his stare tracing my body as I moved. It should creep me out but didn't. Maybe because he hadn't taken advantage of me being asleep to… I don't know. Roll me off the cliff?

"When it happens, it won't be that easy," he said softly.

"What?"

"You know what."

"You a mind reader, now?" I drawled.

"If our positions were reversed, I'd strongly consider it."

"*You* might have murderous tendencies," I said, keeping the edge out of my voice, because I wouldn't be the one to break our truce. "I, however, do not."

"That remains to be seen." He lay down on the ground a few feet away, facing me. "Wake me up with the sun starts to rise."

"I will. And…"

He peered up at me. "What?"

"I'll watch out for you, too."

A pause stretched between us, as if he chewed on my words. Finally, he dipped his head. "Thanks."

I nodded.

His breathing slowed as his body relaxed into sleep. Just like every other guy in the world, he snored, though it was soft and low, not throaty or irritating.

About twenty minutes into his share of the night, he scooted closer, shifting until his back rested against my outstretched thigh. He did it because he was cold, nothing more. And when he rolled over to face me and dropped his head onto my lap, it also meant nothing. It felt damn strange, however.

I guarded our truce, and when something crept close, through the nearby grass, I hefted a stick and waved it in the air. Whatever it was grunted and stomped in the other direction.

I must've drifted off, because I dreamed Feral changed. His face shifted.

No…*we* shifted.

This had to be a dream because I stood on a flat plain covered with tall strands of late-season, tan grass for as far as my eye could see. An opaque, ghostly creature sat on his haunches beside me, his shoulders coming to my waist level and his tawny fur ruffling in the breeze.

An Eerie. Like the wexal cat, the mix of saber-toothed tiger and wraith should only exist in legend. This one, however, was very much alive, if still in spirit form.

He tipped its head back, and his brown eyes met mine.

Feral.

Those teeth…

I was fortunate he hadn't shifted fully in the court-house. But, then, Eeries only changed in their dreams. Except, Feral had partly shifted in real life. How?

A sound, low and muffled, tugged me away from the plain and back to the Darkwater Prison trial.

While I'd dreamed—traveled to another universe?—dawn had arrived, a pinkish haze on the horizon. When I tapped Feral's back, he stiffened and, lifting his head, peered up at me.

He scrambled off me and rose to his feet, then stood over me, glaring. "What did you do?"

I lifted my eyebrows. "Huh?" Jumping to my feet, I stretched again, ignoring his stare. He wasn't watching for any other reason than to ferret out my vulnerabilities.

"You did do something. Otherwise I never would've put my head on your lap."

"Quite a stretch to think I made it happen. Why the fae would I want you to do anything like that?"

"Good question." He shook his finger at me, and I wanted to smack it away but resisted. "I'm watching you."

"Nothing new about that," I said calmly.

His cheeks reddening for no apparent reason, and he turned to face the sea.

"At least I better understand your fangs," I said.

"What is that supposed to mean?"

I shrugged but my smile teased across my lips. Perhaps I'd keep my knowledge of his abilities to myself. I could pull it out when I needed it most.

A howl pierced the air; close enough the shriek rippled across my skin. I whirled to face the forest. Sunlight parted the trees and stabbed light across the field. At least I'd see whatever was coming before it leaped.

Shadows engulfed the sprawling stone prison fortress sitting on the top of a broad hill beyond. My shoulders drooped when I took in the distance I still had to travel. Running in a straight line, I might make it there in fifteen minutes but to get there, I'd have to cross a broad, over-grown field and, if it was like the rest of this place, I'd meet up with dangerous creatures. And, per my grandma, "beings older than the fae".

Something with glowing red eyes watched from inside

the tree line, on the right side of the path leading through the woods and to the prison. A shady thing, it blended in with the thick landscape around it. Except, those eyes... They—

An ear-piercing scream shattered the silence, coming from that direction, and the tops of the trees shifted. My mouth went dry. If it traveled through the canopy, it could drop down on me while I was on the path.

"How fast can you run?" I asked Feral, contemplating the field.

He chuckled. "Faster than you." The look he shot me contained too much smugness. "But since I'm a gentleman, I'll let you go first." His arm swept forward. "Go for it. You blaze the trail through the field. I'll be right behind you."

"A gentleman, huh?"

He smirked. "I'm practical."

"Conniving."

"So much for your truce."

"It's morning."

After scrunching my nose at him, I tiptoed forward, my sneakers snagging on the deep grass. It enveloped me to my waist, the tops of the grass brushing my hips. Seed pods swayed in the breeze. I feathered my fingers across them and studied the area, waiting for what would come next. Rolling my shoulders to work out the kinks, I got ready to bolt.

"You're not going very fast," Feral said from right behind me. "Thought you were eager to reach the prison, where you can hide?"

Tension heightening my nerves to screech, I whirled around and glared at him. "Back off, Feral."

"My name's not Feral."

"If I knew your real name, I'd use it."

"If someone knows your name, they can control your power."

I tapped one of his tennas. "That's controlling your power, influencer boy."

He lifted one eyebrow. "You know I'm not a boy."

For damn sure, I did, but I'd never admit it.

He was too much a man.

Spinning, I darted across the field. He gave chase, keeping up with me until he drew level then passed me with ease.

"Damn, you're slow," he taunted over his shoulder. "Didn't they teach you in Seeker's school not to walk when kertins could be on your tail?"

While I wasn't any more eager than him to meet up with that thing in the woods, I was just as unwilling to be left behind. Growling, I ran after him.

"What's a kertin?" I pushed for speed, trying to keep up with his long strides. *Kertin* sounded like *kitten* but they wouldn't send kittens after us, would they?

"Something that should only exist in a myth but here we are," he said. Bellowing, he leaped up, stretching his right leg forward. As he soared, he pointed downward. "That's a kertin. Don't let it bite."

Something latched onto my ankle, and I tumbled to the ground.

Chapter 10

My chin smacked on the ground, and my breath woofed from my lungs. I flipped onto my back and ripped something off my leg.

Kitty-like fuzzy, the beasty about a foot long had plush, tan fur. Its papery, bat-ish wings smacked against my hands while its claws sank into my arm.

I bit back a shriek while the kertin struggled in my grip. It struck out, trying to bite me, but I shifted my hands and shook it. "Don't!"

Feral's guttural cry suggested he was wrangling with his own kertin, too.

If they had wings, why did they hide in the grass? Except… We wouldn't have come in this direction if we'd seen them. We would've sought a different way around the area. Not through the woods, though. We needed to avoid the woods.

The kertin's claws dug in, and I ripped it off my arm before it sunk its teeth into my flesh. I wanted to fling it away but knew it would fly back at me with a vengeance.

Feral's warning about not letting it bite rang out in my mind.

Climbing to my feet, I kept my hands around its skinny neck and tossing it from one hand to the other to avoid its gnashing teeth. When its fangs grazed my arm, I pressed my thumbs into its throat. With a toss of my head, I flung my unruly hair off my face and glared at it.

So, okay, it was cute. But deadly, according to Feral.

"What happens if it bites?" I asked him, over my shoulder.

"You'll sleep…for…" He grunted. "About an hour."

I was tired, but I had a feeling falling asleep in the deep grass would put me in more danger.

"Once you're asleep, they call…their parents," he said. His coarse growls told me he was still trying to subdue his kertin.

"I assume the parents are bigger," I said.

"Much bigger."

"Not interested in becoming a meal."

"Nope."

Blood trickled down my arm from where the kertin's claws had sunk deep.

Arms outstretched, Feral twirled and twisted through the grass as if he and his snarling, snapping kertin were engaged in a bizarre dance. Laughable if it wasn't so scary.

Taking advantage of my distraction, my kertin slashed my hand with its claws.

Fed up, I snarled and shook it. "You like your head where it is, buddy? 'Cuz I'm beginning to think removing it would make my life a hell of a lot simpler." I dug my thumbs deeper into its throat. "One flick and pop, the lower part of you will be flapping around in the grass, while I'll be kicking your head off the cliff."

The beastie stopped struggling and stared up at me

with tears shining in its big orange eyes. Its silky fur fluttered in the wind, and its papery wings drooped.

By the fae, what was it doing? I felt sad about being mean to it.

"Look," I said, trying to sound reasonable, but really, how could I feel bad for a creature who'd slashed my hand open and was determined to set me up as a buffet for its parents? "Behave, and I'll let you go."

The kertin stopped wiggling and its teeth retracted into its gums. Neat trick. I flicked it up into the air, and it flew toward the forest instead of dive-bombing me with its fangs bared.

"Keep going," I shouted after it.

With a roll of my eyes, I stomped past Feral, who continued to wrangle and flail through the grass with a kertin clutched in his outstretched hands.

"Stop playing with it," I said. "We don't have time for games." Okay, my words came out smug, but jeez, he deserved it after his recent behavior. "Get control of your kertin. Time's awastin'."

I savored the amazement blooming on his face and injected some attitude into my stride. Always needed to keep a guy on his toes, even if he wasn't romance material.

Trying not to come across too conceited, I strutted toward the path, kicking the tall grass out of my way. With three tests down, there was a good chance I'd survive long enough to make it to the prison.

Feral caught up, puffing from his efforts. Kertin-less, thank the fae.

"What did you do with yours?" I asked, snapping my head in all directions, waiting for more batty-things to attack. If they were related to the centipedes, there would be others lurking, poised to pounce.

"Buried it."

I frowned, remembering mine crying. "In the ground?"

"Under a pile of brush."

"You left it enough air to breathe, right?"

He grabbed my arm, slowing me down. "You're worried about the kertin? It was clawing me." Twisting, he showed off scratches on his right forearm. "It almost bit me."

"Nothing I wouldn't do, given the chance."

He snorted. Not a snide snort but one that came out like suppressed laughter.

"Gotcha," I said, pulling my arm from his grip. Touch between him and I was not a good combination. Cursed tingles. They suggested I was *attracted* to Feral, which wouldn't do. I didn't like him. I'd never like him.

He planned to chop off my head. Or something like that.

"Just so you know, I didn't hurt it," he said. "I only put it out of commission for a while."

"Left it for predators, didn't you?" I said to irk him.

When he shook his head, I knew he was shaking off my teasing. "What did you do with yours? And, hey..." He glanced around. "You see any more?"

"Not so far. I spoke reasonably with mine. Asked it to leave."

"Threatened to pop off its head, didn't you?" Restored to his regular, irritating self, his lofty, snooty tone came shining through.

"You overheard me talking to it," I grated out. "You didn't *know*."

"You sure?"

Something smacked into the back of my head. Scrambling through my hair, it worked its way down to my neck. While I squirmed and tried to knock it off, needle-like claws dug into my spine.

Feral turned and released a scowl. "What are you doing? We need to get going."

I drove to the ground and slammed onto my back. Bucking, I tried to crush the creature, but its claws dug in. Deeper, and they'd sever my spine.

Lifting myself, I plunged back down, jarring my brain.

Feral returned to stand over me, staring down with a bemused expression on his face.

"If you ask nicely," he said. "I'll be happy to smack you in the back of the head. I'll do a better job than you are."

"Kertin," I bellowed. "Digging into my back!"

"Why didn't you say so?" He sighed as if greatly put upon. "Roll over, and I'll take care of it for you."

I sprang over, onto my stomach, and Feral wrenched the kertin off my back.

As I rose to my feet, I snagged a stick off the ground. No more dancing around. The kertin had brought war to me, and I was more than ready to battle.

He tossed the creature aside like he didn't expect it to attack again, which it did, spinning in the air and diving over him, toward my head.

I lifted my stick and glared. "Come for me, baby. Go for it." I'd smack it so hard, it would fly past the two moons.

It skidded to a stop mid-flight and hovered, wings flapping while it turned on the waterworks.

"Don't even try that on me again," I snarled, hefting the stick higher. "Not fallin' for it twice."

The kertin whimpered as I wiggled my spine, assessing for damage from the latest attack. The slices stung and blood trickled down my back.

"See? All set." Feral said with a smirk. He fisted his hip again. Damn arrogant jerk. "As you pointed out moments ago, you spoke with them; they'll leave us alone now."

"Incoming," I shouted as two kertin flew toward Feral. That would teach him to mock.

He spun and tried to snatch them from the air.

I brandished my stick and took aim as one of the kertins skimmed past Feral and zoomed toward me. Like with the other, it slowed. About time these beasties learned who was boss.

Around us, a flock of kertins rose from the grass, a horde of supersized nips stirred by us leaping around.

As they dove at us, my stick whistled through the air. Feral leaped and grabbed one in each hand. He squeezed until they stopped struggling then dropped them on the ground. I couldn't tell if they were dead or passed out but as I rushed past him, I didn't stop to see if they needed CPR.

"I'm outta here," I said, keeping my stick aloft while edging toward the forest path. "You?"

"Hell, yeah."

We raced across the grass with more kertins zipping up from the grass to join the cloud diving at us from behind. Feral kept snatching them from the air and squishing them, and I scored numerous hits with my stick. Relentless, the creatures kept coming.

Our breathing ragged, we hit the paved path.

What seemed like a thousand kertins shrieked and flew toward us.

Chapter 11

We bolted forward.

My heart roared in my chest, and I wondered how much more my body could take before it gave up.

When the kertins reached the path, they smacked into an invisible barrier. As one, they dropped and hit the ground. Rising to their clawed feet, they lifted and wove through the air as if drunk, before diving into the deep grass, disappearing like dust in a gale-force wind.

Slowing my pace, I breathed out a sigh of relief.

I'd started forward again when Feral put his arm out in front of me, holding me back.

"Let me go first," he said.

"So that thing in the woods can pick me off while I'm straggling behind you?"

"Sure. That's why." His smile didn't reach his eyes. "Or maybe I'm actually looking out for you."

"You're the one who said the temporary truce was over." I brushed past him. "And who said I needed you to watch my back. I don't suddenly need a hero."

"Good, because you won't find one in me." He caught up and strode a few steps ahead of me.

"Honest," I said.

"Determined."

We moved in silence, and I waited for the shadowy beast to descend. Each section of this island had offered a new challenge, and the path would be no different.

This was likely a taste of what I'd find in the prison.

"This Reformatory Challenge," I said. "Any idea what to expect?"

"From what I've heard, it's a bit like this. A series of tests."

Great. This wasn't going well so far, although I was still alive. I'd always been the one doing the saving, yet Feral had come through for me twice already. Each time I trusted him could be the last, the moment he'd grin and announce the game was over. I'd yet to find a way to prove I hadn't killed his mother, so that couldn't be it.

"What happens to inmates who don't make it through?" I asked.

"Don't take it unless you're confident you'll survive."

"You know I'm determined to survive."

"That's what all the others who failed said."

I paused on the path, frowning. "They died?" What kind of place was this?

"Most. A few get sent back to the prison."

While nobody lived forever, the facility must have a limit to how many inmates they could house. What a grim way to keep the numbers at a manageable level.

Frowning, I kept walking, hovering behind Feral.

A deep mesh of forest grew up to the path and arched over it, creating a gloomy tunnel. While we'd been busy fighting off the kertins, the sun had fully risen. Light barely penetrated the darkness in the forest, however.

Damn creepy place. I couldn't wait to reach the end of the path.

"Why would anyone want to get into the Reformatory, then?" I asked.

"Rumor has it it's a way out."

"Of the prison?" I hadn't heard this before, but my grandfather had said there were options…

"Yup."

Maybe I wouldn't need to fulfill my blood bond promise to get out of prison. "I assume Reformatory means it's a reform school." They must rehabilitate those who made it past the initial testing. "How long are the students in school?"

"One year."

"And they release them after that?"

"So I've heard."

"Do you know anyone who's done it?"

"Nope."

"So maybe the rumor isn't true."

He shrugged. "Then why bother creating a Reformatory?"

"Good question." I was determined to discover the answer.

"Stats for those who make it through the test are worse than for those who are dropped off on the island," he said. "Thought you should know that before you commit to taking the Challenge."

"I'm doing it regardless."

He tossed an odd look at me over his shoulder. If I didn't know better, I'd read interest. Must be curiosity, however. "Why?"

I wouldn't share the whole truth with him. "I don't want to stay here forever."

"Neither do I."

"Which means…" I didn't say it. No need to. Despite working together to reach this point in the test, the rules between us hadn't changed.

He nodded and kept walking.

I stared into the forest, wondering how the next beast would attack. While I'd only caught shadows, it had appeared big. How could I fight something I could barely see?

I gritted my teeth, tightened my fingers around my stick, and pulled my knife. The weapons wouldn't be much in a fight with an enormous creature, but I had nothing else.

Something thundered deep in the forest, making trees fall. The wind groaned, and leaves shuddered. Unease skittered like spiders down my spine, and sweat beaded on my upper lip. I wiped it away and watched for movement.

Feral kept plodding ahead of me, going faster whenever I tried to get close.

The rank scent of fermented vegetation drifted from the woods, carrying the bitter taint of defeat. The scent stuck in my throat like a wad of gum.

"Turn back," Feral hissed.

I ignored him. Walking faster, I tried to catch up, but he started jogging. Awesome. Be that way.

Huffing, I looked around, trying to identify any movement in the gloomy forest, but couldn't see farther than twenty feet. The trees seemed to move, as if they could uproot and scurry sideways.

With each second that passed without an attack, my anxiety grew. My belly twitched, ready to explode.

"Why don't you take the cliffs to the beach and let the vines hang you," Feral said.

"Don't do that," I growled. Jeez it was hard enough

waiting for the next assault. He didn't need to make things worse with taunts.

Grunting in disgust, his arms splayed wide. "Don't do what?"

Sure. Pretend he wasn't playing tricks with me. It stung, because I had been wondering if he was softening toward me.

I was out of my mind to pursue this. Should I turn back? If I could make it back to the beach, I might be able to bribe the ogres into taking me back to my world. Then I could ping my grandfather and beg his help getting out of this mess.

It was mean of him to suggest I end my life. My anger at him grew, shoving aside my nervousness.

"Hold on." I grabbed his arm, but he wrenched away and kept going, stomping up the path leading to the prison. "I know what you're doing. You're trying to influence me." What a coward. Didn't want to do it himself or get his hands dirty. Just make me do it to myself.

I stomped my foot and fumed.

He lifted his hands, and fire rippled across his tennas. "These babies won't let me do magic."

"I'm not returning to the cliffs," I said stiffly. I couldn't face the vines, not again.

His lips twisted. "Seems like a wise plan. I approve."

"I don't need your approval."

He rolled his eyes. "That's not the impression I'm getting."

"Maybe we should be quiet. That screaming thing is around here somewhere." I peered into the woods again but still didn't detect movement. Shivers rippled across my skin, telling me to run, to get out of the forest as soon as possible. My instincts had always been right.

"I'm only talking because you're talking," Feral said in a smug tone. He started up the path again.

Despite my efforts, he remained a step ahead of me. It was beyond infuriating.

"I'm trying not to talk at all since we don't want to draw attention," I said. "I think you need to do the same."

"Go drown yourself in the sea," he mumbled. "It wants you. Needs you."

I raced ahead, wheeled around to block him and, brandishing my stick, glared.

He stopped and put his fists on his hips in his same old, irritating manner he'd used too many times since I met him. "You always such an asshole?" he said before I could rise to his posturing challenge.

"Only on Sundays."

"It's Monday."

"How would I know what day of the week it is? This is your world, not mine."

He stomped right up to me and shoved his face down, close to mine. "Leave my mother out of this. Bad enough you're her murderer. No need to slam through the good memories I still have of her."

"Professor Trarion was a great teacher. She was fun and kind. I'd never say anything mean about her."

"No, you'd just stab her in the back." His gaze shot to the pocket where I'd returned my knife. "Did you use that?"

Like they'd give it to me after I'd use it to kill someone? Fuming, I smashed my foot down on the path. "I told you I didn't kill her."

"You were convicted by the Council."

"I was framed."

"By who?"

My gaze darted from his. "I can't say." Damn blood

bond promise. It kept me from pushing out the words that might help in my defense.

"Why would anyone want to frame you?" he asked.

Great question. And why did the Master Seeker want me to kill Brodin? "Maybe that's what we need to find out."

"I have no interest in doing anything with you," he snarled as he shoved past me and marched up the path. His fists remained clenched at his sides, and I swore smoke poured from his ears. "And stop saying horrible things about my mother."

"I'm not! I just told you I liked her."

"There's a staircase that leads to the top of the tallest turret," he said. "Climb up and jump off the roof."

"I'm not doing it," I shouted at his back. "Where do you get off—?"

"Just..." The gaze he turned my way contained a wealth of rage, enough I'd combust if I was made of paper. "Is that how it was? You enjoyed the feel of the blade sinking into her flesh? Knowing she was hurting, scared?" His voice dropped to almost nothing, and I swore his eyes shimmered. "They said as she died, she whispered my name. And you took pleasure in making it happen." His hands lifted, and he stalked toward me. "No more chances. It's over."

"I'm not..." I backed up until I was engulfed in the woods and my feet crunched on dead leaves. Blinking fast, I lifted my stick.

I couldn't blame him for being upset. If he'd killed my mom, there'd be no first chances from me. He'd already be dead. But to taunt me into taking my life was despicable. My anger with him, with this situation, burned through me, a lit fuse approaching a pile of dynamite. Fury combined with frustration inside me. My knife. I pulled it from my pocket, and it felt good in my hand. The blade popped free at my touch. I stood tall. Strong. Just try me. Come close, and I'll—

Something slithered through the woods behind him. A glassy shade flitting from behind one tree to another. It clung to the bark and, peering around a tree, watched.

It *plotted*.

"You didn't tell me to kill myself," I whispered.

Feral's hands, reaching for my neck, paused. He frowned and shook his head.

The hand with my knife dropped to my side and I stepped around him and left the woods, returning to the path.

Puzzled, he followed.

I didn't stop walking until I stood in the center of the paved surface. I turned to find Feral close enough, I could feel his warmth radiating off his skin.

He smelled good. Like a drink of hot cocoa while I was curled up by the fire with a good book.

"Trust me this once," I said softly.

His shrug shouted uncertainty.

Subtly peering over my shoulder, I watched as the shade crept closer.

"If you want to live," I said. "Cover your ears and run."

————————————

Chapter 12

————————————

Feral and I rushed up the path. Our feet jarred the surface, and our breathing grew ragged.

I prayed we'd be out of the woods soon. There was no way we could last against this latest threat.

Behind us, the creature shrieked, thwarted.

How many prisoners before us had given into its commands? If I hadn't been peeved with Feral, I might've listened to the voice. Because I did feel bad about Professor Trarion, and I was more than uncertain about my upcoming mission.

The voice had been persuasive.

We rounded a bend in the path and the woods split, revealing a broad expanse of grass that meandered up to the tall, imposing prison building.

A fence and a gate stood between us and the entrance, but it wasn't high. If I needed to, I could climb over it with ease. Simple and decorative, it was made of wrought iron, and it encircled the three-story stone building that stretched forever in either direction like a pretty bracelet. This just showed how incorrect appearances could be.

As we fled from the path and started up the hill, our paces slowed.

"You think that's it?" I asked. "Or will it follow?"

"We're here," Feral said with excitement in his voice. "We passed the final test."

Did he plan to kill me, then? Why else would he sound eager?

Feeling assured the shade wouldn't creep into the light, I slowed to a walk and elbowed him in the ribs, making him woof. "See? Told you to trust me. In case you didn't figure it out…" Okay, a bit of conceit came through in my voice. But I'd been an equal partner in this challenge. Two for him, two for me. We were even. "It wasn't you or me back there saying those things."

Hands fisting, he growled. "That thing played with my mind."

Rather ironic. "It's not fun having someone toy with you, is it?"

The look he slanted me led me to believe he'd seen my point, though he didn't comment on how close I'd hit my mark. "The creature told you to kill yourself, didn't it?"

I dragged my gaze from his, not eager to give him a chance to read my secrets. "Yeah. It made sense I'd believe it was you. I thought you'd found a way past your tennas to use your Influencer skapti on me."

"And you didn't say horrible things about my mother or tell me how much you enjoyed killing her."

"I wouldn't say anything like that, and I've told you already I didn't do it." He'd never believe me. I needed to save my energy, stop defending myself, and focus instead of avoiding him. Once I reached the Reformatory, I wouldn't see him again.

"We have no reason to trust each other."

He was right. Whenever I was around him, I'd have to

worry about when it was time to make me pay for my supposed crime. That would be the only constant in our future. We stood on opposite sides of a cavern we'd never dare cross. There was no meeting in the middle.

"It's best if we don't trust each other," I said softly.

"You're right." Regret did not shine in his eyes.

At least I knew where I stood.

Rubbing my chest, I turned away from him and approached the gate. He stayed right behind me, no striding ahead to blaze the trail. What had changed?

We stopped in front of the gate, and I looked for a buzzer or a bell, something I could use to let those inside know we were here. Such an odd way to be sent to prison. But who'd want to remain outside the gate? The night would fall, and I was confident even worse things would be ready to attack.

Two huge square posts flanked the arched gate, and thick, coiled basiliques had been mounted on top, their heads pointed toward the sky and their wings coiled tightly on their backs. As we got closer, their eyes opened, becoming slices of gold on their elongated faces. In unison, they unfurled their wings and stretched outward, before recoiling the leathery segments onto their backs. They slithered down to the ground and straightened, standing at least twice my height. If they chose, they could snatch us up in their teeth and gulp us down with one swallow.

I backed away, my mouth going dry.

Thick bands of tan and brown encircled their bodies. The bands rippled, and the creatures hissed. Smoke hissed from their jagged-toothed mouths.

Feral nudged my back. "Don't stand there gawking." He peered over his shoulder before his sarcastic gaze met mine. "Unless you're up for another round with the forest test."

"I'll pass." I leaned close to him as we approached the basiliques. "I've heard this island is so terrifying, they don't need to lock up the prisoners. If anyone's lucky enough to make it from the prison to the sea, something there will get you there instead." I'd seen a few of those "somethings" already.

"It's true," he said. "The island and the water around it is teeming with beasts."

"Yet we didn't have much trouble getting here today."

"We didn't meet up with the real threats. This was a structured, magical course."

"Yet inmates fail." Like the girl on the cliff.

"A weeding, they call it," he said.

"She was a person, not something to be yanked from the ground and tossed aside."

His lips curled down. "You don't need to tell me that."

"You both have completed the course," the snake on the right hissed out, drawing my attention.

"What if we don't want to go inside?" I asked Feral.

"Your eagerness, I understand. Where I go, you go."

He huffed.

"You're here to kill me, so it makes sense you'll trot behind me through the gate. But me…"

Feral's eyes drilled into mine as if seeking my every secret. "Why didn't you run when you had the chance? You could've left me while I was asleep."

"We had a truce."

He shrugged but said nothing.

"I get it," I said, my throat tight. "You assumed I'd bail on you."

No hiding his wince.

"Just because you might do something like that doesn't mean—"

"But I didn't."

I frowned.

"You slept, and I watched out for you."

Why? It would've been the perfect time to kill me. Because, let's face it, there wasn't anything I could do or say that would convince him I hadn't killed his mother.

"What's driving you to this location?" he said as if he truly needed to hear my answer.

"I… I can't say."

His face tightened. "Okay. I get it. You don't need to share anything with me."

"I can't."

"Won't."

"Why the fae does it matter?" I shouted.

"I don't understand why you wouldn't try to hide from me rather than go inside where you'll be trapped."

"What makes you think I'm eager to walk into the prison?"

His lips pursed and his brow furrowed. "A hunch, I guess. But I'm right, aren't I?"

"We all have our agendas."

"What's yours?"

"Nothing you need to know."

"You want into the Reformatory, which is the only way out, but I think it's more than that. Is there someone there you're eager to find?"

My skin prickled. He was getting too close. Rather than reveal something I'd rather not, I said nothing.

"What's at the Reformatory?" he said.

Peeling my gaze from his, I turned to the basilique on the left. It indurated, its tongue flicking in and out. "Nothing."

The skin around Feral's eyes scrunched. "I'll be watching you. I'm curious to see how you'll try to prove your innocence."

"It's impossible."

"Then you'll—"

"You both may enter," the basilique I'd been studying said in a rich monotone.

The gates slowly creaked open.

I was outta here. No more evading Feral's prying questions. Yeah, I had an agenda. Find Dad. Obtain the missing part of me. Decide whether I had the guts to kill someone.

Other than the murder, all paths led to the Reformatory.

"Pass at your own risk, Tria," the basilique on the right said.

Turning, it slithered back up to the post and stretched its wings again before recoiling them. It settled back into its original position, morphing into stone.

The basilique on the left bowed its head to Feral. "Pass at your own risk, Brodin."

Chapter 13

I gaped at him. "*You're* Brodin?"

How was this possible?

He'd tried to kill me at the courthouse, because he'd "run into" me at the Academy then saw me fleeing into the woods.

"Names have power, remember?" he said. In his case, yes.

The Master Seeker said Brodin hadn't committed his crime yet, but he would. He'd known if I "murdered" Professor Trarion, her son would do something to ensure he was sent to Darkwater Prison, where he could seek revenge.

He wanted to kill me, yet I was supposed to kill him. What a cluster…

Coiling around the post, the second basilique returned to its pedestal and solidified back into stone again. The two creatures stared forward, oblivious to us standing on the ground beneath them.

"You preferred me calling you Feral?" I asked.

He rolled his shoulders. "I don't care what you

call me."

I blinked, totally stunned about this. *He was Brodin.* How the fae could I even consider killing him? Yeah, he irritated me, but being a jerk wasn't a valid enough reason to murder someone.

Like any other time I felt unsettled, I reached for my selection stone set in the pendant I wore around my neck. When students arrived at an Academy, they chose a stone —and the stone chose them—as a place to store their magic.

I sought threads of power, the strands all the Elite used to amplify our skills and conduct magic. Yes, the tennas restricted the use of power, but I could replenish my supply in my stone. Eventually, I'd find a way to ditch the tennas, and when I did, nothing would keep me from casting spells.

"Thread crap won't work here. Tennas, remember?" Brodin said. He started through the gate then turned, smirking to drive his point home.

Scowling, I strode up to him. "Maybe I wasn't looking for threads."

"Get used to having no magic, sweetheart."

Clenching fists, I growled. "Don't call me that."

"You'll have to suffer without magic like the rest of us."

That wasn't quite true. I also knew sketar magic, and that could change everything. Pausing, I closed my eyes and felt for it. Did the tennas block my ancient, sketar magic, too?

There. I found it in the trees, the grass, and even the slabs of stone making up the fortress prison, a deep burgundy mist I could grab hold of and use as my own if...

It slipped through the fingers in my mind. I couldn't latch onto it. But it waited for me. It wasn't the threads I'd practiced with for years; I couldn't store this power. But if I kept at it, I might be able to use it. This could give me an edge.

Brodin studied me. "What are you doing?"

I fed him a smirk. "Not a thing."

"Verifying you can't do anything with magic?" His lips quirked up on the corners. "You're *Sidhe*, not fae. That's what you renamed yourselves after leaving this world, right? While a few fae might've been able to do something with the bits of magic floating around us, count yourself out of that group."

Nope. Count me in.

"The fae and Sídhe are the same people," I said.

He grunted. "Not any longer. While the fae have continued to advance, the Sídhe mixed with mortals, diluting their magical potential. You'd be lucky to host even a simple spell when you're not bound by tennas."

"You're wrong. You don't know anything about me and magic."

He rolled his eyes and, pivoting on his heel, strode toward the prison. "We need to get inside before you draw anything else to us," he said over his shoulder.

"Surely you're not suggesting I am responsible for the creatures that attacked us on our way here."

"If the shoe fits…"

I shoved past him. "Looks like you have memory problems, ghostly-dude."

His footsteps slowed. "What's that supposed to mean?"

I bit back *if the shoe fits*. "Oh…nothing."

"You don't know what you're talking about." Hands fisting, he picked up his pace. "You can't. I'm…I'm *not* a ghostly dude." But his gaze wouldn't meet mine.

Bingo.

He shook his head, making his unruly hair flop

forward. "No one…"

"No one what?"

"Nothing." Pivoting away from me, he kept walking.

As I followed, a glance around told me we were alone. My spine tingled, and I braced myself for a creature to attack. I wouldn't feel "safe" until we were inside the prison, which was a bizarre notion. But nothing rushed us as we approached the front door of the prison—a three-story, imposing thing made up of huge blocks of dusty, tan stones braced together with metal bars.

Brodin frowned up at the building as if he was looking for a way to climb it.

I strode around him and took the crushed stone path leading to the main entrance steps.

Before I could climb them, the front door opened and a man of average build and a tall woman, both dressed all in black, stepped out. The man slunk close to the building and leaned against it, crossing his arms. His gaze remained intent on the woman, as if he awaited her guidance.

The woman halted on the top step and stared down her nose at us.

Somehow, I had a feeling these two weren't the welcoming committee.

Behind them, a knee-high creature slunk through the open doorway. It paused beside the woman and sat on the landing made up of huge slabs of granite.

My breath caught in my throat as I stared at the wexal cat. Unlike the inky black cat at the Seeker's Headquarters, this one's burnished gold coat glinted in the sunlight, like a fox's. Large, pointed ears curled toward me, and its deep green eyes watching my every move while its luxurious copper whiskers twitched. Its long, bushy tail flicked back and forth, scraping the stone in either pleasure or agitation.

"Wexals are extinct," I stuttered, staring at it in amazement. To think I'd seen two within such a short period of time.

"Not here," Brodin said. "Weird to see one at the prison entrance, however. They're shy creatures. They definitely don't come around wizards like you."

"Aren't *you* a wizard?"

"I'm fae. We're…different."

Which said nothing.

The cat left the stoop and sashayed down the front steps, its movements languid and sleek. It stopped and sat directly in front of me, staring up, its coat flickering like fire. Releasing a soft, huffed meow, it rose and bumped my thigh with its head then dropped back down and wove between my legs, rubbing against me.

Brodin watched with his jaw unhinged. "And that's even odder. They…" He shook his head. "This is so weird."

"Lots of wizards and creatures like me," I said. Well, not him. "It's not unusual at all."

His lips curled down.

Scowling, the woman focused her sharp gaze on me.

With a soft meow, the cat put its front paws up on me again and extended its head, begging for my touch.

As my hand reached forward, the man growled and his fingers twitched.

"No!" The woman jerked forward. Her arm lifted and a spear of flames rushed from her pointed finger. It hit me square in the chest, sending me reeling backward, away from the cat.

Snarling, the cat whirled to face the woman, putting itself between us, but it was too late. While it hissed, I gaped at the deep black hole in my chest. It expanded out to my shoulders, a lethal stain. It also dove down, coating my belly. Soon, it would engulf the rest of me, and I'd…

Brodin grabbed my arm. "Tria. Whoa." Keeping his grip tight—and somehow holding me upright—he whirled on the woman. "What the hell is going on here?"

Why wasn't he cheering? His wish for my death was coming true.

The man cackled.

As leisurely as the cat, the woman sauntered down the steps with pure hatred shining on her face. "She can't have him."

"Him?" I whispered. Did she mean the cat, the man by the door, or Brodin?

"He's mine," she snapped. "He'll always be mine."

"So, you did this?" Brodin shouted.

As I struggled to drag in my last breath, I released one word. "Help."

She laughed as I crumbled forward, wrenching free from Brodin's grip. Her legs shifted backward as if she feared I'd get blood or drool on her shoes. The smooth stone slab at the base of the prison steps rose up to greet me. I cried out as I hit, but the pain of my wounded limbs was nothing compared to the agony erupting from the blazing hole in my chest.

Brodin stooped down beside me. "Hang in there, Tria. I'll get…someone." His head lifted. "We need a healer!"

I didn't hear even a hint of concern in his words, and I didn't feel it in his hand when it landed on my back.

I could only stare forward and wait for my death.

The man cackled again, and the sound clawed down my spine.

Creeping closer, the cat sat beside my flexing hand. It meowed again and lowered itself to the ground, stretching across my arm.

Tipping its head back, it growled at the woman.

Chapter 14

I woke and found myself lying on a hard, flat surface, covered with a scratchy blanket. My hands clawed at my prison top, shoving it aside to reach my chest, but when I found only normal skin underneath, I relaxed back on the stone-hard mattress. So, the woman in black hadn't killed me, unless I was dead and this was…

In no way, shape, or form was *this* heaven.

Welcome to Darkwater Prison. I reached into my pocket, relieved to find I still had my knife. I'd have to keep it hidden or someone would take it from me.

No Brodin in sight, however. Which was…a relief? Exciting? Sad? No, *not sad*.

Maybe six by ten, the room had almost no furniture other than the bed. A stinky smell drew my eyes to a chipped white toilet and sink in the left corner. No shower, but I imagined I'd find an open, shared area somewhere nearby. Prison life at its finest.

The slice of a window on the wall higher up and beside me let in only enough murky light to create a shadowy strip on the chipped stone floor. Much of the opposite wall was taken up by a metal door without bars. Was it locked?

Nearby, sketar mist waited for me, a burnished red mass. It wavered, fingers of it darting my way before retreating to merge with the rest.

I should get off the bed and start making a plan to do…who knows what, but *something*. But the mist…

This was also a chance to practice.

Closing my eyes, I called it in, wondering how I could test this form of magic against the tenna magical restraints on my wrists. What if I couldn't do any magic at all?

Come. I coaxed it near, and then sucked it down into my lungs like my stepfather had taught me. It came willingly but that meant nothing if I couldn't use it.

It swirled inside me and, in my eagerness to prove I could do something with it, I grabbed it. It slipped from my hands and dissipated, spent. I huffed out a sigh.

"Coax it," my stepdad had once said with a laugh, during practice. Since I'd started at the Academy, we hadn't made time to play with this form of magic. "Don't be rough. Treat the mist like you would a baby nat." A tree spirit who guarded the environment. They often took on the form of a butterfly.

Instead of slamming my way into the mass of power again, I tugged on it, and when it coiled inside me, I stroked it, working my fingers around it. When it didn't slip away, I eased it out me with a command.

Make the bed soft.

A simple spell that would either work or it… Holy fae, the mattress went squishy beneath me. *Yes.*

It was a little thing, but I couldn't hold back my whimper of joy. Sketar magic could make the difference between—

My heart stalled and my eyes popped open when a soft

shuffle of someone moving above me was punctuated by a scraping sound. A girl about my age slid off the bunk over mine.

Crap. Had she sensed me pulling in the mist?

I swallowed back my fear and waited for her to confront me.

Her shoes thudded on the floor and she turned. A guarded smile rose on her face. "You're awake," she said. "About time. I thought you'd remain locked in the healing sleep forever."

"Um…hi. I'm Tria." I rose onto my elbows but flopped back down when pain shot through my chest.

"I'm Jacey. From that wince, I can tell you're uncomfortable. The pain will pass, most likely by the end of the day. They brought you here last night, by the way, after you were healed."

"That woman dressed in black tried to kill me." Though she'd need to take a number after Brodin. I was racking up enemies by the second.

"That woman is Warden Bixby." Jacey's dark hair shifted across her shoulders as she stooped down beside my bed.

"She's in charge of this place?"

"Yup. Bixby runs the girl's pods, which are residential units, and Warden Duvoe, her brother, is in charge of the guys'."

"They're siblings?" Frowning, I tried to bring his image to mind, but all I could remember was his bone-chilling cackle while the woman shot fire my way.

Face tight, Jacey nodded. "You need to be careful around them. They're nasty, though Bixby is much worse than Duvoe, because she's unpredictable. He's…" She shrugged. "I guess you could say he tries to be fair, if such a thing is possible here."

"Since she tried to kill me, I'll stay out of her way."

"If she'd wanted you dead, she would've left you to die on the front steps." She peered over her shoulder. "Fortunately, she changed her mind. While she was angry with you, she must've gotten over her snit."

"I didn't do anything to make her mad. I just showed up here." One would think she would've been pleased I'd made it past the initial tests.

"Because of what happened, word is already spreading through the network about you." Jacey's sly smile made her eyes gleam. "You're almost a celebrity."

The idea made anxiety spike through me. Whenever someone stood out as different, at least fifteen people were eager to knock them down. "I haven't done anything special."

"You only did something no one else has."

Frowning, I tried to figure out what that could be but came up blank.

"Kai took a liking to you." Her gaze drifted to the end of my bed, where something moved. "I've never seen him do anything like it before."

My pulse jumped, and I sat up fast, smacking my head on the upper bunk. I scooted back against the stone wall behind me and rubbed my aching head.

The wexal cat I'd met at the prison entrance stood. He stretched and swaggered toward me then climbed up onto my lap and curled into a ball. A big ball since he had to weigh at least forty pounds. I'd have a difficult time shifting him to the side. His purr rumbled, vibrating the bed.

"Hi, um…Kai," I said, almost afraid to touch him. Those fangs…

He blinked up at me before closing his eyes, and his purr grew louder, echoing around us.

"Bixby has been trying to force him to like her for months," Jacey said. "Guess he's taken to you instead."

"Maybe?" I said.

Jacey smiled. "He's been guarding you since they brought you here. That speaks volumes."

I stroked his back, and his fur rippled beneath my fingers.

But when Jacey glanced over her shoulder and stiffened, Kai sprang to his feet. His fur bristled along his back, forming hard, segmented spikes like a dragon's, and his lips peeled back. His snarl and gnashing teeth sent anxiety spiking through me.

"A spyling," Jacey hissed, jumping to her feet. Her hands flailed at her sides, but she didn't make any other move.

I scrambled from the bed and stood wavering beside it. My head screamed and my pulse pounded, plus my chest was on fire, but I ignored the pain. "What's a spyling?" I whispered.

She pointed to the upper corner of the ceiling, to the left of the door, where a small creature crawled. About two inches long and an inch wide, it resembled a tan-colored beetle, other than the long, clawed legs.

"The spyling means Bixby's watching," Jacey said close to my ear. "Don't...do anything. Or say anything."

For how long?

Kai leaped off the bed and scrambled up the wall. He latched onto the small creature with his mouth then leaped down onto the floor. His sharp teeth crunched through the spyling like a housecat severing the spine of a mouse. With a gulp, Kai swallowed the creature whole.

Jacey sagged against me. "Whoa. I've never seen anything like that before. Kai's..." She stooped down and held out her hand, cooing. "Come here boy. You're the bestest kitty in the world. Let me thank you."

He sashayed around her and approached me. Sitting on the floor, he gazed up at me. I stooped down to give him a good scratch, and his purr resounded.

"He *does* like you," Jacey said in awe, rising to her feet. "I've never seen anything like it." Standing, I staggered back to the bed and sat on the side, and she followed to stand beside it. "Welcome to Darkwater Prison, by the way. This is Pod D, and you're my new roommate."

My chest spasmed where the warden had burned it, and I rubbed it carefully.

Her gaze dipped down my front. "Rest up today. Things are tricky here at Darkwater. Our fellow supes love to see how far they can push us, and you may not be strong enough to fight them off yet. For them—the guards and the wardens, that is—this place is a game. For us, it's about survival." Jacey settled onto her butt on the floor and extended her legs underneath the foot of my bed. Tucking the long sleeves of her dark gray jumpsuit up past her elbows, she leaned back and propped her palms on the floor. The tops of her shoes scraped across the springs as she shuffled them back and forth. "It's eat or be eaten here. That's why I'm getting out as soon as I can."

"How?" Although, I suspected what she meant. Darkwater Reformatory.

"There are ways. I have too many things left to do. For one, I need to…" She closed her eyes tightly for a moment and, when she opened them, they shimmered with tears. "Someone I… Anyway. You know what I mean."

I didn't, but I wouldn't press her to say anything else, not if it caused pain. "So, I need to watch out for Bixby…" I ticked them off on my fingers. "Guards, and spylings.

Anything else?" Well, Brodin, but I'd almost become comfortable with the idea he wanted me dead.

"The warden's no treat, as you've already discovered. Duvoe... I'm still trying to figure him out. As for the general population, it depends on who you kiss up to and whose hate list you make it onto first."

"Hazing, you mean."

"It's not too bad. The best thing to do is make friends because they'll watch your back while you learn how to watch ours." Her head dipped in a nod. "Like me."

"Thanks." I couldn't deny how relieved I felt to find a friend already. "How long have *you* been here?"

"A month."

"What did you do to…"

"Nothing." Her growl shot across the room. "Except refuse to marry an old guy who's known for killing off his wives."

"They put someone in prison for something like that?"

"The fae king gave the command. I…chose someone else." Her face tightened. "Someday, I'll kill the king."

"After you get out of here."

"Yeah."

I rubbed Kai's head. He tipped his face up and licked my finger.

Jacey's lips twitched as she watched. "Because of Kai, you've made a mortal enemy in Bixby. But don't worry. I'll do all I can to protect you."

She looked about five feet tall. Lean. What kind of protection could she provide against the woman who ran the prison? I had a bad feeling about this, despite the fact that she'd survived here for a month.

"For the best chance to live, you'll need to join a triad. I happen to know of one with a few openings."

"What's a triad?"

"Three inmates who group together for protection."

"Like a gang?"

"Sort of."

After what I'd heard, it was hardly surprising.

Our door banged open and three women who looked about our age sauntered into the room.

While the short blonde shut the door, I got to my feet.

"So…Tria's awake," the one with dark, glossy hair hanging down to her butt said as she advanced toward me.

"And up on her feet," the blonde said, her gaze pinning me in place.

The third, a redhead with a billion freckles, giggled for no apparent reason, but her attention had locked on Kai. "Was kinda hopin' she'd still be asleep." The grin she slid toward the girl with dark hair could only be described as slick. "Right, Sheera? Then we coulda…" The sharp look she sent me made it clear I wouldn't have enjoyed whatever she'd planned. "But it's okay. Her punishment will perk things up."

"What kind of punishment?" I asked.

The blonde purposefully widened her eyes and rubbed her hands together. "Oh, goodie. You don't know. Newbie initiation. Newbie initiation!"

After feeding a scowl at the blonde, Jacey leaned close to me. "I'll explain later."

Sheera's gaze darted to the door, and her lips curled up in a way that could only be considered sly.

"Why are you here?" Jacey grumbled, crossing her arms. Her foot tapped on the floor.

Sheera stiffened. "Mindi, Kimmie, and I live here."

"Not in this room," Jacey said. "You only come here when you want to make trouble."

Mindi posed daintily, with her hands cupped beneath

her chin. "Us?" Her posture loosened. "We never make trouble. That's your role."

"And running," the blonde shouted. "Oh! And leaving friends behind."

"I didn't run!" Jacey said.

"Hell, yes, you did," Mindi said. "You killed Kylie."

Jacey's fists clenched at her sides. "You know I don't remember what happened, but I know for damn sure I didn't kill her."

"Who's Kylie?" I asked her.

"My former roommate. She… She wanted into the Reformatory but she didn't make it through the Challenge." Jacey quivered, overtaken by intense emotion.

Her roommate had taken the Challenge? I needed to quiz Jacey about it ASAP.

"You murdered her." Sheera stomped closer to Jacey. "She trusted you and you left. Her. To. Die!"

"Killed your boyfriend, too," Kimmie said in a perky tone.

Mindi snickered.

Jacey stormed past Sheera, and Mindi slunk behind Kimmie.

Sheera smirked. Placing herself between Jacey and the other girls, she held up her fists. "Try it," she whispered. Her grin rose. "You might find it hard to walk for a while after we're done with you, though, so think twice."

Face florid, Jacey pointed to the door. "Out."

"So sad about what happened to the rest of your triad," Kimmie said, emboldened by Sheera's presence. Though she slapped her hand over her mouth, her fingers didn't hide the subtle lift of her lips. "Now you're stuck here with us."

"Your boyfriend, Rohnan, was hot," Kimmie said,

adding fuel to the fire. "Thought I'd make a play for him but, well…we know how that turned out."

"Things took a dark turn for you three in the Challenge, didn't it?" Mindi said with secrets flitting through her eyes.

Jacey's face darkened. She stomped around Sheera to get closer to Mindi.

Enough of this. I tugged in sketar mist and sent it toward Mindi.

She's going to destroy you.

Gulping, Mindi stumbled backward, smacking into Kimmie. Her eyes widened for real this time.

"You have any information about this you'd like to share?" Jacey ground out at Mindi.

"No!" Mindi blinked fast. Her gaze shot from Jacey to Sheera then Kimmie. "I don't, do I? It's…well, we aren't supposed to say, but Jacey just told me she's gonna—" A frown rose on her face. "Wait a second here." Gaze clearing, she tossed her head back, and I could tell she dumped my spell along with the shake. "You didn't say anything. What did you do?"

"Me?" Jacey looked bewildered. "I didn't do anything." She lifted her hands. "Tennas. Remember?"

The tension in my gut uncoiled because I'd found a tiny weapon in sketar magic that could make a difference.

"Back off," Sheera told Jacey, pushing her to the side. Her evil gaze turned my way. It was all I could do to keep my expression neutral. I loved that… Wow. I still had power! "We just stopped by for a visit. To say hi and get to know your new roomie." Her voice dropped so low it grated across the floor. "We heard all about her."

"Funny." I pushed for a smile, though I knew the gesture held no kick. "I haven't heard about you."

Sullen silence ruled.

"I was joking," I said.

Sheera's lips squished together, and she started to say something but her tongue stalled when her attention fell on the cat lounging on the bed. Kai had uncurled and stretched out, his body reaching from one side to the other. "You better get that thing out of here before Bixby sees it."

"She's on her way. She's on her way." Mindi bounced on her toes and clapped her hands. "Inspection time for the newbie, and Tria's gonna get into trouble!"

"Fuck," Jacey said. As Mindi, Kimmie, and Sheera scooted from the room and the door banged shut behind them, Jacey whirled around and raced to the bunks. She stuffed her foot beneath my mattress and rose to straighten her blankets. After dropping back to the floor and giving the bed a satisfied nod, Jacey's attention fell on mine. "Fix yours. Fast."

"But—"

"Now!"

Fear bolting through me, I nudged the cat to the side and yanked on the blankets. Kai blinked up at me. He stretched and yawned before hopping off the bed and scooting underneath the frame.

As I smoothed the blanket, I said, "I take it those three girls are a triad."

"What gave it away?" Jacey fiddled with the already neat piles of clothing in the small wall closet. From here, it looked like we had plenty of cotton undies, dingy night-gowns, and multiple steel-gray jumpsuits. Everything the best-dressed prisoner could need. At least I wouldn't have to pour through my clothing options in the morning, unable to decide what to put on. Jacey closed the cabinet with a bang.

"Why do they hate you?" I asked. "I get the mean girl thing. Kinda clichéd but expected."

Silence ruled long enough I turned, and my fingers froze on the blanket.

Jacey had squeezed her eyes shut. Her arms hung like sticks at her sides, and pain emanated from her frame. "My roommate was Sheera's sister."

"So this wasn't motivated by simple mean girl malice."

"Revenge is Sheera's goal, and she's happy to twist the screws until she finally achieves it. She has a valid reason to be angry."

"You said you don't remember what happened during the Challenge, which we need to discuss, by the way. But I doubt you were responsible for what happened to Kylie."

"That's just it." Stark pain tightened her face. "She and Rohnan didn't make it through the test, and I…" Eyes swimming with tears, she gulped. "They say I ran." Her fingernails raked down her arms, leaving red streaks. "I must've, because I woke up back here. Alone. I can't believe they're dead. I've got to get back into the catacombs and find out what happened."

"Catacombs?"

"That's where the Challenge is held. Only triads can apply to take the tests. I've been waiting…"

"For someone to arrive to form another triad."

She winced. "Maybe you, um…Maybe you'd be willing to consider forming a triad with me?"

"Can I think about it?"

Her shoulders slumped. "Sure."

I felt bad turning her down, but I needed to look into the situation before jumping into a triad. I wasn't even sure what it entailed other than providing each other protection.

Stomps outside the room drew our attention.

"Bixby!" Panic suffused Jacey's face. She rushed to the

middle of the room and stood with almost military precision. "Come stand beside me before she gets here."

Joining her, I mimicked her posture. "Anything I need to be aware of? Other than, well, dodging fire she might fling at my chest?"

"Keep quiet and let me do the talking."

"I can behave." Mostly.

"Please. If something happens to you, too, I…" She blinked fast, and I knew she was remembering Kylie and Rohnan. "Just don't…talk back or act cocky."

"I'll do my best. Promise."

"Good. Because next time, she might not let a healer near you."

Chapter 15

The door swung open and crashed against the wall.

Warden Bixby strode into the room with tousled hair. A red, splotched face. And a bony body trembling with fury, which had to be bad news for us.

Warden Duvoe slunk in behind her and shut the door. He stood beside it, his intent gaze focused on me.

Great.

As if she enjoyed channeling Maleficent, Bixby still wore all black, from her flouncy top to her snug, black leather pants. Who wore something like this in a prison? Heels and black chunky jewelry livened up the stark look. Frankly, the black lipstick and nail polish were overkill. Only her green eyes broke through her dark persona.

"Where is he?" she demanded, her head jerking back and forth.

Warden Duvoe, dressed in a robe similar to the kind our professors had worn at the Academy, studied her every move, almost as if he'd never seen her in action before. But he had, at least at the entrance when I arrived.

"Who are you talking about?" Jacey said in a reasonable voice. "It's just me and Tria here."

Bixby stalked closer. She latched onto Jacey's shoulders and shook her. "You know who I mean. Kai." Releasing Jacey, Bixby's voice went high-pitched, cooing. "Kai, baby! Where are you? Come to Mama."

Had she seen him on the spyling?

When Kai didn't appear, Bixby stomped her foot, the force of her heel cracking the stone. "Kai!" Any hint at sweetness and cream fled, replaced with a snarl worthy of a slork, a mountain creature with the bad habit of chomping on wizards. "Kai! You better not be in this room or I'll…" Her gaze turned my way, and she advanced toward me with a sniff. "Woke up, did you?" She slithered around me, studying my body as if she hoped to find blood gushing from multiple wounds or a wince of pain on my face when I took in a deep breath.

Duvoe's thin lips curled back in a devious smile. Jacey might think he was a decent-enough guy—for a warden— but I wasn't convinced.

"If you've done anything with him, I'll get even," Bixby sputtered in my face.

I cringed. If "getting even" involved fire arcing from her finger, I'd pass. Should I thank her for making sure I was healed when she'd been the one to deal the fiery blow? The wild look in her eyes suggested no, as did Jacey's subtle jerk of her head.

As always, Duvoe watched. There was something odd about him…

When Bixby snarled, stark fear slunk down my spine, spreading goosebumps wherever it touched. In my old, confident days as a Seeker, I would've stood tall and told her in no uncertain terms to stand down, and she would've done it. But here, she and her brother ruled. I was a powerless, disbarred Seeker who was scrambling to come up with some sort of magic I could use in defense against a bunch of cut-throat supernatural inmates.

"I don't like you," Bixby finally said, her nose twisting as if the place stunk. She acted like a rabid trana, and I had a feeling she hadn't been bitten. "You'd best behave, missy." Pivoting, she stalked over to the bunk bed, her shoes thundering on the floor and her butt swaying. She leaned forward and scrutinized my blankets. "What's this?" She plucked something off the bed and stalked toward us. Pinched between her fingers, she held a solitary, coppery hair. Short, like Kai's. "Neither of you have hair this color or this length."

"I do," I said in a reasonable tone that I thought did a decent job of masking my inner tremor. My mind kept flashing to her pointing her finger at me and the pain in my chest when her magic made the impact.

Bixby's eyes jumped to my head. "Black hair. Black!"

"Not where the sun don't shine." I grimaced when Duvoe's eyes widened. "I...umm," Ugh. "Dyed it."

Crap. This might be the wrong move on my part. What if she asked me to show her? If I had to, I could use sketar magic to... No, no, no. I wasn't going to change the color of *that* hair with magic.

She flicked the strand up into the air and growled. "Don't think I won't check."

Double cringe. I held my face impassive, because in no way was I eager to press this.

"But I can't do that now." With a huff, she swept around grandly and minced toward the door, not stopping until she stood in the opening. "Brother?"

He nodded, but his gaze swept across me before he turned in her direction.

Bixby's hand rose to clutch the trim. She posed, though

her grip was tight enough to crumple the metal. "I'll be watching you, Tria."

And I'd be watching out for her, which shouldn't be too hard. She'd stand out like a bat in the field of gray-clad supes.

This proved it was even more imperative that I get into the Reformatory. I needed to do whatever I could to escape their clutches.

The door shut, and we were left alone.

I wanted to sag onto my bed and catch my breath. Plus find a way to make my freakin' fingers stop shaking.

Jacey whipped around and grabbed my arms, holding me upright. Bouncing, she squealed. "You were awesome! I know I told you to keep your mouth shut but that was inspired. I never would've thought of saying anything like that." Her gaze swept to the door. "That woman scares the shit out of me."

"Probably everyone else, too."

"Most of them. Maybe not the Crew but they're in a class all their own."

"Who's the Crew?" I asked.

"The in-group to avoid, because we'll never be welcome."

I wasn't sure I cared to be "in", anyway.

"They're unique. A quadrad instead of a triad, which usually isn't possible but they somehow made it happen."

"Four wizards."

"Four powerful shifter wizards."

Shifters, like Brodin. Would he hang out with them?

"The leader, Titan, can change into a raptor."

I held up my arms. "Don't the tennas keep them from shifting?"

"Shifting is part of their innate makeup. Tennas don't interfere with that."

"They have an advantage over non-shifters, then." And I assume the wardens and guards had the magical advantage over them, which kept them in line. But it would be a free-for-all for the rest of us. "They sound deadly." All I could think of was a T-Rex trying to fit inside one of these tiny prison rooms.

"Titan's a bambiraptor. Sounds warm and fuzzy but when he changes, he's more vicious than a pit-bull on steroids. Twelve feet tall, claws longer than my forearm." She grimaced. "You get the picture."

"Someone to avoid."

"The other three are just as bad." She ticked them off on her fingers. "Lars—who has an ironic name—can shift into a larbeera."

A creature with scaly wings, long, sharp claws, tusks, plus thick, armored skin. I wouldn't want to meet him in a dark alley.

"The other two can shift into a lizard and a chiema."

I wasn't sure what a chiema was, but… "Lizards aren't always scary."

"Micah is. He's a lot bigger than a croc."

Shuddering, I turned and flopped on my bed.

Jacey followed and stood beside me. "The other three aren't as powerful as Titan but together, they're a force that could take down an army."

"How will I know who they are, because I'm eager to stay out of their way."

She tapped her chest. "Stick with me. I'll point them out the first chance I can and steer you in a different direction."

Kai slunk out from underneath the bed and jumped up beside me. He snuggled against my hip and purred.

I scratched his neck and his chest rumbled with pleasure. "You're going to get me into trouble, aren't you, boy?" I squinted up at Jacey, who'd stepped backward and leaned her butt against the sink. "I don't want to push him away, but what am I supposed to do with him?" I'd never had a pet or anyone who seemed to like me this much outside of my parents, sister, and grandfather.

"Ask him to hide, and he will."

"Like, under the bed again? That won't hold up if the room inspector decides to drop onto her knees and lift the edge of the blanket."

"Can't see Bixby sticking her ass in the air to do that but what do I know?" The smile Jacey released held secrets I could tell she was eager to share. "Try it, though. Ask Kai nicely to hide and see what happens."

No harm in that, I supposed. "Hey, Kai. Would you mind, um, going somewhere else?"

He disappeared.

I bolted upright, almost smacking my forehead on the bunk over mine again. "Where did he go?" Funny how I missed him already.

She nudged off the sink. "He'll come back when you call him. I think you're his, now."

I tipped my head. "What exactly does that mean?"

"He chose you, so I assume he'll be here for you like he was with the spyling."

Crunch, crunch. If he took care of the pests, he'd be welcome. But I didn't want anything happening to Kai because of his association with me. Bixby was on a rampage.

Jacey came over and offered her hand to pull me off the bed. "Come on. It's time to go eat." She started toward the door. "I'm famished. After we do that, I'll show you around. The unrestricted areas, that is."

My belly rumbled on cue. "Sounds great."

We walked out into a long hall with a high ceiling and

two floors on each side. A set of metal stairs rose to the second level on my right, and a narrow walkway with a steel railing spanned each side of the upper story.

"In each of four pods, there are twenty rooms with two inmates," Jacey said, sweeping her hand toward the upper areas. "All of this section is Pod D. Pod C is down there, through the door." She pointed to our right.

"So, one hundred and sixty prisoners. Sounds like a small number to house every Sídhe and fae criminal from the combined worlds."

She winced. "You're right. And we're not even at full capacity. Bixby needs to lighten up on the weeding."

Brodin had mentioned the term.

"There are a lot of accidents around here," Jacey said in explanation. "Falls on staircases. Falls through windows. And…" She glanced around, seeking threats, even darting her eyes toward the ceiling, before her shoulders relaxed. "Everything that goes on here is a game to them. A deadly game."

"Bixby?"

Biting her lower lip, she nodded. "Fellow inmates and guards, too. You'll need to watch your back." She started down the hall, and I followed. Other women joined us, leaving their rooms, aiming in the direction that I assumed led to the cafeteria. "I'm sure there's an official name for what happens, but weeding fits."

I'd need to be careful until I could reach the Reformatory. I'd hate to come this far only to die before I had the chance to take the test.

Jostled by others, we headed toward an open doorway on the farthest end of the hall from our room.

The skin between my shoulder blades twitched, and I turned. No one seemed to be paying any attention to us, but that meant nothing.

A flicker of movement drew my attention to the back, upper corner of the residential wing. Something… I squinted then huffed. I hadn't seen anything moving there, had I?

Jacey latched onto my arm and whirled me around to face her. Her wide eyes met mine. "Don't. Look."

"What…?" I started to turn, but she wrenched me around.

"You caught the attention of a…" She leaned in close and dropped her voice below a whisper. "A gorelon."

A mythical being that hunted wizards. Nothing new for a prison, but…

"It's watching," she hissed in panic. "Hoping you'll turn. Once it locks onto you, it'll wait until it finds you alone, then attack."

Chills rippled across my skin. "How do I avoid them?"

"Stay with others at all times. Don't look them in the eye. And form a triad, because the members watch out for each other. Gorelon's are less apt to strike when you're with friends."

We moved forward again, but I couldn't get rid of the clawing sensation on my back.

Mindi, Kimmie, and Sheera left a room on our right, the last at the end of the residential area, and crowded in behind us.

Jacey rolled her eyes. She leaned in close to me as she opened a door and we walked into a hall. "I thought we'd lost them, but no."

"Witch," Kimmie hissed.

"Murderer," Sheera added.

Blinking quickly, Jacey picked up her speed, almost to a run, hurrying down the hallway. They kept pace with us like predators on the hunt.

Mindi cleared her throat and raised her voice. "Like I

was saying, Sheera, I think new girls should be required to shave their heads. They might have nits, and I don't want them spreading." Her snarky giggle burst out, raking across my nerves like barbed wire. "Maybe we can make it happen tonight, after lockdown."

"Love how you think, sweetheart," Sheera's voice boomed.

Would they truly try to shave my head? I smoothed my hair, then tucked it forward, over my shoulders, as if that would protect it from shaving.

Okay, so I was a little more than weirded out by this. Who knew what went on here at night?

The gaze I turned to Jacey did not contain fear. I hoped it didn't, anyway, because that could give me away to the girls behind us.

"They can't do it," she whispered as we exited the hall and walked out into a big open area. Three stories high, one wall was made up entirely of glass and looked out at the woods behind the building. She tugged me past a bunch of people and to the side of the room. The threesome followed, though they hovered farther back, watching. "One, our rooms are locked at night—*magically* locked so there's no coming in or going out. And two, Mindi doesn't have the guts." The scowl she shot them would've made me back up more than one step. They flounced but remained in place. "Get lost."

"Oh, burn! Not." Kimmie rolled her eyes. Mindi giggled.

"We're going to get something to eat," Sheera whined. "You two are in the way."

They pivoted in unison and, heads close together, wove through the room toward the cafeteria archway. Not-so-yummy smells floated toward me from that direction.

This room around us was filled with a sea of gray. My

fellow inmates, and at least eighty of them. I could pick out shifters, slakes, and even a few demons; a decent mix of magical abilities.

The realization of my vulnerability was messing with my mind. Despite being manacled, everyone around me seemed to have full command of this world, while I floundered, trying to decide if I dared keep testing my sketar witch skills. "How do we survive here without power?" I asked Jacey as we walked toward the cafeteria entrance.

"You learn how to stay out of others' way fast or…" Her grimace made tension spiral through me, a sensation that was becoming my norm.

No need to point out the obvious. "I need to watch out for stairs, the windows, and the shadow creature." I wouldn't use its real name, to keep from drawing it to me.

Jacey pointed her finger at me. "Exactly." Standing on tiptoes, she tried to see around people shuffling ahead of us and through the cafeteria entrance. "We're part of the second serving line for our meals, which means seven a.m. sharp for breakfast, twelve-thirty for lunch, and five-fifteen for dinner. If you're late, you don't eat."

"How's the food?"

"Not so good."

Only now was it sinking in how wonderful I'd had it at the Academy. I could come and go as I pleased. I'd been respected as an apprentice Seeker. More than one person had covered my back.

"I've eaten better, but I don't starve," she said.

Great. I'd always been a foodie. Having a Level Five Chef at the Academy had spoiled me.

"Only Level Two chefs here," Jacey said as if she'd read my mind. "And I think they've stretched their credentials. This is the first place where I've eaten mac 'n cheese that was pasta baked in milk with hunks of processed cheese floating around."

I shuddered.

We moved slowly toward one of two narrow slots in the wall where someone pushed out a tray of food as people passed.

My turn. Stooping down, I peered through the hole. Inside the large kitchen on the other side, a bunch of gargoyles stomped around the room. One slapped trays on a conveyor while others added plates and eating utensils. The trays slid magically along the smooth surface, passing in front of a series of cooking stations where other gargoyles worked grills and dipped their arms into big pots on stoves. Others plopped various food items onto the plates, also with their hands.

Not feeling too hungry at the moment.

A loaded tray spit out through the hole, smacking me in the belly, and I grabbed it before it fell onto the floor. Shuffling away from the window, my insides spasmed as I studied my meal. I'd be famished tonight at bedtime because…how could I eat this?

"This way." Jacey nudged her shoulder toward an empty metal table and four chairs—bolted down—near one wall, in front of a bank of normal-sized windows. A glance told me we'd sit on the opposite side of the room from the mean girl triad.

No Brodin, but I didn't want to see him, anyway.

Following her, I dropped my plastic tray on the table and studied the congealed brown mass oozing over what looked like a splat of grayish boxed potatoes. Not that I'd eaten boxed potatoes before but I'd heard about them from Fleur.

"Ah, stroganoff," Jacey said, sitting and shoving her

plastic spoon into the mound on her plate. She grimaced. "Utterly delightful."

Other than the steel table and chairs, everything else was made of flimsy plastic.

"But…" I grimaced and pretty much threw up a little, though I swallowed it back down. "The cooks were using their bare hands."

"Gross, for sure. But here, it's either be picky or starve. There won't be anything else offered."

I sat across from her but didn't touch my food. I needed to work myself up to the idea before I could put any of it into my mouth. "So, um, you should know, since you've offered me a spot in your new triad." Lifting my fork, I dragged some potatoes through the sauce. "Bixby isn't my only enemy."

"You work fast. Who else could you have offended?" Shoving in a bite, she spoke around it. "You just got here and you've been unconscious since you arrived."

"Brodin."

Her brows drew together. "Don't know him."

"The guy I arrived with."

"Oh, the hot guy, right?" Jacey said, swallowing. "I saw you two together out front, right after Bixby… you know. From the way he hovered over you, I thought he was your boyfriend."

My fork clattered on my plate. "You thought I arrived here with a boyfriend?" What were the odds of that happening?

"You wouldn't be the first. I did." Sadness came through in her voice, telling me she was thinking of her boyfriend, Rohnan.

"Brodin's not my boyfriend," I said.

"Did you two hook up on the way here then, because…?"

"Because what? And wait. Where would anyone hook up?" Like I'd do anything with a guy—let alone Brodin—while centipedes crawled all over me? Or on the cliffs with the attack vines and a dead body dangling nearby? The kertins wouldn't back off long enough for something like that, and who knows what the shade would suggest if we'd stopped… I rolled my eyes. "Didn't happen." Would *never* happen. "Why do you think it did?"

Her gaze softened. "I could swear there was something between you."

"He hates me. He wants to kill me."

Lips curling down, she sighed. "Like I said, he appeared concerned about you. And he's cute. Muscular. Tall. Natural bed-head hair. What's not to like?"

"His personality." I huffed. "I just met him yesterday. We're never hooking up."

"Who's not hooking up?" someone asked from behind me.

Ugh. Brodin.

Chapter 16

"Go away," I growled, looking up at him.

"I just…" His gaze drifted across my face.

"What?"

Jacey grinned and winked at me.

No. There was nothing between us.

"Just wanted to make sure you were still alive," he growled. Cranky, but there was nothing new there.

"Aww," Jacey sighed as if we were talking about making out.

"I am alive, thanks," I said stiffly.

"Well, good. Glad to hear it." After giving me a stiff nod, he took his tray to an empty table halfway across the room, where he sat alone.

"You should've asked him to sit with us," Jacey whispered, leaning across the table.

"I don't want him to sit with us. I just told you he hates me."

She snorted. "Didn't look like hate to me."

"He growled."

"Guys. Who can figure them out, right?"

"You're wrong," I ground out, hoping she'd let this go.

"He came over here to ask how you were doing."

"He came over to make sure I'm alive so he can kill me."

"He could've done that from across the room." Her head tilted. "Why does he want to kill you?"

"I can't say."

"Okay," she said slowly. Her attention fell on my mostly-full plate. "You done?"

I pushed my tray away. "Yes."

Standing, she lifted hers. "Then let's ditch these and take a tour of the unrestricted areas."

We left the cafeteria and went left across the great room, then walked down a hall with a steel door at the end.

"This part of Darkwater is three stories tall. We're allowed in our own residential area—no one else's—the great room and cafeteria, the yards, sometimes the court-yard, and a few areas on the second floor. We're not allowed to go anywhere else, hence my showing you around."

"Why just sometimes in the courtyard?"

"Titan hunts there, mostly at night, but sometimes Bixby gives him free rein during the day."

"I assume we become the hunted."

Her face fell. "Yeah." Shaking her head, she continued down the hall. "They built this place in the usual fae structure of a square with the large garden-strewn courtyard in the middle. There are also outside exercise areas where we can hang out during free time, the yards. Warden Bixby thinks fresh air and sunshine will perk us up and keep us tame. I've yet to see it happen."

"We built our academies in a circle with inner gardens,

too," I said. Like the fae. But then, we used to be the fae, too.

"That's how the capital is set up. The walled city, it's called." She waved toward the main staircase. "Upstairs, you'll find the wings housing the guy pods. We can't go in that direction, but there are classrooms up there, too."

We went through a door and approached a set of stairs opposite an exit outside, then climbed to the second floor, where we paused on the broad landing with a few sturdy chairs and random bookcases with dusty volumes. Not exactly a cozy nook where someone could sit and read, but this could be all I'd get.

"Darkwater is made up of three campuses," she said, clutching the wooden railing. "The Reformatory, which I've heard is a youth correctional facility, though no one truly knows, because it's hidden beyond an impassible mist."

"A mist?" Was there some association with sketar magic? No one knew where the magic came from. It just *was*.

"It's actually a weird fog that drifts off the ocean continuously, from the north. It creates a barrier no one can pass through, not without the right kind of magic. The Reformatory is the only way off this island other than by dying, but how they release anyone isn't known. Once someone makes it there, they don't come back to share stories."

"Meanwhile, we all wait here to die from Bixby's weeding process."

"She likes keeping the population down. And it's not like you can do much about it. We can stay here and risk weeding, or try to get to the Reformatory." Turning, she pointed to the right. "Over there, you'll find the guy's pods." Shadows crept across her face. "My boyfriend stayed there before…" She choked back a sob. After staring up at the ceiling while blinking fast, she sighed and turned to our left. "I'll take you past the classrooms."

"We have classes here?"

"Not many but I guess they want to keep us busy."

"No classes in how to use magic, I assume."

"With tennas, it's impossible." Her gaze drifted forward, down the long hallway stretching in front of us. "The only magic left is…" She bit her lips together, before taking a big breath. "You'll be sent a schedule. Math, science, fae languages, etc. The general subjects."

"Sounds exciting." Though it wouldn't be bad to learn fae languages, which I hadn't taken at the Academy.

"Inmates over twenty-two are shipped directly to Dark-water Penal Colony," she said. "Called the third campus. They separate the younger crowd from the older inmates, as if they think it'll keep us from turning completely hard-core. But I've found age doesn't discriminate when it comes to committing a crime, so you'll need to watch your back."

Those stats Brodin had mentioned ran through my mind.

"I'm going to take the Reformatory Challenge as soon as I can," I said.

"You're bold." Pausing, she leaned against a wall beside a closed metal door labeled 5B, and her arms linked on her chest. "Since the odds aren't in our favor, most wizards wait before applying, if they choose to do so at all."

"You didn't wait."

"I…had reasons."

So did I. "I need to get into the Reformatory as soon as possible."

"Lots of us try. Very few succeed."

"The tests are tough?"

Her lips tightened. "They're horrible."

I had to take the Challenge. It was the only way to reach my birth father and the only reason I was here.

"The tests take place in the catacombs beneath the prison," she said. "The catacombs are a series of ever-changing, magical chambers, and were discovered ages ago and infused with magic. Each time a group goes down there, the tests change." She tilted her head, and her brows drew together. "Personally, I think the catacombs learn."

"As in, it's a living entity?"

She nodded. "From what I've heard, and it hasn't been easy to obtain information, the catacombs come up with different tests for each group that goes down there."

How was I going to get through something like that? I'd hoped to ask around to find out what to expect, but if no one came back—other than Jacey with no memory—and the tests changed, I was in for a bigger challenge than I'd assumed.

"I could be mistaken. It might not *really* be alive." Her face smoothed, but tension remained locked in her brown eyes. "But who knows with Darkwater? You'll find things here you've never seen before."

My grandma's words passed through my mind. She'd known. Had she been incarcerated here at one time herself?

"As for failing the test, it happens all the time, unfortunately." Her palms raked down her face, leaving pale lines behind. "Most die, or we assume they do. Maybe they make it to the Reformatory alone. Anyone sent back here —like me—has no memory of what happened. The warden calls it another form of weeding but…" Her voice broke. "It's not right. You know what I mean?" Her face stark, she bumped off the wall and continued down the corridor.

This didn't sound easy, but what choice did I have?

"Don't forget. You'll need a triad to enter the Challenge," she said, but held up her hand. "No pressure. You already know my offer remains open."

I couldn't keep my lips from quirking up. "Once we find a third, we'll have a full triad."

Complete joy replaced the sorrow on her face. "You mean it? You're in?"

"We're getting out of here."

She wouldn't need to face the mean girls, the wardens, the guards, and gorelons alone any longer, not while I was here to stand with her.

"Thank you. You don't know how much this means to me."

"You offered me friendship without knowing anything about me, which says a lot."

"We just need a third." Tapping her chin, her eyes sparkled. I knew just who she was thinking about.

"No." I walked past her but turned, because I didn't know where we were going. "Pick someone else." Anyone else. Even the raptor dude would be a better choice.

"My reputation precedes me, and no one will consider forming a triad with me." She tilted her head and frowned. "Maybe give him a chance. He seemed pretty concerned about you for a not-boyfriend."

"If you saw something that suggested he was protective, it was only because he wants to make sure I'm healthy enough before he kills me."

By the fae, would he do his own version of "weeding" and push me down a staircase? If so, he'd beat the gorelons to it.

Jacey continued down the hall, and I walked with her. She paused outside a door marked 2A. Her hand reached out, toward the knob, but she snapped it back. Turning, she continued walking.

Why stop here then keep going? I peered back at 2A as I followed her, but didn't see anything unusual.

We passed classrooms on either side, ten total. Exiting through a door at the end of the hall, we entered an open room much bigger than the one downstairs, outside the cafeteria. This room spanned the entire back portion of the building and—

My eye was drawn to the symbol magically imprinted on the back wall.

By the fae, it was a—

"Oh, no," Jacey said with horror lacing her words.

I yanked my gaze away from the symbol and followed to where she looked upward.

A man had been impaled to the ceiling with a fillinette —a rare Seeker's wand that was purported to enhance magic.

Chapter 17

I grabbed Jacey's arm, and we raced out of the room and down the classroom hall. We hit the top of the staircase at a full run and kept going, not slowing until we reached our room.

Inside, we took a quick look around to make sure there weren't any spylings watching, then stood facing each other, our breathing ragged.

"Dead guy," I said, my voice alight with shakes.

"Really dead guy," Jacey said. "Really dead *guard*, actually. Jared, one of the mean ones."

"He pushed you on the stairs?"

"From a window."

I wasn't going to ask for specifics, but sympathy rushed through me. It must be scary facing this place all on your own. Her blank, cloudy gaze was going to haunt my sleep tonight.

Dropping to the floor, she leaned against the wall beside the door.

I joined her, and we curled our legs up and hugged them in unison.

"What are we going to do?" I said, picking at a loose thread hanging off the knee of my prison jumpsuit. "We need to tell someone."

"Sure, how about we stroll into the Bixby's office and let her know?" Jacey said, gnawing on a fingernail. "She'll be happy we stopped by."

The guards were out. Duvoe gave me the creeps. Our fellow inmates? If I mentioned this to Brodin, he'd accuse me of doing it. Nope.

"We don't tell anyone, then," I said. Warden Bixby would grill us, and if she discovered I could use sketar magic, she'd be convinced I was somehow involved. The guy had been impaled with a fillinette. As a Seeker—apprentice, that is—she'd automatically suspect me. Never mind that I'd only seen a fillinette once in class. Only the elite of the elite were allowed to touch them, though I'd heard wizards with other skaptis also had access to them.

"He was a big guy," I said. "The ceiling was awfully high. Wouldn't they wonder how we were able to get him up there by ourselves?"

"Still."

Our door banged open, making us both jump.

A two-foot-tall frog hopped into the room. Its tongue flicked out to grab a fly from the air, and it gulped it down.

"Herald," Jacey said. She leaned in near to me to whisper. "One of the wardens' minions."

Dark green and wart-encrusted, the frog hopped further into the room. Turning toward us, it hacked and heaved and then spewed vomit onto the floor.

While I blinked and swallowed hard, the frog turned and leaped from the room.

Jacey got up and shut the door.

I stood and backed away from the pool of sludge coating the tiles. "What the...?"

Squatting down, Jacey studied the puke. "Bixby wants us all to attend her in the main hall ten seconds ago."

Tiptoeing over to stand beside Jacey, I carefully avoided looking too closely at the smear on the floor. "How do you know that?"

She straightened. "I read the message."

"There's a message in the vomit?"

The bilious circle disappeared as if it was sucked down into the floor.

"See?" she said. "Bixby knows we received it." Reaching out, Jacey opened the door. "Let's go. We're already late."

She dragged me from the room while I peered over my shoulder at the blank floor.

We hurried to the big open room outside the cafeteria.

Other inmates rushed into the room and we mingled, no one saying much but whispers abounding.

Wardens Bixby and Duvoe appeared in the middle of the room and, like they were all compliant sheep, everyone sat on the floor. Arms crossing on my chest, I didn't play along, not until Jacey yanked me down beside her.

Soaring back and forth as if powered by jetpacks, Warden Bixby hovered at a height of about three feet above the ground. Probably so she could look down on all of us. Her face redder than the sketar mist I called, she came to a stop and whirled on us, snarling.

A few people nearby gulped and scrambled backward.

Warden Duvoe followed her like a faithful puppy, almost as if he had no life of his own outside of one standing in her shadow. He'd yet to say much of anything, let alone act, when I was around.

"Who is responsible?" Bixby shouted in the growing silence.

Everyone looked at each other and soft, speculative

murmurs erupted as they all tried to guess what she might be talking about. Since I assumed she'd found Jared dangling from the ceiling, I studied each face, wondering if the murderer was among us and if they'd give themselves away. Well, Jared's murderer, that is. There were probably multiple murderers here. This *was* a prison.

"Not willing to talk?" Bixby shrieked. With a flick of her arm, three animal skeletons appeared in front of her.

Warden Duvoe stepped back, taking a place beside the wall, his rapt gaze remaining on the creatures.

"Are those horses?" I asked Jacey. And why call them here?

"They're sort of elk." She shuddered. "Screechers."

"Screechers?"

"You'll see. "

I watched as they pranced in front of Bixby, their loosely jointed limbs shifting and slipping as they moved.

"And why are sort of elk skeletons here?" I asked.

"Watch."

I wasn't excited about this.

After Bixby flicked her hand to release them, the elks leaped around the room, darting among us, their hooves clattering on the floor and their limbs shifting like segmented rubber bands. They'd stop and sniff the air, which was odd since they didn't have lungs, let alone noses. No tendons or muscles, either. It was anyone's guess how they held together and didn't crumble into a heap of bones on the floor.

One stopped and sniffed me, and I cringed but remained motionless.

My gaze was drawn to Duvoe, who studied my interaction with the screecher.

With a snort, the creature galloped around me, nearly

trampling the guy sitting on the floor at my back. He gulped and dove to the side.

The screechers worked the room, sniffing everyone until one released a barking-grunt that rose to a high-pitched shriek.

"See?" Jacey said. "Screechers."

Duvoe and Bixby leaned forward, their rapt gazes trained on the animals.

The other skeletons echoed the ear-piercing call and converged with the first. They surrounded Brodin, who sat with a bunch of other guys on the floor. The guys melted away from him, leaving him exposed to the skeletons.

I started to get up, not sure what I'd do, but Jacey yanked on my arm. "Don't," she hissed. "Going over there won't help him."

"But he's—"

The sharp jerk of her head, plus the stark fear in her eyes, made me sink back down beside her. While frustration roared through me, and I itched to bolt in Brodin's direction, I held myself still.

"Wait. What…?" Brodin shouted.

Leaping on top of him, the elks drove him to the floor.

Struggling, he broke free and, leaping to his feet, bolted, but they galloped behind him and soaring through the air, toppled him to the ground again.

A pop and the elks and Brodin disappeared.

"That was close." Jacey shook her head. "You were almost swept up with him."

I shouldn't feel worried about him. I didn't *like*, like him. He was a jerk. He wanted to kill me. He…

My shoulders sunk. Crap.

The wardens popped from the room.

"What do they want with Brodin?" I gnawed on my lower lip.

"Yes, why *did* they take Brodin?" she asked, leaning back to peer at me with speculation in her eyes.

"We're not together. I told you that already."

She stared at me, her brows drawn close, saying nothing.

"We're not," I said. By the fae, I couldn't even convince myself!

"I can understand why you're worried."

"Look at me." I tapped my cheek. "This isn't a worried face."

"Maybe leave your poor lip alone, then."

I forced myself to stop chewing on it. "I'm not concerned in the least."

Standing, Jacey offered me a hand to pull me up off the floor. "If you say so."

"I do say so."

I hurried behind her, and we left the main hall and hurried to our room. Once inside, she climbed up onto the top bunk and flopped on the mattress.

"What will they do to him?" I asked. Okay, so I *was* concerned. A little.

"You told me you weren't worried. Yet… Here you are. Worried."

"It's… I'm just expressing the usual concern someone would have for a fellow wizard."

"Sure." She leaned over the side of the bed, grinning. "Why not just admit it. You like him."

"I don't."

"Not even a little?"

I groaned. "How can I? He wants to kill me."

"So you keep saying, yet here you are, alive."

"He said he'd give me a chance to prove I didn't do it."

She squinted my way. "Do what exactly?"

"Kill his mother."

"Well that's…" She laughed.

I growled. "It's not funny, but… You believe me?"

"You said you didn't do it. That's enough for me."

"Wow." While I could see why Brodin wouldn't trust me, it felt good to have someone on my side. "Thank you."

"In a place like this, you need friends. That's you and me."

My heart warmed.

She cleared her throat. "How do you plan to prove to him you didn't do it?"

"That's just it. I have no idea how I can. See, the thing is, it looks like I did it. He saw me inside… Then she was dead. I ran."

Confusion filled her face. "This sounds complicated. He saw you kill her?"

"No. He was inside the Academy."

"Parts are missing from this story."

I tipped my head back and studied the rusty spring coils on the bottom of her bunk. "Have you ever heard of a blood bond promise?"

"Unfortunately, yes." She hopped off the bed and sat on the floor beside me.

"I agreed to one, which means I can't tell you or anyone else what happened."

"Which also proves you didn't do it." She dipped her head once. "You could tell him there's a blood bond, even if you can't share the details."

"I could, but I'm not sure it would be enough to convince him. And… I guess I'd like him to realize I'm not the kind of person who could've done this."

"Good people do bad things all the time."

"True, but when you get to know someone, you build trust." Would it be enough? I was banking my life on winning him over with no not-so-stellar personality.

Her half-smile hinted at sadness. "I wish you luck." At my nod, she added, "I don't think you need to worry about Brodin right now, though."

"Will Bixby hurt him?" I shouldn't care. He was irritating. Way too cocky. And beyond arrogant. But that didn't stop my belly from churning.

"Most of the time, she releases us after questioning."

"What if he killed Jared?"

"Do you think he did?"

I shrugged. "I can't imagine why he would, but who knows what his agenda is outside of eliminating me?"

"If they don't let him go by tomorrow, we'll go after him."

I blinked. "We can do that?" Who was this girl and how did she hold this kind of power?

"Witches don't fare well under lengthy questioning."

"He's fae."

She paused. "Interesting."

"Why?"

"No reason."

Not an answer but I'd let it go for now.

Rising to her feet, she brushed off the seat of her prison suit. "If he didn't do it, she'll let him go and hunt for new blood after that."

"*We* didn't do it either, but I'm still worried the screechers will sniff us out. Bixby won't be able to tell we saw the guy there, will she?"

"Nope." There was no disguising her grim tone. "I didn't see any spylings around."

My stepdad had once taught me a spell… Did I dare try it? I had to. We needed protection.

Trying to act casual, I got up and strolled over to the cupboard storing our uniforms. While my back was turned, I drew in some mist, then sent it out with a command.

Glamour us so the screechers don't smell anything about Jared.

Jacey shuddered. "What did you do?"

Looking down I saw nothing unusual about me. Really not rockin' the gray uniform, but who would? They might as well dress us all in shapeless sacks.

Had I done something or was it wishful thinking on my part?

She paced over to me and scrutinized my face. "Tennas block magic."

"Yup. You're right. I can't do magic." Gulp. *Please, don't question me further.* I didn't want to lie to her.

"If I didn't know better, I'd think you'd cast a spell on me."

"Can't." I held up my wrists. My tennas flickered, and fiery sparks drifted to the floor. They were sucked down, disappearing. "And besides, why would I?"

Her posture eased but her gaze remained alert. "You're right. You can't. Because… If you could, there might be a way to break that blood bond. I can't any longer." She held up her wrists. "My tennas were enhanced."

"What does that mean?"

"I used to be able to do more than thread magic."

Did I dare ask if she meant sketar? Not yet. I trusted her but this was my only source of power. I wouldn't share it with others easily.

"We could break a blood bond with a different form of magic?" Could I find a way to do it myself?

"Sometimes…"

"It's an oath."

"All promises were made to be broken."

Oh, yeah? I wasn't so sure about that. "I wasn't forced to make the bond."

"Most involve some sort of manipulation"

I growled, remembering. "I…There was something I needed. Information. I thought I'd be willing to do anything to obtain it but…" I shrugged. "He took advantage of that."

"You were naïve, like most people are when they need something. I understand desperation."

"Nah, I was stupid."

"It's hard to see past something you've wanted for a long time." An echo of pain filled her voice, making me wonder what she longed for more than anything. She'd acted this way before, as if a part of her was missing. "But it's silly to keep talking about it because, as you said, we're wearing tennas."

If I broke the promise, I could tell Brodin the truth. The big question was: would he believe me?

We opted to hide in our room for the rest of the day other than for dinner. No need to draw screecher attention.

It wasn't a silly fear on our part. The skeletal beasties clattered past our room more than once before lights-out.

After midnight, their shrill cries dragged me from sleep. I lay on my bunk, half asleep, hoping the door wouldn't bang open to let them inside, where they'd leap on me and haul me away to be questioned about the Seeker's fillinette.

That's why, come about two in the morning, it didn't make sense for me to consider leaving my room.

Chapter 18

I couldn't stop thinking about the Seeker symbol I'd seen magically imprinted on the wall near the dead guard. A message was waiting. Would it lead me to who might've used the fillinette to kill the guard? Assuming they were connected. I kept thinking about the information mentioned in my classes, how fillinettes were primarily used by Seekers but how a few wizards with other skaptis—though I couldn't recall which—also occasionally used the device.

Regardless, I needed to look into it.

Once I placed my hand on the symbol, I'd know… something, assuming the tenna bracelets didn't block the message transfer.

Of course, I'd have to get past the lock on our door first.

Pulling sketar power, I twisted it and, with my hand over the mechanism, carefully fed my spell through my fingers.

Open.

I turned the knob.

Nothing.

It was all I could do to bite back my growl. But slamming around would get me nowhere. I had to keep trying.

I gathered more magic and directed it onto the lock.

The mechanism clicked.

Yes! I danced in place.

When Jacey rolled over on her bed, I stilled. Holding my breath, I waited until I was sure she was still asleep, before carefully opening the door and creeping outside. The lock engaged behind me, but I'd deal with getting back inside later.

They'd dimmed the lights in the three-story room, and I stubbed my toe on the wide base of a support post before my eyes adjusted. Hopping and muffling my curses, I squinted around to pin down landmarks so I didn't hurt myself on anything else. No spylings so far. I wouldn't want Bixby seeing what I was up to.

A slithering sound sent me scooting left, toward the door to the hall that led to the big open room outside the cafeteria. I reached the panel and tugged it open. After sliding through the gap, I carefully closed it behind me then tiptoed down the hall to the great room. As I skirted the big open expanse, my skin crawled with fear. What would I do if a guard saw me? If I ran, he'd nail me with magic then haul me to Bixby's office where she'd do horrible things to me, while Duvoe watched.

Hovering close to the rail, I crept up the stairs to the second floor and down the hall to the left, passing the classrooms. I stopped when I reached 2A. Jacey had paused here, but why?

After I read the Seeker symbol, I'd stop on my way back.

Turning, I continued down the hall and went through

the door on the end, entering the room that spanned the back portion of the building.

Scooting around the outside of the room, I passed a long bank of windows overlooking the backyard, where scruffy grass grew in perfusion, peppered with spindly, new-growth trees. No one had mowed the lawn for ages, and the forest was reclaiming the field.

A movement drew my eye, and I leaned against the glass, squinting.

Clouds blanketed the sky, hiding the stars and moons, and making it a challenge to see, but I spied…

Kai.

He slunk across the back edge of the lawn, hugging the trees, moving from left to right, toward a gazebo. He crept up the crooked stairs and entered the rickety wooden structure overgrown with vines. Something… no, *someone* waited for him inside, a person who remained hidden in the shadows. The bulky form suggested a man. A few moments later, Kai backed away and, pivoting fast, leaped from the top step to the lawn.

As he rushed away from the gazebo, his head lifted, and I swore his gaze found me where I stood motionless, watching.

Eyes gleaming, he changed course, aiming for the building, but he stopped and peered over his shoulder, back toward the gazebo.

I inched away from the window and, turning, ran toward the wall.

Out in the hallway, something shuffled, like a foot dragging across the floor.

I froze. My heart leaped up into my throat, and I squashed down my breath to remain quiet. I needed to read the mark and get out of here.

Scooting to the wall, I placed my palm against the symbol, closed my eyes, and whispered the spell.

Words echoed in my mind.

Your contract has not been fulfilled. Do it!

Gasping, I yanked my hand from the wall and cupped it with the other, pressing both of them against my chest.

Damn Ramseff. Why leave me a message here? How did the message involve the guard who'd been impaled to the ceiling?

If only I knew what this all meant.

Kai could be heading this way. I was surprised he hadn't flitted here already. I needed to get back to my room before he—or a guard or, shit, one of the shifters—found me out of my room.

I hurried to the door and peeked out into the hall. Seeing nothing, I dashed forward, but I stalled outside 2A again. A squirming feeling between my shoulder blades told me to look into this before returning to my room. Peering around, I made sure I was still alone. Only silence and a muffled tick-tick-tick reached my ears.

I expected the door to be locked, but it gave way at my touch. Murky darkness greeted me inside, but I could pick out long tables set up in a row with chairs on all sides.

While I couldn't see a damn thing, I didn't dare turn on a light.

Moving left, my foot caught on something, and I tripped, flying forward. I tumbled onto the floor and hissed when my knees slammed into the unforgiving surface.

I groaned and pivoted around, trying to see what I'd stumbled over. The shadowy blob in front of me gave nothing away. With a huff of frustration I rose and returned to the open doorway, where I flicked on the light.

Kimmie, Sheera's sidekick, sat slumped in a chair, facing me. I must've caught my toe on one of her outstretched legs. While her gaze remained focused in my direction, her milky-white eyes didn't track movement. Her jaw had slid downward, leaving her mouth slack, revealing her swollen, protruding tongue.

I crept closer and stooped down, hoping to find her lungs lifting and falling. Reaching out, I laid my finger on her wrist, but couldn't feel a pulse. When I dropped her arm, her head lolled forward. Her chest followed, and she started to topple from the chair. I grabbed her arms, but the breath whooshed from my lungs when I spied the fillinette sticking out of her back at the right height to hit her heart.

A shriek burst from me and I reeled back in horror, unscrambling my limbs from hers. She continued to fall. With a wet smack, she hit the tiles at my feet.

I gulped and covered my mouth while my stomach revolted. Spying a trash bucket in the corner, I ran to it and skidded onto my knees in front. I hurled, my belly erupting into the can, spasming over and over until it felt like everything I'd eaten over the past week was gone. Sinking back onto my butt, I shuddered.

Glancing around, I looked for another Seeker's mark but didn't find one. The fillinette said the two murders had to be related, yet why no mark?

Subtle tick-tick-ticking drew my eye to the opposite side of the room. Something moved, slithering up the wall and onto the ceiling. It oozed toward me...

A gorelon.

What if the Master Seeker had left the mark and the fillinettes were not related? After all, other wizards used them, too.

That could mean the gorelon...

It slithered closer.

I leaped up and rushed toward the door but tripped

over Kimmie again. Sprawling across her, I gulped and wheezed, struggling to lift myself off her cold, stiff body. She squished beneath me, and bile rose into my mouth again. Flailing off her, I bolted for the door. It banged against the inner wall as I raced into the hall.

Fleeing, I didn't stop running until I'd reached my room. With tears streamed down my face and my sobs echoed around me, I called sketar power to use on the lock, but the magic kept slipping through my mind's fingers.

Afraid to bang on the door to beg Jacey to let me in, because I could draw the attention of guards, I slunk into the shadows and settled on the floor, pressing my back against the wall. I drew up my legs, wrapped my arms around them, and rocked. Whenever I closed my eyes, I saw Kimmie's blankly-staring face. The fillinette wedged into her back. The gorelon creeping closer.

"Hey," someone said softly from the entrance into this section of the prison.

My pulse skipped, and I leaped to my feet as they approached. Crouching, I assumed a defensive posture. But I relaxed—somewhat—when Brodin strolled into the wedge moonlight streaming in through an upper window.

"What…" Straightening, I gulped and swallowed, struggling to regain control of myself. "What are you doing here?"

"The screechers spit me out."

"They ate you?" My jaw dropped, but why should I be surprised? That was how I'd arrived in the fae kingdom. Regurgitation must be the norm for creatures here.

"Not yet, but maybe tomorrow." Brodin paused beneath one of the dimmed lights. One corner of his mouth lifted before his lips smoothed. "For now, I'm free to wander around inside the prison walls."

Tension eased from my shoulders, though my hands

still trembled. I swiped away my tears, pretending they were strands of hair caught on my face. But as he came closer and his face tightened, I could tell he'd been clued into my crying.

His hand reached toward me. "Anything I can…" Growling, he yanked it back and pressed his palm against his thigh. "Are you okay?" The last bit came out stilted. He had no reason to care if I was upset.

I flicked away his question with a wave of my hand. "Did you kill the guard?"

"Why would I do something like that?"

"Not an answer."

His jaw twitched. "It's the only one I'm giving."

"The screechers thought you were involved."

"They were mistaken."

Were they? Other wizards had access to fillinettes. Did Influencers?

"Have you heard of fillinettes?"

He frowned. "Can't say that I have. What are they?"

"Nothing."

"Nothing, but you asked me about them," he pressed.

"If you don't know, it's not up to me to tell you."

"We're back there again, are we?"

"Last I knew, we hadn't left. You're the one who wants to kill me, remember? I have no reason to act any other way but defensive with you."

"You forget I'm letting you prove to me you didn't kill my mother." Steel edged into his voice.

"How gracious of you. I told you I didn't do it. That should be enough."

"Not for me."

"Then we've reached an impasse." My gaze darted to the entrance. "Why don't you go wander somewhere else? The guys' rooms are in another part of the building. You're not even allowed in this section of the prison."

"I was looking for…" He shook his head, making his hair flop forward, covering his face. What was he hiding? "I saw you run through the great room and followed. What are *you* doing out of your room? It's late."

Sharing anything could take away my advantage. "It's none of your business, but I…went for a walk. Funny thing, my door was unlocked."

He reached out and tested the knob. "Funny thing, but it's locked, now." No hiding the sneer in his voice.

Battling with him all the time only made me feel exhausted. And damn my eyes for stinging with tears again. "Go away."

He studied me for a long time, though I kept my face in shadow, before he dropped to the floor and leaned against the wall.

I stared down at him. "I said go away."

"Warden Bixby is something else, isn't she?" With a jerk of his head, he flicked his hair off his face. "And Duvoe. What's up with him, anyway?"

Grumbling, I sat on the floor, opposite him to keep a decent distance between us. "I've thought the same thing."

"They go everywhere together."

"They're brother and sister."

"And adults."

I shrugged. "Does it matter?"

"I guess not." He stared up at the steel-beamed ceiling. "This place isn't anything like what I assumed it would be."

"It seems prison-like to me. What were you expecting?"

"I don't know. My mom…" His face softened. "She used to tell me stories about the fae kingdom."

"*You're* fae. You grew up in the air here, remember?"

"I'm half-fae."

"On your mom's side."

"Dad's like you." His lips twisted.

"Scum because we didn't grow up here?"

"I don't think you're scum."

"Just a murderer."

He got to his feet. "That remains to be seen, doesn't it?"

I also rose. My head tilted, and I studied his face but he'd discovered my shadows and was using them to his advantage. "Are you truly giving me a chance to prove my innocence or is this all a game?"

He started to walk away, toward the exit into the hall. "I guess you'll find out."

Growling, I chose not to run after him.

As soon as he'd left this area, I pulled in sketar magic. When I pushed it out, the lock granted me entrance. Tiptoeing inside, I undressed and climbed underneath my covers.

While my panic had fled, I couldn't stop shivering. I'd assumed the Master Seeker killed the guard, leaving the body as a gruesome reminder of our contract. But if he could kill a guard, why not eliminate Brodin himself? Short of playing manipulative games, he had no reason to involve me. But no second mark near Kimmie suggested the murders might be independent of the Seeker's mark; a coincidence. Fillinettes, while rare, could be accessed by wizards with other skaptis.

The gorelon… Had it killed the guard and Kimmie?

My shivering intensified until I worried I'd shake the bed hard enough to wake Jacey.

Swirling thoughts kept me awake, but sometime during the night, Kai appeared on my bed. He padded up the mattress and butted my shoulder as if to say, *I know what you were up to but we'll talk about it in the morning.* He purred while I patted him because, how could I resist? Curling in a circle, he settled at my side. He winked up at me for a long while before his eyelids slowly drooped, and he slept.

I did, too.

I woke when narrow bands of steel snapped free from the mattress on either side of me and slapped down across my chest, pinning me to the bed.

Chapter 19

Releasing a shriek, I yanked on the steel claws biting into my chest. They loosened, and I scrambled out from beneath them and leaped from the bed.

Kai had disappeared sometime as I slept. Lucky him, because he'd avoided impalement.

I stood beside the bed, panting, while the claws retracted into the frame surrounding the mattress.

My freakin' bed was alive! How was I going to go to sleep on it again?

Jacey groaned and sat up, rubbing her chest where she'd been poked. Scooting to the end, she hopped down and came over to stand beside me. "Takes getting used to, doesn't it?"

I advanced on my bed but saw nothing amiss any longer. "What was that? It's… It's…"

"Yeah. Creepy." She opened the cupboard and pulled out two clean prison uniforms and undies. "You've just met our alarm clock. Effective, huh?" After tossing some of the clothing at me, she hurried to the door. "Come on. Be quick."

"Why?" I said, watching the bed over my shoulder as I joined her at the door. "Will it attack again?" Would it chase me out into the hall? I shivered. It was clear I wouldn't stop shaking until I'd left this place.

"Not until tomorrow. It already did its job for today." She swung open our door but I tapped her arm, then tugged her back inside and closed the panel.

"This won't take long." I filled her in on what had happened the night before.

Her eyes widened. "Kimmie's dead?"

"Yup." Eyes wide open, blankly staring at the wall. Chest not moving. Her limp body splayed wide then collapsing onto the floor… A shudder ripped through me. I'd fallen on top of her! "A gorelon was in the room with her."

Her lips parted. "No."

"It…" I frowned. "Does it make a tick-tick-tick sound?"

Arms wrapping around her waist, she nodded. Fear flashed in her eyes. "Did you make eye contact?"

Had I? I didn't think so, but it was hard to tell.

"What happened next?" she asked.

"It crept toward me, but I bolted and didn't stop running until I got here." No need to mention Brodin. Our encounter meant nothing.

"You didn't touch Kimmie, did you? Otherwise, they'll know you were there."

"Yeah, that's the problem."

Her hand slapped over her mouth before dropping to her chest. "You didn't."

I winced. "It was dark. I tripped and fell over her. After hurling out my guts in the trash bucket, I saw the gorelon and stumbled over Kimmie again, landing on top of her."

"So, this isn't good." Jacey paced the room. "But we'll figure it out. Somehow."

"Bixby's going to send screechers after me, isn't she?"

"Maybe. Maybe not. A dead guard is different than a dead girl. The latter happens often enough it barely creates a stir among the inmates."

"What should I do?" No hiding the tremor in my voice.

"Hope she doesn't care. That she doesn't call the screechers to sniff Kimmie."

I swallowed, but the lump of fear in my throat wouldn't go down. My pulse thundered in my ears. "If they question me, I don't know anything. That won't be a lie."

"You…should be okay, then."

Ugh. This was going to be awful.

Stopping, she grabbed my forearms. "We need to get out of here. Taking the Reformatory Challenge is the best option." Her soft sigh huffed out. "That must've been scary for you."

"Very."

"Could you tell how she died?"

"She…" For some reason, I didn't want to mention the fillinette. Maybe because it was a Seeker's thing, even if I was no longer an official Seeker. But Jacey needed to know some of it. "She was killed the same way as the guard."

"With a spear."

I wrenched my gaze from hers. "Yeah."

"Could be the same murderer."

"Or a gorelon, assuming they use spears to kill."

"I haven't seen them use one yet, but why not? It's just another way to achieve the same result."

"A dead inmate."

"And guard, in Jared's case."

"So… I won't worry about Bixby until I need to. If she questions me, I'll deny being involved."

"And she'll probably let you go."

"Probably" was not something to look forward to.

Jacey stepped away from me. "How did you get out of the room?"

"It was…" I scrambled for a lie. "Unlocked." I shrugged. "The bolt mustn't have engaged at lockdown."

Her frown smoothed. "Why did you leave, then? I mean, anything could've happened."

And a lot did.

"I… When we found the guard, I saw a message on the wall beneath him. It couldn't be read unless I touched it."

"And you know this because…"

"It was a Seeker's symbol. A way for a Seeker to leave a note for…someone." I couldn't tell her I was a Seeker.

"Huh." Her head tilted. "What did it say?"

The words hovered on the tip of my tongue, but no matter how hard I tried to spit them out, they wouldn't come. "I… can't."

"This is related to the blood bond."

"The message was a reminder." It told me the Master Seeker was watching. How far did his evil reach?

"Of the task expected of you." She shrugged. "It's the norm with this kind of bond. My uncle… Let's just say he was often tasked to secure them for the king."

I wasn't sure how I felt about that. My blood bond experience had made me leery of them in general, and I couldn't see how they could be used for good.

Jacey stared off into space for a second before growling. "So, a Seeker's mark. Do you think the person who left the mark also killed the guard?"

I shrugged. "Kimmie, too? No mark there."

"It could be someone else, then. Maybe they're not related."

Except for the fillinette…

"The only thing we can do is take this as it comes. But for now, we've got to hustle." Jacey opened the door and turned right outside our room.

I hurried beside her toward a chamber at the end of the open dorm area. "Why do we need to be quick?"

"If we drag our feet, all the individual shower stalls will be taken and we'll be stuck using the community showers." A shudder rippled through her tiny frame.

After the "alarm clock," I could only imagine.

No one joined us as we entered the area made up of five individual stalls and one open chamber with multiple showerheads with no partitions between them.

Pausing outside one of the separate stalls, Jacey frowned. "Will anyone else be able to tell that the Seeker's message was for you?"

"It disappeared immediately after I absorbed it."

"Good." She handed me a towel from the stack on a table near the door. "You should be safe, then."

After showering and dressing, we went to breakfast.

"After we eat, we've got indoctrination, then classes," Jacey said.

I dragged a hunk of sausage through the syrup left from my pancake and popped it into my mouth. While it felt like I was chewing a tire, hunger made everything palatable. I wiggled my neck to make the hunk go down, and frowned. "Indoctrination?"

"That's what I call it. The Warden calls it a general meeting. She holds them twice a week, after breakfast, to harp on the rules." Sitting back, she dropped her fork on her empty plate.

"This place doesn't seem to have any rules."

"More in the vein that we must be mindful of others' space and remember that we're here to coexist with each other for the remainder of our imprisonment." She huffed.

"Which means until we're killed by something outside or inside the prison walls." Looking up, she grinned as someone dropped their tray onto the table to the right of me and sat.

I bit back my groan.

"They let you go free?" Jacey asked Brodin.

His gaze cut to me. "Yeah. You didn't know that?"

"Why would I?" She smiled and, reaching out, tapped his forearm. "Good to see you're still bruise-free."

He'd pushed up the sleeves, showing off his muscles. Not that I was noticing.

"I didn't get the idea you were worried," he said to me.

"Not in the least."

He fed me a crooked grin. "It's okay for you to admit it."

By the fae, if I didn't know better, I'd think he was flirting. Why?

"I wasn't worried."

Jacey's head snapped from me to Brodin then back again, and her smile grew bigger with every jerky motion.

"Bixby couldn't hold me because I didn't do anything," Brodin told Jacey.

"Why did the screechers grab you, then?" I asked.

He shrugged and, lifting his fork, dug into his meal.

"Tria here has been telling me all about you," Jacey said.

I glared at her but she just winked.

Brodin sent a sly look my way. "Anything good?"

Jacey's humor-filled gaze darted to meet mine. "Only the best."

The delighted sound he released grated on my nerves.

"Can't you sit somewhere else?" I snapped.

"Why? Are you feeling unsocial?" he asked around a big bite of pancake.

"You two are so cute," Jacey said, beaming. "It's like a rom-com. Hate to love, I think they call it."

"Ugh. I don't love him," I shouted.

Brodin—Feral—smirked and slapped his hand to his chest. "You're woundin' me."

"What the hell is going on here?" I asked him. Had he changed his mind about me? I couldn't imagine what I might've done to make him believe I was innocent, however.

"I'm just being friendly."

"Why?"

His fork stalled on his plate. "Because we're eating together?"

"Exactly," Jacey said. She nudged aside her half-eaten tray, proving our convo must be much more appealing.

"You're not helping," I said, my face growing hot.

"Oh, I think I am." She propped her chin on her palms, with her elbows on the table. "Tria was telling me you'd be the perfect third for the triad we're forming, and I agree."

I gulped. "I never said that."

He frowned and his concerned gaze flicked my way. "A triad? I assume you mean you, Jacey, plus…"

"Tria, of course," Jacey said.

"Okay. Hmm…"

Jacey's face fell. "Don't feel pressured."

"I don't." His back straightened and he blew out a big breath. "Sure, I'll join your triad."

So he could kill me. Silly of me to believe, even for a second, that he'd changed his mind.

"You're only said yes so you can watch me," I said.

"So sweet!" Jacey said with a chuckle. She waved her spoon at Brodin. "Keep going. You're doin' awesome."

"He isn't doing awesome," I said, horrified she was gushing all over him. "I told you he wants to kill me."

"Do you?" Jacky asked, completely serious for one second. "'Cause that would ruin my rom-com."

He turned a scowl my way, and his gaze traveled to my right arm. I'd pushed my sleeves up to my elbows. "Would you be willing to—?"

A crash erupted at the entrance to the cafeteria, and we jolted apart.

Staring past me, Jacey's mouth slid open.

Brodin peered over his shoulder.

A voice boomed out. "I smell a fuckin' Seeker."

Chapter 20

Jacey's eyes blazed. She reeled backward as if she expected to see a herd of centaurs galloping across the room.

Brodin's spine jolted, and his hand dropped to his side, seeking a weapon.

I tried to slink underneath the table.

"I'm gonna kill me a Seeker," a guy said in a gruff voice.

I'd made a mistake thinking I could slip past everyone's notice.

"Did you tell them?" I hissed at Brodin.

He shook his head, but I wasn't sure I believed him.

"Titan," Jacey whispered in horror, staring past our shoulders. "He... I..." Her panicked gaze met mine. "Don't turn. Don't say a thing. He'll leave us alone." She swallowed and grimaced, as if something wouldn't go down. "I wouldn't want to be that Seeker, though. Bad day for them."

"Reveal yourself, Seeker," Titan shouted in a growly voice. "Or it'll be worse for you once I hunt you down."

My pulse going triple time, I remained frozen on my

cold metal stool. It looked like I wasn't going to live long enough to take the Reformatory Challenge, after all. Twenty percent odds now sounded fantastic compared to my chances of getting out of this room alive.

Brodin's broad shoulders tightened. He turned and stood, his chin solidifying into granite. "I'm your Seeker." Even his voice didn't waver. "What of it?"

"He's so brave," Jacey sighed. "You didn't tell me he was a Seeker."

"Because he's not," I said.

"Then who is?"

"Me."

She plunged backward in shock. "No!"

"Yes."

"How?"

I shrugged. "The usual way? I had the skapti and got the training. I'm almost a Level Five." Well, I'd once almost been a Level Five. Who knew what I was now.

"Why are you doing this?" I yanked on Brodin's jump-suit. "Sit down."

He tugged free and stepped forward. "I'm the Seeker you're looking for, Titan."

Brodin was going to get himself killed. According to the Master Seeker, that was my job, not Titan's. Not that I had any solid plan or interest in doing it, but still.

I stood and turned.

Titan was a beast, even in people form. At least six-seven, he sported hulking shoulders and thighs that would fit well on a T-rex. Which must be the point, since he was one in his other form. He stomped closer, flanked by a guy almost as big as him—six-six if I had to guess. Two other, equally tall guys, though lean and muscular, rather than bulky, guarded the rear, their long blond hair swaying across their shoulders.

Titan stopped a few feet away from Brodin, and a slick grin rose on his face. "Not many Seekers make it through the challenge outside. Those who do, the ones who enter the prison…" His smirk widened as he took in other wizards fleeing the room to reach the relative safety of the outer hall. "Those who make it this far? They don't last more-an-a-day." His chuckle rang out. "Lots of accidents happen here, especially to Seekers."

"Oh, scary," Brodin said, seemingly unfazed by Titan's blustering fury. "You might want to try harder."

Why was Brodin taunting him?

Fists formed at Titan's sides. "What did you just say?"

"Sounded clear to me," Brodin said. "You're all show. No action."

"By the fae, he's totally awesome," Jacey said. "You sure you don't want him?"

Growling, I turned away from her. While I hadn't yet figured out why he was doing it, I still wasn't letting Brodin take the fall for me.

I wedged myself between them. "Hold on a sec, guys." Sort of guys. Titan was a bambiraptor. Brodin? How could his Eerie abilities help him here?

Titan pushed me aside as if I was fluff. "Out of my way, peanut."

By the fae, I hated nicknames. A spark of anger lit inside me, aimed at Titan. It combined with confusion, because I couldn't figure out what Brodin was doing.

When I jumped between them again, Titan bodily lifted me and dropped me about three feet to his right. "I said to get out of my way." His jaw elongated, a scaly, beastly structure jutting out from the bottom of his head. "I'm gonna rip me apart a Seeker."

Would he shift into a raptor right here in the cafeteria? Raptors were hunters. And while I wasn't a peanut, I might be the equivalent of a rabbit. He'd chase me down and claw me to shreds.

Teeth popped out of his jawline, long and sharp, and beyond deadly. This wasn't looking good for me or Brodin. Why was Feral so eager to play the hero?

"Let's be reasonable," Brodin said softly, his hands splaying wide. "We can take this outside."

Perhaps he planned to get Titan outside and leave him to the island elements. Was that why he'd stepped between us?

"You don't want to hurt anyone," Brodin added.

Rationalizing would do nothing for a monster like Titan. But maybe…

Sketar mist drifted around me even here, inside the cafeteria. My eyes closing, I sucked it in and made it my own. It charged through my veins. As if they sensed what I was doing, my tenna manacles tightened to pinch around my wrists, eager to suppress the magic. But my power came from a different world. Not Sídhe. Not fae.

"You should leave, Titan," I said, infusing a hint of power into the command. I'd have to be careful, or someone would notice I was doing magic. "You're tired. You need to lie down."

He blinked at me. "What?"

Brodin slanted me a confused look.

Jacey rose from her seat, her mouth twitching.

I added a bit more sketar power and shouted, "Go. Lie. Down."

Titan's jaw jolted back into his head. His eyes glazed, but only until one of his sidekicks bumped his ribs with an elbow.

"Dude," the guy growled while a ruffled golden mane sprouted from his head. "You're… What are you doing? We were going to kill a Seeker. I was looking forward to it."

Leaving Titan's side, he stomped closer to me, but Brodin stepped between us. The guy slammed into Brodin, who didn't shift an inch. He didn't even flinch. Who was this guy? A totally different person stood beside me, trying to defend me when he shouldn't. It… I wasn't sure how it made me feel.

"I can't believe you're willing to challenge Titan," the guy said. His arm swept out to encompass Brodin and Jacey. "All three of you must be lookin' for a quick death."

"You only want me," I said, stepping between Titan and Brodin. "I'm the Seeker."

"Peanut?" Titan barked out. He laughed, a belly shaking, roaring chuckle.

I stomped my foot. "Don't call me peanut."

He ground his face close to mine, while his friend wrenched away from Brodin's grip. "I'll call you whatever I damn please." His hands wrapped around my throat, and his face grew ruddy. Mine must be going red, too, because I couldn't breathe. Couldn't speak, which meant I couldn't use sketar magic on him to make him let go.

Grabbing my knife, I clicked free the blade and slammed it up into Titan's forearm.

Releasing a high-pitched bellow, he stumbled backward, his hand slapping over the slice. Blood trickled past his fingers and plopped on the floor.

Brodin growled and rushing forward, rammed his head into Titan's side.

Gasping and choking, I clutched my throat. Freed, I drew in mist power, sucking and pulling it in until it must glow beneath my skin.

Kai appeared beside me. When he leaned against my leg, heat and flames charged into me, cauterizing my bones, my skin, and setting me alight. The magic grew stronger inside me.

I combined the power he'd given me with sketar mist. My insides vibrated like an earthquake as a massive bolt of energy roared up through my body and out to my fingertips. I shot the invisible power at Titan with my command.

"The four of you are tired," I shouted. "And hungry." I pointed to the window where filled food trays popped out at regular intervals and shot across the floor. "Get some food." I sucked a breath of air in through my swollen throat. "Eat it. Then go back to your room." My sweeping hand took in the entire quadrad. "All of you."

Titan pivoted and strode over to the window where they dispensed meals. A tray loaded with breakfast popped out, and he grabbed it. Stumbling behind him, his entourage did the same. They took seats and proceeded to mechanically shovel food into their mouths.

I hoped they were eating gargoyle fingernails.

With a feline smile of satisfaction curling his kitty lips, Kai revealed long, sharp incisors. He meowed at me then disappeared.

"That…" Brodin's eyes met mine. "I'm not sure what you did or how you did it but that was…"

"This is why we three need to form a triad, right, Tria?" Jacey said, coming around the table to stand with m. "You both…" Her arms wrapped around me in a big hug. "You and Kai were awesome. You did something, didn't you?" Releasing me, she smacked Brodin's arm. "Way to go bold, dude. With Tria's…" She coughed down whatever she'd started to say. "And you, with your—"

"*My* skapti is Influence," Brodin said.

I crossed my arms and smirked. "Yet I was the one doing the influencing."

"I was warming up."

"With your tennas?" I said. "You *were* standing up for me, though, and I appreciate it."

His head drew back. "You do? I mean…really? Why?"

Jacey linked her arms through ours and drew us close to her sides. "Guys. We are going to be the best triad ever."

Brodin spoke over the top of Jacey's head. "What did you mean?"

"What did you mean? Why did you say you were the Seeker? You challenged Titan on my behalf."

"I…" Color filled his face, leaving me completely confused.

Maybe he half-believed me.

"You do have a hero complex, don't you?" I said.

His head dipped. "No, I don't."

"So, triad?" Jacey said. "Guys, pay attention. This is serious business."

"Yes," I said. "How soon can we——?"

A bellow rang out. Oh-oh.

The quad got up, leaving their trays on the table. Titan shuddered and shook; the movement making the floor waver underneath him. Turning, he glared in my direction.

"You did something to me," he roared, his gaze pinning me in place.

A flash and a twelve-foot prehistoric predator stood inside the cafeteria. He tipped his head back and, slashing at the air with his arm-length claws, he roared.

Chapter 21

"Holy fuck," Brodin said, his eyes widening.

Hyperventilating, I floundered backward, banging my hip on the table. But I couldn't let Titan hurt my friends. Well, Jacey. Brodin was… That was still undecided.

I ran forward, and my hair crackled around my face as I gathered more sketar power from the air around me.

"That won't work when he's in raptor form," Jacey said shrilly, snagging my arm. "We've got to get out of here!"

Despite my taking care, she knew I'd tapped some sort of power. Crap.

Brodin's frantic gaze swept across us. "You two get over by the wall. Stick close to it and make your way to the door. Run to your room. Hide. I'll provide cover."

Against raptor teeth and claws? I gaped at him. "I'm not going anywhere." I turned to Jacey, who looked like she couldn't decide who to listen to, Brodin or me.

Resolve filled her eyes, confirming she hadn't abandoned her roommate and boyfriend in the catacombs. Something else had happened there, and I'd help her find out. We'd do it together.

Taking her hand, I squeezed tight. "Triad, right?"

"Soon."

"Is there another exit?" I asked. Titan's friends had shifted and blocked the doorway.

"Nope, and the quad won't let us escape. Titan's on a rampage and we're about to become dino fodder." Her narrowed gaze flicked to the raptor. While his roars were no longer stabbing my ears, he was now dragging his claws across the floor, creating deep furrows in the tile. Must want to make sure we were truly terrified before descending on us to slash us to pieces.

We didn't stand a chance, but I wasn't hanging around to calculate the odds.

The chiema tipped its three heads back and each shot flames toward the ceiling. It had a body like a goat's except I'd never seen a goat with massive claws and a long, spiked tail. The lizard roared, displaying jagged teeth, while Lars expanded his scaled wings. His armored skin gleamed in the overhead lights.

I wasn't embarrassed to admit my entire body shook at the thought of taking on the quad.

Abandoning ripping up the floor, Titan stomped toward us, a towering hulk of rage. His friends lumbered behind him.

Brodin put himself between us and the raptor as if he could defeat the enormous predator with his bare hands alone. His body shimmered as his hands lifted, and I waited to see if he'd shift into an Eerie before my eyes. Impossible. He could only do that in dreams.

Clenching my jaw, I tightened my grip around my knife. It wasn't much, but if I infused it with sketar power, I could leave a few wounds of my own before I was killed.

"Window," I said, pointing to the bank of them behind Jacey. "We can get out that way!"

"It's worse out there than in here," Jacey said. Her spine stiffened, and she pressed herself up close beside me. "No matter what, we'll go down together."

How could outside be worse than facing these ferocious shifters? We'd be mounds of bloody pulp within seconds. My heartbeat thrashing in my ears, I ran toward the windows while Brodin stalked toward Titan.

Foolish hero. He'd be chomped to pieces in seconds.

The window opened. But then, why use locks when worse things waited for inmates outside?

"Brodin," I shouted, and he darted a look over his shoulders. I tipped my head toward the opening, and he nodded. "Come on, Jacey!" I shot my leg through the opening and scrambled across the jamb.

Jacey peered outside and her face scrunched tight. "All right. Let's do this." But she nudged my backside and laughed. "Get going before Titan chomps on us."

Brodin ducked beneath a swipe of Titan's claws and ran in our direction, his body giving off a burnished glow and his fangs on display.

I tumbled onto the lawn, barely missing being impaled by a thorn bush. Rising to my feet, I brushed off my jumpsuit as Jacey and Brodin joined me.

Inside, Titan roared. While he wouldn't fit through the window, I doubted that would stop him. He'd take down the wall to reach us.

"Where to?" Brodin asked Jacey.

"No clue." Frantic, she shook her head. "I don't come out here."

Kai appeared to my left and meowed shrilly, before disappearing.

That was enough guidance for me.

"Time to find out what this place is all about." Grabbing both their hands, I dragged them in that direction.

"I think there's another entrance around the side of the building," Jacey said. "I saw it…" She frowned. "Some-time. Anyway, be super quiet. We don't want to draw atten-tion. If we're lucky, they won't know we're here."

"The quad?" Brodin said.

"Them, too," Jacey's face tightened. "Don't touch anything."

Hard not to do that when my feet were hitting the ground.

We ran along a rough slope covered with knee-high grass, and I prayed we wouldn't stir up kertins. One bite and we'd be laid out as a snoozing, raptor buffet. The bank sloped downward to our right. Not much to worry about touching so far, but we were approaching a cluster of big trees. That area could prove tricky.

Breaking apart, our lungs raging from the exertion and a healthy dose of fear, we wove through the wooded area. Behind us, Titan pummeled himself against the inside cafeteria wall.

A roaring snarl was followed by a crumbling sound, and a glimpse over my shoulder showed Micah—the giant lizard—had squeezed through a window and was in hot pursuit. His clawed feet churned up the soil as he scram-bled after us, his long teeth dripping saliva in anticipation. The three-headed chiema galloped at his heels, his necks stretching forward. Lars soared above them, his broad wing-span blocking the sun.

We had to hurry if we wanted to escape but would returning inside be enough? How could we keep them from following and killing us there?

"Keep going!" Jacey said. "We've got to get to the other entrance before—"

I slammed into a tree. Turning, I pulled in sketar mist.

Too much! It overwhelmed me, consumed me. I was going to drown.

Kai appeared at my side. The wind swept up his fur, whipping it around him, but he bent into the gust and leaned against me, staring up with support in his eyes. His spiked fur bristled on his back, and his lips peeled back to release a snarl.

"Help," I stuttered, not sure who or what I called for. But I'd overdone it with my magic. And like I'd worried, it had backfired on me. Wild and untamable, it would scorch me from the inside out.

Kai keened, a scratchy-plaintive meow.

"Get behind me, Kai," I said in desperation. "Run or disappear again. It's too dangerous here!"

As the sketar magic sunk deeper into me, heat and flames roared through my veins, burning me. No! Gulping, I tried to push away the magic but more joined what I'd hauled in, spiraling into me like red-hot lava. I couldn't handle it. I'd explode.

"Please," I whispered, slumping against the tree. "Help my friends. Help Kai."

Titan thundered closer, his shifted buddies on his heels.

Staring up at the tree, Kai howled again before he nodded at me and winked out of existence.

The branches of the tree overhead reached down and grabbed me.

Chapter 22

The branches yanked me upward, into the leafy canopy. I grabbed my knife from my pocket, but it slipped from my grip and dropped to the forest floor. Awesome. Now, I was defenseless.

Jacey snatched up the knife and whirled to face whatever came next. Her hair flew around her head, and her guttural taunts to the shifters made me proud to call her my friend. I'd never had anyone eager to defend me before; I'd always been the defender.

The branches dropped me onto a limb, far enough out from the trunk, I worried the branch would break and I'd plunge to the ground. Then the leaves pummeled me, smacking my arms, legs, face, and the sketar magic I'd sucked in dissipated. When the leaves retreated, I started climbing down, but the leaves returned and hit me again. This time, I swore they told me to behave. A tree. Was telling me to chill. And diffusing the sketar magic I'd recklessly pulled inside.

The branches that had hefted me into the sky wrapped around Jacey. While she remained strangely still, they hauled her up and deposited her onto a branch close to mine.

Brodin stopped about a hundred feet away. Spying a rock on the forest floor, he grabbed it and braced over his head. "Come at me. Just try me!"

"What's he doing?" I shrieked at Jacey, but she gave no reply.

Lars landed on the ground and tucked his wings against this back. His beaked head darted toward Brodin, who smacked him with the rock. Shrieking, he backed away while the three-headed chiema and lizard stomped closer. Brodin was going to get himself killed, and I wasn't sure I wanted him dead. He'd gone from irritating to intriguing me.

Jacey wrapped her legs around the tree branch and—more surprises—tipped her head back and closed her eyes. Was she scared? She didn't seem to be but it was hard to tell.

"Work your way backward," I whispered, hoping to reassure her. "Slowly. When you hit the trunk we'll be together. You've got this!"

I inched backward, and she did, too.

On the ground, Brodin remained strong, his legs spread and his rock poised over his head, ready to smack whoever came near. Stoic and resolute. Despite my eagerness to dismiss him, I felt a hefty dose of respect for him instead. And damn, too much attraction. It made me feel giddy. He shouldn't cause so much conflict inside me.

My butt hit the tree trunk. Beside me, Jacey did the same. Our legs brushed, and she nodded, though I wasn't sure what she was agreeing with. She kept her eyes close, and she…hummed.

"What are you doing?" I asked.

Her humming grew louder. She leaned back against

the trunk and her voice vibrated through the air. It sunk into my skin and lulled me, but only for a moment.

Heavy thuds rang out on the ground as the shifters drove Brodin closer to the tree with us sitting above him.

Turning, I stretched my leg toward a branch below me. He wasn't going to face the quad alone. If anyone was going to be pulverized, it would be me. I'd drawn them to us.

Branches attacked, smacking my back and head, but I fought them off and dropped, working my way toward the ground.

Titan—in raptor form—scrambled up to Brodin and, tipping his head back, roared.

Brodin swung his rock, and it smacked into Titan's side. The raptor bellowed and reeled backward while Brodin grabbed the rock and hefted it again.

I was halfway down the tree when limbs plunged toward me again. They snatched me off the branch and, hauling me up, deposited me beside Jacey, who continued to hum.

My growl of frustration ripped through the air.

"Hey, tree," I said softly, and I swore the branches that had finally stopped smacking me stilled. "My friend…" Okay, Brodin was not quite a friend but…an acquaintance? No, he was Brodin. A *hot* wizard—per Jacey—and maybe a little bit per me. He was in a class all by himself. "Anyway. Tree. Brodin could use some help. A quadrad of shifter dudes are about to pulverize him. I don't suppose you could lend a hand? Or, a branch or two. Haul him up here with us?"

"Don't talk to me. I'm busy."

I turned to Jacey. "I wasn't talking to you."

"Huh?" Jacey asked. Her eyes remained closed.

Reeling around, I stretched my leg out again, aiming for the lower branch.

"I'm doing all I can."

Frowning, I gazed up at Jacey. "I know this is hard for you. We'll find a way out of this."

She frowned again. "You do realize I'm not humming because I'm scared."

My fingers tightened on the branch I'd been sitting on. "I'm not sure why you're humming."

"Do it with me before it's too late."

"Humming with my eyes closed isn't going to help Brodin. I've got to get down to the ground." Shouts rang out below. Brodin swung his rock and Titan ducked. They were playing with him, each taking a jab before backing away to cheer for the others. When they grew tired of the game, they'd end it. "We need a miracle, not a concert."

"Tria."

"What?" I cocked my head at her.

"Get back up here before the tree does it for you and hum! Closing your eyes is optional."

I huffed, but what the hell. Scrambling back up beside her, I joined in on her song. It wasn't much. By the fae, I shouldn't sing, because my voice was awful. But I tried, softly at first, my lower tone mixing in with Jacey's much-nicer, higher-pitched voice.

Like David with Goliath, Brodin remained upright and confident. Titan towered over him.

"Louder," Jacey whispered, and then resumed humming. "It's working."

Branches flicked downward and wrapped around Brodin as Titan's claw-encrusted paw struck out. It swiped through mid-air because Brodin had left the scene.

In seconds, he had been deposited on top of the branch to my right. His rock fell from his hands and clunked on the lizard's head. Knocked out, the creature tumbled to the ground and lay still.

Eyes opening, Jacey sat up and brushed bark bits off her chest. Her smile lifted when she saw Brodin sitting with his mouth open, on the branch beyond me. "Nice of you to join us."

"The humming," I said.

"It's an old trick." Her lips curled down, and sadness filled her eyes. "My uncle taught me." She waved to the trunk. "Our song called her."

"We were…rescued by a tree," I said, unable to believe it. "Thanks, tree."

A look down showed me the three remaining shifter guys had turned back into fae. They huddled together like dudes at a ball game, consulting before a major play, while the lizard lay on the ground unmoving, beside them.

"Finally," a voice said softly behind me. "Until I was acknowledged by you, I wasn't allowed to speak."

I twisted around because… "Is the tree talking to me?"

Brodin's attention remained on the shifters. "If the tree's talking, I'm not hearing it."

"It's okay," Jacey said. "I hear, and we're all that matters."

A tree limb smacked Brodin on the side of the head. All color fled his face. "What was that?"

"The rules say I can't reveal myself unless I've been truly seen," a voice said from all around me. Overhead, the leaves rustled like pedestrians scurrying along a sidewalk in a storm. "And that doesn't happen often."

"Rules were meant to be broken," I said.

"They weren't," Brodin said. "That's how we ended up here. We should've stayed inside."

This situation would be comical if it wasn't so scary.

A chiema could climb trees.

"Go," Titan said, slapping Micah on the back.

Micah shifted back into his chiema form and his claws dug into the trunk as he ratcheted himself upward, toward us.

I cleared my throat. "Now would be a good time to—"

Above me, a form made completely from bark oozed out from the trunk, turning into a complete, almost-human-looking being. It leaped down and landed on my branch, making it shake. Like a tree trunk, the creature's lower body was thicker, though split into "legs". The legs shifted into roots that clung to the branch. The being's body narrowed as it rose toward the top, and it had multiple branch-like arms, a head much like mine, and green, leafy hair.

As I gaped, the bark split on the head-ish top, and a grin filled the creature's face, though it was made up of creased bark. Widely spaced blue eyes watched me with eagerness.

The chiema continued to climb and I was grateful this was a tall tree, reaching at least forty feet into the air. Fear climbed up my spine like a cluster of spiders.

"Welcome," Jacey said, nodding at the tree creature. "I've rarely had the chance to harmonize with a tree nymph. My uncle told me you're keepers of the forest."

The nymph curtsied at Jacey then my way, her leafy branch arms flicking sideways like a ruffled green skirt. "I am Akimi."

"Nice to meet you," I said in awe.

"Who are we talking to?" Brodin asked.

Branches flailed his arms and back but rather than cower, he fought them off and glared at me.

"I'm not responsible," I said, my words sounding defensive.

"Thank Akimi for her help, Brodin," Jacey said. "Or she might toss you back on the ground."

"Thank who?"

"Just do it," I said.

He smirked said he was doing it only to humor me. "Okay. Thanks, tree."

Akimi dipped toward him. "You are welcome."

"Whoa," Brodin said. His back smacked against the trunk. "Where did you come from?"

"Everywhere," she replied, releasing another barky smile.

"And…you saved me. Thanks." True emotion infused his words.

"She wished and thus, she receives," Akimi said, her branches dipping my way.

Brodin studied me. "You asked her to help me?"

"Well, sort of?" My face overheated. "I just felt…" I shook my head. "Never mind."

"You felt what?" he asked, his gaze intent on my face. But I had no interest in revealing secrets. "Tell me."

I crossed my arms on my chest and leaned against the tree trunk. "Nope."

He shrugged. "No matter. I'll get it out of you eventually."

My snort of derision ripped between us. "Dare you to try."

The grin he shot me made my toes curl. "Just watch me."

"Hey, guys," Jacey said. "You two might be having fun flirting, but…" She pointed down. "We've got a problem."

The chiema's long teeth dripped as he came closer, his claws shredding the bark as he shimmied up the tree.

"Fear not," Akimi's lofty voice said. "Allow me to assist." She swirled down around the tree like leafy ribbons.

When she reached the chiema, she paused and glared. She spoke, but while her mouth moved, I couldn't understand what she said. It seemed the chiema did, because he darted us a panicked look and started backing down toward the ground.

This wasn't enough for Akimi. Branches plunged down and flailed his back, hurrying him along. About twenty feet from the ground, he let go. With a twist, he landed on the ground, his claws digging into the soft soil.

Akimi flowed down behind him. She reached the bottom and, with a spring, did a flip in the air and landed in front of Titan.

Again, I couldn't hear what she said, but there was no missing the blanching of his now-human face. After shooting us a scowl that promised retribution, he and his buddies shifted back into their original shapes and, after grabbing the lizard, ran toward the prison entrance.

Akimi swirled back up to where we waited. "You see now?" she chirped once she'd perched on a branch. "I was able to assist."

"What did you say to him?" I asked.

"Shifters are simple beings. To work with them, one must drop to their level. But there is a price to be paid for pursuing such as this." Her eyes twinkled. "If they refused to back away, I offered to enter their rooms this eve and sever their balls."

Balls coming from the lips of someone who sounded like the lofty ruler of an elite kingdom, made me laugh.

"You didn't!" Jacey said with a grin.

"Cool bluff," Brodin added, his fingers relaxing on the branch.

Akimi's lips curled up with grim satisfaction. "'Twas not a bluff."

"I should've thought of that," Jacey said.

"You can do something like that?" I asked her.

Her eyebrows drew together. "Not in the same way Akimi can, but I have my ways."

"I need to learn these ways." They could come in handy.

"As to the debt to be paid," Akimi said to me. "I have saved your boy and—"

"He's not mine," I grumbled.

"I'm not a boy," Brodin said at the same time.

Akimi's head tilted, and her leaf hair rustled. "No?" she asked me. A thin branch rose up to tap the place where she sort of had a chin. "Silly child. All is clear to me. You feel *something*."

Brodin backed into the trunk, putting space between us. "What *do* you feel?"

"Nothing for you." The words shot from me but they lacked their usual kick. Something was changing between us, but I couldn't define it.

With his hands cupping the back of his neck, he leaned against the trunk, lifted his legs, and crossed them at the ankles. "Akimi, why don't you tell me all about Tria's feelings. I think this could be interesting."

After shooting him a glare, I leaned close to her. "Please don't say anything."

"You should share," she whispered and it came out like a light breeze fluttering across my face. "There will come a time when this knowledge could mean the difference between life and—"

"He wants…" I began by rote, but if he wanted to kill me, why did he keep putting himself between me and danger?

Her barky lips twitched. "Perhaps he does not."

"I didn't finish my sentence."

"Yet I heard."

So much, I wanted to believe his plan had changed, that he'd decided I wasn't someone who could've killed his mother.

"No matter what," I said. "I owe you for what you did for us." I placed my palm over my heart. "I swear, I'll pay back the favor." We'd be dead without her intervention. "Just name it."

Her pleased gaze took in Brodin and Jacey. "The time soon comes when the debt will be paid in full."

I lifted my eyebrows.

"For now, I shall hold your promise close and will reveal it when the time is nigh."

"When would that be?" Brodin asked.

"'Tis a secret." She clapped her branchy hands together. "Secrets haunt us all, even you three."

I wasn't sure I liked where this was going.

"In what way?" Brodin asked, his voice taking on an edge I swore sounded like fear. Right from the start, I'd suspected he was hiding something. His Eerie ability or something else?

Akimi's mouth curled up on one side, almost conniving. "As for you, my fine friend, Jacey, yours shall be revealed soon."

"You're lying," Jacey snarled, pressing herself back against the tree. "Please...I..." Her eyes closed and her hands trembled. "I'm not sure I'm ready."

What was she talking about?

Akimi turned to Brodin. "Your secret shall be your strength. Do not be ashamed of it. 'Tis a part of you that will one day be more valuable than anything you have treasured in the past. Release it, and it will be your savior and that of those you cherish."

Did his secret somehow relate to why the Master Seeker wanted me to kill him?

"As for you, Tria," Akimi said with a soft smile, turning to fully face me.

I wasn't sure I wanted to hear any more.

"Take care with that which only you are able to do."

My mind immediately went to my sketar magic.

"I'm not sure I'll dare use it again," I said.

"Care does not mean inactivity."

"All right." I'd practice when I found a free second that wasn't spent running from raptors and gorelons.

Standing, Akimi flipped over me and, when she impacted with the trunk, she sunk back inside.

"Well," Jacey said. "That was…interesting." Her gaze flicked toward the ground. "We need to climb down, which might be a problem."

Before we could start in that direction, branches snatched us up and deposited us on the grassy slope.

As I gazed up at the tree, Jacey nudged my side with her elbow. She waved her hand toward the prison. "We need to get back inside before something else comes after us."

In the woods to our right, a beastly howl echoed.

Chills rippled across my skin, and I raced after her, with Brodin right behind.

Chapter 23

As we wrenched open the door and tumbled inside the side entrance, something big rushed through the woods toward us, sending trees toppling.

We slammed the door behind us and magical locks clicked into place. Not to keep us in but to keep other things outside. For now, anyway.

The creature's echoing howl of frustration blasted against the steel door as I collapsed against the inside wall. I swiped my hair off my face and took in faltering breaths. Damn, that had been close.

Heavy stomps fading told me the beast was retreating.

Jacey wavered on her feet, her lungs heaving from the run. Brodin behaved like his usual self, standing tall while watching the area around us for threats. I was almost getting used to him acting protective.

"No wonder they don't worry about us leaving the building," I said. "Other than Akimi, the island surrounding this place is one big trap."

"Don't even start thinking you've got this place figured

out yet," Jacey said. "You haven't taken on any of the magical tests."

"You mean something other than the centipedes on the beach, the kertin in the deep grass, or the mind-confusing creature in the woods?"

"Those were warm-ups."

"For what?"

"The Reformatory Challenge."

"How do they differ from what Brodin and I encountered on our way here?"

"I imagine they're worse."

Awesome.

"I know what you're thinking," she said. "But the tests are ticking bombs. Complete some of them within the allotted timeframe, or else. And solving one riddle or climb or puzzle will result in another."

I tried to read from Brodin's expression what he thought of this discussion but couldn't tell. He watched me. Was he doing the same thing, trying to understand my motives from my reactions?

"What have you heard about these challenges?" I asked him.

"Not much. I haven't been here before." Yet his eyes didn't meet mine, implying he was hiding something.

I shrugged, dismissing the idea. He'd arrived with me. If he'd been here in the past, he'd still be here. If he'd already gone to the Reformatory, he would've told us.

"In many ways, what waits for us outside the prison walls is better than in the catacombs," Jacey said. "Ironic, huh?"

"Yet, here we are, planning to form a triad and take the Challenge." Would I survive long enough to confront my father, or would I disappear, like Jacey's roommate and boyfriend had?

My glance took in the long, white-painted hall with dim lighting that revealed stains on the square tiled floor.

Tick-tick-tick.

Crap. I knew that sound. The gorelon slunk across the ceiling like a crab across dark sand. Its gleaming yellow eyes turned to me, and it grinned.

I saw it.

And it saw me.

What have I done?

I wanted to slap my hands over my eyes, but it was already too late.

The creature melted into the wall, leaving behind dark stains in smeared splotches. And … I jerked my head in that direction but found nothing. A shiver scraped down my spine. Was my mind playing tricks on me?

The stains called to me again, and I flicked my hand that way, not sure I wanted to know but I felt compelled to ask. "Something's…" Horror seared through my veins, but it wasn't hot enough to beat back the chills climbing up my spine.

Jacey turned, and her lower lip trembled as she studied the end of the hall. "By the fae," she said in a shaky voice.

Brodin strode down the hall, evading Jacey's hand that sprang out to snag him as he passed. Stooping down, he studied the stains, though he didn't touch. When he returned to us, his grim expression didn't invite questions.

Jacey stared at Brodin for a long moment before they both nodded in silent communication.

"Did you find a," my gaze darted to Jacey, "spear?" I'd almost said fillinette, but wasn't sure I wanted to fill Brodin in on my suspicious—that the Master Seeker hadn't killed the guard and Kimmie, but the gorelon. Or something else.

Brodin frowned. "No spear."

I advanced toward them. "The gorelon was here." I gulped. "Our eyes met."

"Shit," Jacey said, her hands fluttering in agitation. "We need to form the triad now and get out of here. It'll track you, hunt you, and then kill you."

"That's my job," Brodin said, though only humor shone in his voice.

"What did you see at the end of the hall?" I asked, staring that way. Something—not a gorelon—shimmered on the floor.

"It's wet," Brodin said.

"Fresh blood, right?" There was no swallowing back the fear lodged in my throat.

His gaze met Jacey's. "It's not the usual color."

I ran down the hall and studied the spray. From the amount, it was clear something vital had been severed. Arterial, since it had squirted. The blood had a purple tinge I hadn't seen before. I bled red. If my ancestors' blood hadn't changed through the years we'd mingled with humans, would it match this color?

Jacey snatched my sleeve and tugged me toward the other end of the hall. "We need to leave. Now."

We rejoined Brodin.

"Tell me what you think happened," I said, grabbing her arm and pulling her around to face me. "I can't handle this unless I understand what's going on."

"From the color of the blood, I think the gorelon killed Austin."

"Who's Austin?" I asked, looking back and forth between them.

"The chiema," Brodin said grimly.

I shuddered and peered at the blood. At the rate the gorelon was killing, the prison would be vacant soon. It must've killed Kimmie and the guard. Who else could've done it? "Where's the body?"

"Good question," Brodin said.

Jacey shook her head. "All I know is we can't remain here any longer. The gorelon will be watching Tria, waiting for us to leave her vulnerable. The three of us might not be enough to protect her, not until we form the triad. If we're around others…" She shrugged. "It won't dare slink close."

Brodin pulled opened the door and indicated we should go ahead of him. He darted another look toward the end of the hall. "The blood is gone."

Moving around him, I strode to the other end of the hall but found nothing other than tiles with fine cracks created by age and wear. What the hell? I returned to them, taking in Jacey's wide eyes and twitching fingers.

My skin itched, and I had to hold myself back from running. Not that I had anywhere I could run to, but I hated feeling as if I was waiting for the next horrible thing to happen.

"Let's go out in the yard," Jacey said. "We'll be safe there as long as there are others around."

Speculating in muffled whispers, we hurried through a series of passages leading to the big main room outside the cafeteria. Which… A glance showed it was as seamless as before we'd leaped through the window.

"It's bespelled," Jacey said, taking in my raised eyebrows. "The entire prison repairs itself if need be. Makes things simpler."

"Like when Titan breaks down a wall," I said.

She nodded. "Exactly. We can talk about forming our triad while we're in the yard. If we hide in a back corner, no one will overhear us."

Everything had come down to avoiding becoming raptor or gorelon bait.

"Will Titan find us there?" Brodin asked before I could, his intent gaze studying everyone we passed, still assessing for threats. I found it strangely reassuring.

"He avoids the yard, and Bixby lets him do it," Jacey said. "While Akimi made him back down, I can't believe he'll leave us alone for long. We need to come up with a permanent strategy, and that's the best place to do it." Her lips thinned. "Which means…"

"Entering the Challenge," Brodin said.

I nodded. "The sooner we get out of the prison, the better." This assumed we'd make it through the Challenge. But we had to try; remaining here wasn't an option.

We crossed the large room packed with supes standing in clusters, talking. A few studied us, and I rubbed my chilled arms.

"Over here." Jacey waved to a door on the opposite end of the room. "We'll be safe for a few minutes at least. While the quad gets away with shit, much more than the rest of us, Titan would rather go to the inner garden, where he can hunt."

"Hunt what?" Brodin asked, scowling at a fellow prisoner who came too close to us. The girl backed away, hands raised, then scooted around us and dashed into the cafeteria.

"You'd be surprised…" Jacey shook her head, and her dark hair flipped past her shoulders. "Or maybe not, after what you went through to get here. All kinds of creatures live in the arboretum. Warden said Titan and his friends help keep the population down."

"Just the population of the inner garden?" I asked. I didn't like where my mind was taking me.

"Let's…continue this conversation outside," Brodin said, staring toward a guard who watched us with intensity.

We hadn't done anything, but the guard wouldn't care. With a growl, he started stomping our way.

My back prickled. Would he call the screechers?

Because I couldn't think of anything else to do, I grabbed sketar mist and infused it into a flick of my fingers.

Coming to an abrupt stop, the guard frowned. He looked around as if trying to remember what he'd been about to do, then turned and strode toward a door on the opposite side of the room. He opened it and strolled into the corridor.

"So, we need to talk about that, too." Jacey held up her hand before I could speak. "Hold that thought. We'll discuss it outside."

I projected innocence. "What are you talking about?"

Her lips thinned. "Soon."

I couldn't keep this secret for long. She'd quiz me until I spilled my guts. But maybe it was time to share.

Leaving the big room, we entered a hall and, at the end, opened a door that let us outside and into a yard about one-hundred feet long and fifty feet wide, encased in a stone wall that had to be twenty feet high. It was covered with shimmering mesh that flickered with blue and red magical current. A large bird circled overhead and, as if spying us below and deciding we'd make a tasty snack, it swooped lower. When it tried to pass through the mesh, it burst into flames. Dark gray smoke, all that was left of it, was picked up by the wind and swept away.

"Like I said." Jacey grimaced as she stared upward. "It's relatively safe out here. You can ignore the island fluff for now. When you're in the yard, the only thing you need to watch out for is what comes at you from inside."

The courtyard was made up of dirt, dirt, and more dirt, with bits of straggly grass growing here and there. No flowers, not that I'd expected any. The only shade was provided by a few trees, plus shadows created by the wall.

"Over here," Jacey said, snagging my sleeve and pulling me off to the side, beneath a scruffy tree that had lost most of its leaves, their dry husks scattered on the ground underfoot. They crunched like tiny bones when I stepped on them. "Let's…" Awe and what almost sounded like hope filled her voice. "A triad. Never thought I'd form one with an Influencer and a Seeker."

Ex-Seeker.

The sun shone down and the day had warmed up to a temperature no one would ever call pleasant. Within seconds, sweat trickled down my spine, and my prison uniform rubbed in all the wrong places.

We passed other inmates huddled in small groups, standing around. A few glared our way, and Brodin's spine ramrodded as if they'd yelled slurs.

Other than the questionable meal, threats from Sheera and her triad, plus the Warden, well, and Titan and crew, it was an okay day. If only I was back at the Academy, hanging out with Fleur.

But then I wouldn't be closer to confronting my father.

When I was just a baby, he stood over my crib and like a slake, siphoned off part of my power, the core essence of my magic that could never be replaced. Who knew what my potential could've been if he hadn't stolen that spark from me?

I wanted it back.

Assuming he still had it. What would I do if he told me he'd wasted it or, worse, lost it? Mom told me once he'd poured it inside a tiny vial, that he might be storing it for a special occasion. Had he already drained it? By the fae, he might not remember taking it from me. After all, I wasn't his only child. He'd been with Fleur's mom not long after mine. We could have other half-siblings. Although, as far as I could tell, he hadn't taken anything from my sister.

My grandfather loved his son and said he could do no wrong. I hadn't told him the truth. How could I hurt him? Because I loved my grandfather, I let him hold onto the son he remembered, the kid he said was kind and caring. The sun to his angry brother Blaine's moon.

But my birth father was no better than his despised twin. They both embraced the endless night.

While Jacey leaned against the wall and fanned her face. Brodin turned to take on any challenger from the inner courtyard with a scowl and clenched fists.

I stood beside him. To form a barrier, not because I wanted to be near him.

"Back to what we were discussing," Jacey said. "Our triad." Her head tilted Brodin's way. "He said yes!"

"Who said yes to what?" someone asked from my right.

Sheera and her sidekick, Mindi, stood about ten feet away, watching us with matching smirks on their faces.

Why did these girls appear at the most inconvenient times?

Sheera sauntered closer with Mindi flanking her, mimicking her swaying moves. It was like watching a pair of hyenas moving toward a kill.

Not today, girls. In fact…

"Now Sheera, I know you're excited to see me, but you need to give it up," I said.

Frowning, Sheera stalled. "What do you mean?"

"I'm with someone already." I slid my arm around Brodin's waist. He stiffened and his eyebrows shot up as he stared down at me. "You're going to have to let this go. I'm not going out with you."

Her face flushed, and her body stiffened. "What the hell are you talking about?"

Jacey snickered, her gaze darting between us.

The other girl gawked at Sheera.

"You *like* her?" Mindi asked. Her eyes filled. "Why didn't you tell me?"

"I don't like her," Sheera said. Wheeling around to face me, she glared. "You are so going to die."

I shrugged. "Take a number."

Fuming, she stomped over to the entrance and, hauling the door open, fled inside with Mindi. Anticlimactic, actually. I'd looked forward to her taking on my dare.

"Thanks," I said to Brodin, removing my arm and putting two—no, three—steps between us. He smelled too good, that was why.

No, wait. He smelled sweaty.

Just keep tellin' yourself that.

"When did we start dating?" he asked, and I swore laughter came through in his voice, but that would be a wild notion on my part.

"Tria," Jacey said, while I stared up at Brodin. He was cute. Too bad everything between us was still unsettled.

"Create a shield, will you?" Jacey said. "It'll keep everyone from listening in."

A quick, careful tug and I'd pulled in a small amount of sketar mist then flicked it out, dropping a magical curtain between us and the others in the yard.

"Knew it," Jacey said smugly. She poked my side, and I dragged my attention from Brodin's eyes long enough to glare at her for disturbing my…

Shit. What the fae was I doing, staring at Brodin? And I'd just used magic at Jacey's suggestion.

"You…" I scowled at her. "What did you do?"

Her lips quirked up. "I knew you were using some sort of power, and you confirmed it."

When in doubt, play dumb. "I didn't."

She lifted one eyebrow and tapped her foot on the ground.

"Okay, so maybe I used a little bit of magic."

Brodin's sharp inhale rang out between us. "None of us can do magic." He lifted his hands and hints of that irritating, snide tone I abhorred slipped into his voice. So much for our unspoken truce. "Remember? We're wearing tennas. Besides, you're a Seeker. No seeking to be done here. And you and I both know that you don't possess—"

A pull of mist and a flip of my hand, and I'd zipped his lips. Literally. While he cupped his face and mumbled, his eyes blazing above his hand, I turned to Jacey.

"It's sketar magic," I said. "My stepfather taught me. I wasn't sure it would work with…" I scowled. "With my Seeker skills and the tennas, but it does. In a limited way."

"I, uh." She lifted her chin. "You need to keep this quiet. Don't tell anyone else." She slanted a stern look Brodin's way but he just emitted muffled grunts. "I also used to use sketar magic but Bixby found out and added another component to my tennas." Lifting her arms, she grimaced. "Now I'm blocked fully, like everyone else. But you!" Her eyes lit up and she grabbed my wrists. "You're our secret weapon."

"Ha." I frowned. "What exactly do you mean by secret weapon?"

"You can do things Bixby won't know about. We won't let on and thus, we'll have the advantage."

Brodin groaned, and Jacey tapped his lips with her finger. "Just a minute."

"How is it even possible?" I asked. "I mean, I'm shocked that I can do anything with the tennas in place."

She bobbed her head. "Old stuff can often circumvent modern magical tech."

"Kind of like your humming."

"A little trick my uncle taught me. It's an older component of sketar magic, called skeitse magic." A frown descended on her brow. "Bixby didn't realize I could do it, or she would've blocked it, as well." Her arm linked through mine. "It'll be our little secret."

Brodin flailed, his muffled groans interrupting us.

"You should unzip him," Jacey said, though hesitancy shone in her voice. Her eyes gleamed, and she couldn't hold back her smile. "Maybe? I mean, he's fun this way, too."

His eyes bulged.

"Do I have to release him, Mom?" I whined.

She chuckled. "While I understand why you did it, yes. You do have to release him."

A flick of my hand and the zipper disappeared.

He latched onto my shoulders and pressed me against the wall. "Never. Do. That. Again."

"Stop acting like snide and I'll leave your lips alone."

His gaze dropped to my mouth, where it lingered.

I didn't like the tingles gliding through me at the thought of his mouth dropping onto—

"Guys?" Jacey said. She chuckled. "Hold this for later, huh?"

Brodin wrenched his fingers off my shoulders, hissing as if burned. He stalked around behind Jacey and leaned against the wall, where he watched me with too much interest.

I struggled to keep my knees from shaking. This guy was lethal.

Maybe I *would* have to kill him.

Chapter 24

"Tell me more about triads," Brodin said, his voice deep and husky—totally the wrong tone when talking about triads.

Wait. He… Nah. He wasn't as unsettled about me as I was about him. He hated me. He wanted to kill me. He… His gaze fell on me and I swore I read longing. But it couldn't be.

Could it?

More than anything, I wanted to believe he'd changed his mind.

"Is everyone here in a triad?" I asked, wrenching my attention from him to Jacey. Once we were done hashing this out, I needed to run… No, walk, but get away from Brodin, as fast as possible.

"Some are. Many have lost members from…" Her lips thinned. "You know."

"Getting too close to something inside or outside."

She pointed her finger my way. "Got it. We'll do the triad ceremony as soon as we get permission."

"From Bixby," I said, not needing to ask the question.

"Does she grant it easily?" Brodin asked, his arms crossed on his chest and his tone suddenly serious.

"From what I've heard, yes."

"But you've been in a triad already. Didn't you need permission to form one then?"

"We…" Her gaze flicked to the door, where a guard watched us. "We kind of bypassed Bixby last time."

I nudged her arm. "You skipped the formalities and jumped into the Challenge?"

She nodded.

"Then why don't we do that? If we ask her, who knows what she'll say? She's not exactly a member of my fan club."

"We *have* to ask. Even if she says no, we need to follow the usual procedure. Last time…" Her sigh went on for a long time. "Last time, we jumped in without following the proper steps. Who knows what would've happened if we'd done it right? We'll ask her."

"And if she says no?" Brodin asked.

"*Then* we'll talk about alternatives," Jacey said.

"What does forming a triad entail?" I asked.

Jacey's sly gaze slid between us. "The catacombs are the true parallel universe and, once we're a triad, we'll challenge them together, with our combined magic."

"How does a triad combine magic?" Brodin asked, his gaze sliding to me before dashing away. His attention kept going to my right upper arm, which made it itch.

"Once bound, triads can share some of their skapti skill," Jacey said. She reached out and nudged Brodin. "Like your influence skill, which is a rare ability."

His arms linked tightly across his chest. "And I'll be able to use Seeker skills?"

"There must be something you could use Seeker magic to find," I said.

"I want some," Jacey said with a laugh. "No hoarding."

If I guessed right, she'd use my magic to locate Rohnan. I just hoped we weren't led to his bones when she sent out feelers.

I held up my wristlets. "Won't these keep us in check?"

"All they do is suppress skapti magic," she said. "Triad magic is different."

For the first time since I'd connected to my Seeker skapti, I felt sad. I'd been proud of the career I'd chosen, proud of how I'd been able to use my growing skills to find wizards and creatures who'd been lost. But a skill like that would be useless in a prison.

"What's your skapti?" I asked Jacey.

Her gaze shot to me, and she paused before nodding as if to inner thought. "I'm a healer."

Brodin leaned forward. "I'll be happy to tap into that ability."

"Are you the one who healed me after the warden's attack?" I asked

"I heal whoever the Warden gives me access to."

"Which I assume isn't many," Brodin said grimly.

"She…enjoys the games played here, plus those thrown at us by the island."

Games of death. "How did a healer end up in prison?"

"I healed the wrong person." Her lips crimped as if to hold back any further comment.

I didn't get it. "How is that a crime?"

Her pause went on so long, I suspected she wouldn't answer. "I'm the one who healed Rohnan."

Brodin's lips parted. "Whoa. I know who you are! You the one who healed the son of the fae king's sworn enemy."

"I can see why that could get someone in trouble," I said.

"Especially when the king dealt Rohnan the lethal blow," Brodin added.

"The king had you convicted and sent here after you healed Rohnan?" I asked softly. Shadows lurked in her eyes. This conversation was hurting her deeply.

"Immediately. He..." Her shoulders fell. "He murdered my uncle, and I was sentenced here for my crime."

Fire rose inside me and scorched through my control. "You know what?" Storming back and forth inside the tiny magical space I'd created, I fumed. "I'm beginning to think the entire fae world is fucked. We have the prison." I shot my hand toward the building. "With a warden who keeps the population numbers down by encouraging us to kill each other. Add to that guards who add to the body count by pushing us out windows and down stairs. Then there's the rest of the island outside the prison, which makes the inside look like a kid's birthday party. But let's not forget. We can take the Reformatory test but that's deadly, too. However, if you happen to luck out and escape this hell hole and find your way into the fae kingdom, someone's waiting to finish you off."

"That sums it up nicely for me," Brodin said, leaning against the wall again. His gaze darted to the sky before returning to my face.

To say I was surprised to see him agreeing with me was an understatement, but I pressed on. "What happened after you got here?"

"Rohnan was sent here with me," Jacey said, staring past my shoulder. "But he's gone. Dead or... I don't know, but I need to find out."

I rubbed her shoulder. "I'm sorry."

She stared forward blankly and released a heavy sigh. "Sometimes I still feel him. Almost as if he's alive."

"Who told you he was dead?" Brodin asked.

Jacey wouldn't meet his eye. "We entered the test. We weren't inside long. It was dark. I couldn't see! And the screams... The screams..." Her body quaked. "Bixby says I ran, that I abandoned my roommate and Rohnan, but I didn't." Her voice rose to a shout. "I wouldn't do anything like that. We were engaged."

Brodin's eyes widened. "That means you're..."

She nodded.

"It's an honor," Brodin said with everything grave in his voice.

"What am I missing?" I asked, glancing back and forth between them.

"Jacey's father is the king's vizier, his closest advisor."

I'd heard about him somewhere...

Something smacked into my shoulders. My yelp burst out as a coarse bird call echoed above me. Slaws pierced my skin, and I was lifted into the sky.

Chapter 25

Brodin jumped and grabbed onto my legs. "Gotcha." He glared up at the bird, as if his stare alone would make the creature drop me.

Sort of a bird. Almost the size of a car, it had two heads with amber beaks, a wide wingspan, plus four legs with long, deadly claws. With Brodin's weight added to mine, the claws dug in farther. I squirmed but was unable to break free.

Its enormous wings flapped, taking us up through a hole in the magical mesh that was supposed to keep creatures like this one out. A gust of wind wrapped around the prison and buffeted me, making me sway. The bird's claws sunk deeper into my shoulders.

Brodin's hands tightened on my ankles, and he kicked out, rocking and swinging.

"What are you doing?" I shouted as I was moved along with him. The claws… Agony exploded in my brain, and the world spun around me. I bit my lip hard, hoping the new pain would keep me from passing out.

"Trying to get it to let us go."

It was all the bird could do to carry our combined weight, but it flapped harder. Dipping to the right, it soared toward the building so fast, I thought we'd smack against it. But before we hit, the bird lifted us up, and we coasted over the roofline.

I pulled in sketar magic, being careful to balance what I needed with what was available. A world full of magic called to me, but like with anything in life, it was better to savor one bite than swallow the entire cake. The mist flowed into me, filling me, and the moment it hit my belly, I tugged it back up and out.

Release me.

The bird cawed in protest, but its claws yanked out of my shoulders.

Brodin and I fell.

As the bird dove down at us again, claws extended, we smacked onto the metal roof and slid, tumbling together, a mix of grunts, groans, swears, and coarse bird rage. As we approached the edge of the roof, my hands locked onto Brodin's arms. We were swept off the roof and went airborne. The yard approached like a freight train on a collision course with a solid brick wall.

The bird swooped above us, raking my back with its claws but not finding purchase.

As I cried out at the searing pain, Brodin and my gazes locked.

"Sorry," he said.

For not believing me? Or because we only had seconds left to live?

No.

Hauling in sketar mist, I bent it and sent it back out into the world. Without a command; just a wish.

Our descent slowed, but not enough.

Brodin twisted just before we hit the ground, putting

himself beneath me. The ground rushed up to us, and he landed hard on his back with me flopping on top of him. His woof mixed in with the bird's cry of anger.

Jacey hurried over to us, arms lifted to scare off the bird. It cawed again then flew away, thwarted for now.

Stunned and windless, I couldn't move.

"Are you two alive?" Jacey asked in terror.

"Yes," I groaned. Gathering up my strength, I sat, and my legs straddled Brodin's waist.

"Can I...?" His hand rose toward my right arm.

I shook my head, unsure what he was asking, but he must've taken my confusion as consent.

Tugging up my sleeve, he bared my upper arm. A long sigh rushed from him. "Knew it." He stared up at me with an expression I'd never seen before. I couldn't analyze it and, from the way my heart hitched, I wasn't sure I dared try.

Unable to sustain eye contact with him, I flopped sideways and onto my back on the dirt beside him.

Normalcy returned to the world. My shoulders stung and throbbed, and I still couldn't catch my breath.

"Hey, Brodin," someone called out from the prison.

Rolling onto his side, he rose onto his elbow and stared down at me. "It wasn't—"

"Brodin!"

Jolting, he wrenched his gaze from mine to the guard standing in the opening.

"Get your ass off the ground," the guard said. "Warden Duvoe wants to talk with you." He glanced over his shoulder and, for some reason, grinned when he faced us. "Now."

Why not send a frog with the message, unless vomit wasn't "readable" on the dirt?

Brodin dragged his palms down his face then rose to

his feet. Without hesitation, his hand jutted out to offer me a lift off the ground.

Flustered by feelings I couldn't define—though they all centered on him—I took his hand, and he tugged me up off the ground. We stumbled together, and his arms went around the back of my waist.

My knees were shaky, and it wasn't just because of what had happened with the bird.

"What—"

"I need to—"

We both spoke at the same time.

"Brodin," the guard yelled again. "Now."

Brodin's hands dropped to his sides. "I'll come back as soon as I can."

I took his words as a promise.

Leaving me, he went inside, and the guard followed.

"You sure you're okay?" Jacey carefully took my arm and tugged me over to the wall, out from underneath the hole in the mesh. How had we missed it when we came outside? Jacey carefully pulled my prison top to the side and peered beneath. "You're bleeding."

I rolled my shoulders and winced at the sting. "I'll be okay."

"I'd heal you if I could."

"I know." I doubted Bixby would suspend her tennas long enough to repair the damage, but I'd heal.

We found a spot underneath a broad tree and backed against the trunk. At least we'd see whatever came at us next.

"Some major move on Brodin's part," Jacey said.

I expected to find her smiling and braced myself for another rom-com joke, but her lips remained flat, and her eyes expressed only concern.

"It was too close. The bird…"

"You got free."

"I used magic," I said softly.

"Thought so. I…saw you pull it in and use it." Her gaze cut around the yard but everyone else had gone back to talking and ignored us. "Not sure if anyone else did."

I watched the entrance door that remained open, expecting to see Brodin appear soon. "Yeah, that would be…"

Mindi and Sheera exited the building and walked toward us.

My belly sunk. The warden wanted to speak with Brodin, huh? Now I understood why a frog hadn't arrived with a message.

"Incoming," Jacey said. "Let's go to our room."

"Good idea, but what can they do?" I asked. "Two on two. We can fight them off. They're not shifters, are they?"

"No, but your shield has fallen, and they're dating guys in the quadrad."

Whose numbers were dwindling.

Before we could scoot around Sheera and Mindi, they stopped in front of us, blocking our escape.

"Couldn't help overhearing you talking about a triad," Sheera said as she sauntered forward.

A quick movement on the fence drew my eye. Damn spyling.

Mindi's snort shouted pure malice. "You'll never make it through the test."

"You haven't been here long," Sheera said to me with a flick of her hand, as if suggesting I scoot through the door and leave Jacey. "So I'll excuse you for now. You haven't had a chance to learn the rules of Darkwater."

My eyebrows rose to my hairline. "And they are?"

"Keep to yourself." She grinned at Mindi, who

crowded near and nodded. "Defer to the quad and their friends."

"The quad is, um…" Should I mention the chiema's death? I pictured Sheera going out with Titan, but wasn't sure about who might be with Mindi.

"What?" Mindi asked.

"Nothing."

Sheera frowned but continued. "Also, stay away from…" Her nose wrinkled as her gaze fell on Jacey. "Her."

"Why?" I asked, stepping forward.

"Because her lifespan's limited."

Mindi laughed shrilly. "Very limited. Like… hours, not days."

They'd only get to Jacey by going through me. Stepping between them, I palmed my knife but kept it close to my side.

Sheera's gaze followed the movement. "You don't plan to use that on me, do you?"

"Be careful." Jacey tugged on my sleeve. "Tria. Step back. I can handle this."

Tension spiraled through me, and my face grew hot.

"Worried about your roomie?" Sheera sneered. "Not wise on your part. She'll abandon you like she did my sister."

Jacey's face colored, and her hands fisted at her sides. "I didn't, and you know it."

"Facts say you did, but I didn't come out here for that." Her gaze fell on me. "I came to talk to the Seeker." She smirked. "You know what we do to Seekers around here?"

"Kiss their feet?" I said. No idea why I wasn't running, other than the fact that I was tired of this place already and I refused to leave Jacey. My gaze cut to her. "Let's go somewhere that doesn't..." I scrunched my face and ran my gaze down Sheera's front. "Stink like raptor shit."

"I could kill you right now and no one would stop me," Sheera said, stomping closer to me.

I sighed. "Didn't you hear? Mean girl tactics went out at least twenty years ago." I shoved past her. "Find someone else to bother."

"I'm going to kill you," Sheera shrieked at my back.

"By the fae, announce it, why don't you?" I said, pivoting to face her.

"Out of the way, Sheera," Jacey said, skirting around the tall girl. "Comin' through."

"Running, Jacey?" Sheera flapped her hands at my roommate. "Go. Scurry inside, you coward. I'll find you later." Her gaze flicked to me, and she stalked my way, her hands lifting. "I'm going to have a little fun with the Seeker."

Mindi pounced on Jacey and dragged her to the ground, pinning her in place.

While Jacey bucked and shrieked, Sheera paced up to me.

I backed into the wall beside the entrance.

Sheera dug her arm into my windpipe. Her hand stuffed into her pocket, and she pulled out a mesh of thin ropes. They came alive and snapped around my right hand. Snaking out, others wrapped around my left wrist, then bound my hands together.

I slammed my knee into Sheera's belly but she must have abs of iron, because she didn't flinch.

While I fought, more ropes spiraled around my ankles, lashing them together.

Angry tears leaked down Jacey's face, and she struggled to get out from underneath Mindi, who quickly secured her with snake ropes.

Kai appeared at my feet and thrust himself between me and Sheera. His lips curled back, and a snarl erupted from his chest.

Mindi stretched out her fingers, cooing. "Here, kitty, kitty, kitty. Come to Mindi. Get away from the nasty girl."

Kai hissed and his claw snapped out, almost ripping off her nose. Shrieking, she fell backward. She rose and, growling, rushed at Kai.

With him distracted by Mindi, Sheera moved in for the kill. Her foot swept out and connected with Kai's chest. He yelped and tumbled sideways. While I bellowed and wrenched at the ties, Kai landed in a heap on the ground. He didn't move.

"Where's your protector now?" Sheera jeered, glancing around. "Brodin? Oh, Brodin? Funny how guys always bail when we need them the most, huh?"

"What did you do to him?" Rage roared through me. I'd rip her head off.

She propped her hand on her hip and sneered. "Me? Why do you think I'm involved in something like that?"

"If you hurt him," I growled. "I'll make you pay."

"You may be a Seeker but you have no power in the fae world. Here, you're worth less than the slime underneath my feet." Turning, she lifted my knife off the ground and waved it in the air near my face. "I'm going to cut you, Seeker. Maybe I'll start with your eyes."

Fear jolted down my spine, and my heart slammed against my ribcage.

Bucking and grunting, I strained against the ties, but they tightened around my wrists and ankles, biting deeply. I tried to pull sketar magic but was too scared to focus.

My gaze fell on Kai, who still hadn't moved. A heavy feeling rose inside me, aching to be set free.

"Or..." Sheera shared a grin with Mindi, who joined

her. "There might be better options for carving." Grinning, she turned toward Jacey.

Thrusting my arms forward, I yanked one wrist from the bindings, then the other. Superhuman strength filled me. I broke the ties holding my ankles and roared toward Sheera, my arms extended.

She swung the knife toward Jacey. "For my sister," she hissed. "And for Kimmie."

I leaped forward, thrusting myself between them.

The blade drove into my belly.

Tick-tick-tick.

My head jerked up, and I spied a gorelon clinging to the upper part of the wall, a shadowy ooze of greenish-yellow slime. A vague, head-like mass shimmered in the center.

It grinned at me.

Chapter 26

Someone kept squeezing my hand. It felt good. Reassuring.

"Hang in there," they said. "Warden Bixby's on her way."

Bixby. How could that be comforting?

"You'll be healed soon."

It couldn't be Brodin squeezing my hand, let alone giving me verbal encouragement. It must be Jacey. I was mishearing the voice. Because I wasn't sure where I stood with Brodin. Why had he wanted to see my right upper arm?

I opened my eyes and heat slammed through me when I remembered. Squinting toward the wall, I relaxed when I didn't find the gorelon waiting. Had it driven Sheera's motions or were they pure Sheera?

Jacey paced by my feet, her face tight, her hands writhing with anxiety.

Brodin knelt on the ground beside me. He was the one holding my hand. Never thought I'd see the day that would happen.

"Where's Kai?" I tried to sit up but couldn't fight off the pain enough to move.

"He disappeared," Jacey said.

"Dead?" I hated to say the word. It couldn't be true!

"He woke first."

I wasn't sure that was reassuring.

A rock underneath my spine made me shift my hips, and I couldn't hold back my gasp. Damn, my belly hurt. My free hand rose to touch, but Brodin reached across me and nudged it back down by my side.

"Don't," he said. Jaw tight, his gaze drifted to my abdomen, and he paled. Great. I shouldn't look, then. "Help's on the way."

"Bixby won't…help," I grated out. "She'll…finish me off."

"If I can talk her into releasing my tennas, I can heal you" Jacey said, tears overflowing her eyes.

"By the fae, it hurts."

"It's gonna be okay," Brodin said. He traced his fingertips across my brow. I must be dreaming. I wasn't sure how I felt about him touching me with kindness. Him being nice battered against the walls I'd built to protect myself from him.

"Maybe you should…" I grunted and gathered some wind to speak. "Should keep Jacey from healing me. It'll be…over faster that way."

His brow furrowed. "You think so?"

My chest pinched. "Why shouldn't I?" I drew my knees up to take some pressure off my stomach but the movement shot pain through me, and I gasped. "It's what you want."

"I…you don't know what I want."

"Because you haven't told me." My head thrashed on

the ground as I struggled for control. "You're confusing me, Brodin."

"Good, because I'm confused, too."

I started to sit up but ground my teeth together to hold back my scream. Damn, damn, damn.

"Hey, hey," he said, bracing my shoulders that still ached from the bird's claws digging in. I was a wreck and things were not going to get better. "Hold still. It won't be long now." Supporting me, he helped me ease back onto the ground.

"The gorelon was here," I said softly. It had not made a reappearance.

Brodin reeled back and scanned the area. "I don't see it here, now."

"It'll be back."

Jacey's grim gaze met mine. She started to speak, but the door to the prison entrance banged open, and Bixby strode down the steps and over to me. Duvoe followed, rubbing his hands and grinning with glee.

Brodin stood and put himself between us.

Sashaying around him and stopping beside me, Bixby raked me with her gaze. "You sure get into a lot of trouble."

Duvoe cackled as if Bixby was a stand-up comic putting on a show. He leaned against the wall and assumed his usual position with his arms crossed, his fingers flexing.

"Sheera did this," Jacey said. "Please. Release my magic so I can heal Tria."

The warden's lips twitched. "Sheera? Now isn't that interesting." From her excited tone, I expected she'd give Sheera an award.

"She stabbed her!" Jacey blurted out.

"With what weapon?" The warden's gaze swept the area before focusing on a section near the fence. She minced in that direction and presented her black, leather-clad butt our way as she stooped down to delicately pick up the knife with her thumb and finger. "And this is interesting as well." She reeled around and stomped back over to us. "Where did it come from?"

"Let me heal her." Jacey's jaw trembled. "Please."

Bixby growled and tapped her foot on the ground. "Answer my question."

"It's mine," Brodin said, holding out his hand. Did he think she'd hand it over to him?

"It isn't his. It's mine," I pushed out through gritted teeth. "I brought it with me."

Duvoe's gaze narrowed on my face. "It's hers."

"Tria…" Brodin said softly, but he couldn't think I'd let him take the blame for this, could he?

"No weapons are allowed at Darkwater," Bixby shouted.

Duvoe watched our interaction. No, he watched me. It would take me years to interpret the look in his eyes… It couldn't be concern. Anger, I'd understand. I'd broken a rule. But that wasn't it either. He…was enjoying watching Bixby grill us. Jacey's distress. And me, bleeding onto the ground.

Bixby handed my knife to Duvoe. He stared down at it lying on his palm, and when his gaze lifted and met mine, the enjoyment I'd seen there had turned to fear.

Why?

He cupped his fingers around the knife and pocketed it.

"Let Jacey heal Tria," Brodin said. His back stiffened. "Please."

"You, too?" Bixby asked with twisted concern. "A third interesting component I hadn't expected."

"If I don't heal her soon, she'll die." Jacey's fingers worked into knots. "Unlock my magic, please?"

Bixby stared toward the wall for too long, while blood trickled down my sides and pooled beneath me. It had soaked the back of my prison uniform. My wound burned all the way to my spine. Anything more than shallow pants made my lungs ache. I wanted to curl on my side and let the world slip away again, but I worried I might not wake up.

As if someone hit a switch, Bixby startled. Her head jerked left and right, and her hands fisted at her sides. "Where's Kai?" she grunted.

"The wexal cat?" Jacey said. "I haven't seen him in…a long time." But she gave me a subtle wink and mouthed *he's okay*.

"You can't have him," Bixby told me. "He will always belong to *me*. I made him what he is, and I control him in every form. I own him."

I bit my lip, holding myself back from confronting her. Once healed, she'd be fair game.

Duvoe shifted off the wall and moved up behind his sister. She glanced over her shoulder at him but then whirled back to face me.

With a growl, she waved her hand at Jacey, and gold rippled across my roommate's tennas before they dimmed. "Get it over with. Fast."

Jacey bent down beside me. "I'm sorry," she said softly. "Sheera hurt you because of me."

"Nah," I huffed out. "She hates everyone. I'd do it again…in a second. We're good." A groan worked its way up my throat as Jacey placed her hand over my wound.

"I'll pay you back."

"Already did. Two healings. You're…ahead."

"A debt owed will be squared." Her eyes closed, and she hissed.

The ache in my belly eased and, when I rose up onto

my elbows, I watched as the slice in my abdomen sealed closed beneath her fingers.

Jacey tucked her hand against her own abdomen, and her body slumped forward, but she righted herself. Her eyes opened, and the echo of my pain was reflected in the depths.

A flick of Bixby's hand and Jacey's tennas burst into color again, the magic-draining energy renewed. Returning to the entrance, the two wardens left us. Jacey called out to them before they went inside.

Bixby turned and posed in the open doorway.

"I…" Jacey gulped, and her gaze darted to me and Brodin before returning to Bixby. "*We*, that is. *We'd* like permission to form a triad."

"You and…" Her sullen gaze drifted to me and then Brodin before taking in other inmates watching the exchange with rapt attention. "Come to my office after dinner this evening, and we'll discuss it."

"Thank you," Jacey said pleasantly enough. But when her gaze fell on me, I read justified anger there.

Brodin stood and extended a hand to me. No hugs this time when I got to my feet.

We went inside to find inmates clustered near the entrance. They parted to let us through, and their hoarse whispers ricocheted off the ceiling as we walked their gauntlet.

Brodin followed us through the great room and down the hall. He held the door to the residential area open for us, then kept pace as we walked through the high-ceilinged area.

It was a toss-up who walked slower, me or Jacey.

We stopped outside Jacey and my room.

"About the gorelon," I said. I hadn't sensed it nearby, not so far. "Will it follow us inside?" How could I sleep?

"Use your sketar magic to ward the room," Jacey said.

"Awesome idea." I pulled in the power and spun it into a tight ball, then sent it out, creating the protective ward. My shoulders sagged, because I'd spent what little energy I had left after being wounded.

At my nod, Brodin opened our door and gestured for us to enter ahead of him. He hovered behind us and would've entered if Jacey hadn't turned and held up her hand. Her smile took the sting from her words. "You're not allowed in the room. Bixby's rules. Come get us later, before dinner? We'll eat and strategize, then go to the warden's office together."

He nodded, and his concerned gaze swept over me before he slipped away.

Jacey shut the door then dropped back against it. She swiped her long hair off her face and sighed, but when her eyes met mine, I humor blazed through. "No matter what you say, I'm still convinced he likes you."

"What gives you that idea?"

"You should've seen him when you were unconscious."

"He…held my hand. Reassured me." And while I had hope, I wasn't sure what it meant. "I was injured. Give him time, and he'll revert to his usual snarky self."

Would he tell me if he was softening? Impossible. Yet…his face.

Jacey joined me in the middle of the room. "You should lie down and rest. Let the healing magic finish doing its work."

"You should, too."

Her head tilted. "Why do you think that?"

"You took my pain when you healed me. Don't tell me you didn't."

"Part of it, but you're right. I do need to rest."

While I collapsed on the bottom bunk, she hauled herself up onto the top and flopped down, groaning.

"Some of the pain gets diffused into the air," she said. "The patient keeps some but the healer takes the rest."

"Why keep it all to yourself, right?" I tried to laugh, but my belly still hurt too much to go along with the jerky motion.

She snorted. "Healers are selfish like that."

I could help her, like she'd helped me. A small favor in return for two healings.

Burgundy sketar mist waited for my call. Would it fail me like it had before or would it bend to my command? If there was ever a time for a spell to work, it was now. Closing my eyes, I put everything I had into my wish and sent it up, toward her.

"Whoa," she said. "What did you do?"

While laughing might tear through my insides, it didn't hurt to smile. "Better?"

"Hell, yes." Her voice...

"You okay up there?" Damn, had I made things worse by softening her mattress? I'd been trying to—

"Yeah." She sniffed. "I'm fine." The strain came through in her words. "Thanks. I've..." Her sigh puffed through the air. "It's been hard facing everything here alone."

"You're not alone any longer."

A long pause followed before she spoke. "While I'd never wish this place on a friend, I'm grateful you're here."

And I was glad I could help her, even a little bit. Other than my sister, I hadn't had a solid friend for a long time. Realizing that made me want to share some of the burden I'd carried forever, but should I? I hadn't dared tell Fleur, who wanted to believe our father was a good man. Who was I to convince her otherwise until I'd determined the truth?

"The blood bond..." I said. "I made it because I needed information." So far, the bond was allowing me to tell Jacey these details. "My father is here."

The bedframe squeaked as Jacey shifted to lean over the side. Amazement filled her face. "He's here at the prison? Who is he? Please don't tell me he's a guard."

"I was told he works at the Reformatory. I don't know anything else."

"No wonder you want to get there as soon as possible." Sadness came through in her voice. "You must miss him."

"I've never met him."

"Then you're desperate to finally meet him."

"Yeah." Desperate wasn't quite the right word. "In some ways, we share a common goal: we both needed to get to the Reformatory because it's one step on our separate paths."

"Where will your path take you?"

"The same as yours, toward revenge."

"Ah. Hmm." She lifted up and dropped back onto the bed.

"You want to make the fae king pay for your uncle's murder," I said defensively. "I'm going to take back something my father stole from me. What else I'll say to him at that time remains to be seen."

"Do you want a relationship with him?"

"It's hard to say. If he offers, if he's excited to see me, I'll..." My growl of frustration shot across the room. "It's stupid to let myself go down this path. I can't trust him after what happened." Only a monster would do something like that to his own child. There was no excuse he could offer that I would accept.

Silence grew between us, and I drifted to sleep, where I

chased an Eerie through a series of tunnels, each narrower and tighter than the last…

I woke to someone knocking on the door, and Brodin's voice rang out. "Guys? Dinner?"

Jacey stirred in the bunk above mine. She hopped onto the floor then grinned as her gaze swept to my side. "Kai. Welcome."

"Kai!" I sat upright. "I'm so glad you're okay." He purred and nudged my hand with his nose. Delicately taking my fingers in his mouth, he directed my hand to his side. "You want pats, do you?" With two hands, I gave him a kitty massage. His eyes closed and his purr rumbled louder.

"Guys?" Brodin called out. "You okay in there? If you're not at the door within three seconds, I'm breaking it down."

"Guess we need to let him in," I said.

Jacey smirked then walked to the door to open it.

Brodin stumbled inside like he'd backed away and rushed it at that moment. His gaze landed on me, but I couldn't read his expression. Relief or irritation? I'd have to wait for him to speak to find out.

But he said nothing, just leaned against the wall.

"Food?" Jacey asked, walking through the open door. "Then we can go beg Bixby."

"I hope it won't come to that," I said, scooting out of the room behind her.

Brodin followed, shutting the door.

We hung out in the big open area until it was our time for dinner, but it was crowded, and we didn't dare talk about anything important. Like murder. Our triad. Why Brodin had shouted *knew it* after looking at my right upper arm. Or the gorelon hovering up near the ceiling, watching me. Unless it got bolder, it wouldn't come near until I was alone.

Chills wracked down my spine. I'd have to find a way to eliminate this threat.

Brodin followed my gaze and stiffened. "Mine," he growled, his fangs popping free from his gums.

The gorelon slunk from the room.

I stared at Brodin in amazement, relieved he'd sent the gorelon away, but… "I'm not yours."

He winced but his back remained tight.

Before I could open my mouth to demand answers, Jacey tugged on my sleeve. "Dinner time."

We walked inside the cafeteria, and I couldn't take my eyes off Brodin. What had he meant by his comment? After we'd taken a seat at a table with our food—sauce-covered, gray meat I hoped wasn't chiema—rice, and limp green beans, I leaned across the table. "Before we meet up with Bixby, can you tell us what we need to do to form the triad?" I asked Jacey.

"It's another trial," she said, fear slicing through the words.

"Attacking creatures?" Brodin asked. "Someone trying to mess with our minds?"

She picked up a green bean with her fingers and popped it into her mouth, speaking around it. "It's hard to say."

"But you formed a triad already," I said, poking my meat. The rice seemed innocuous enough, so I ate a bite. "That should give us an advantage. What did you have to do?"

"The test we'll need to pass to form a triad shifts constantly."

"Sounds like the catacombs we'll need to get through for the Reformatory Challenge," I said.

"Where you've also been," Brodin said, eating a forkful of meat. He chewed slowly. "Tell us what you can."

"That's just it. While I remember the test for the triad, where we had to solve a series of riddles together, I don't remember much about what happened in the catacombs." She frowned. "We entered, and it was dark. Kylie ran ahead of us, though Rohnan and I weren't far behind. We were all eager to get it over with."

I waited, giving her time to share this at her own speed.

"Kylie screamed, and I froze," she gulped out. She pushed her tray aside, leaving her meal unfinished. "Rohnan…"

"What happened?" Brodin asked. He shoveled in the rest of his meat, and I wished I could separate my emotional pain from my physical needs, too, because my belly rumbled.

"Rohnan yelled." Urgency pushed the words out of her. "He was hurt. I had to reach him. Help him! Something grabbed me. Choked me. I…" Her voice drifted to almost nothing, and she stared down at her tray. When she looked up at us, her eyes swam with tears. "I woke up in my room, alone. I haven't seen or heard anything about Kylie or Rohnan since."

"I'm sorry," I said, leaning across the table to rub her shoulder.

Brodin carefully lowered his fork beside his plate, and I didn't miss the slight shake of his hand. "The entrance to the Challenge is in the arboretum," he said softly, and I wondered how he knew this when he hadn't known the rest.

"Titan's hunting grounds," I said. "But he won't be there, will he?" This was sounding scarier by the minute.

Jacey wiped her eyes. "One other thing."

Of course. There was always one final thing. The killer rule. I waited for it, holding my breath.

"In the triad test, we'll have to work together. This forms the bond."

"We don't have magic," I said.

"Your sketar power won't work, either," she told me. "Mine didn't. And then Bixby locked it down after I woke up, back in my room. I'd pulled it in while running through the arboretum, and she must've felt or seen it."

I ate a few mushy green beans to placate my stomach.

"We'll only be able to use magic in the Challenge," Jacey said.

"Each other's." Brodin's gaze slanted to me, but I couldn't tell what he was thinking.

"We'll both be able to use his ability to influence," I said to Jacey. "And Brodin and I will access my Seeker skills and your healing, which I hope we'll never need."

"You need to know one more thing." Jacey fiddled with her fork, not looking up. "I'm not just a healer."

Brodin and I shared eyebrow-raised looks.

Jacey leaned forward and whispered. "I'm also secretly a necromancer."

Chapter 27

We walked down a hall toward the warden's office, which was located at the end.

"How did you end up with two skaptis?" I whispered. A quick glance told me we were alone. No spylings. Or the gorelon. Yet.

"Necromancy is a special skill combination, one common in my family," Jacey said softly. "But I was raised to host the skapti."

"What does host mean?" I asked.

"When I was born, I showed the mark. At thirteen, the ability was brought to the surface, and I began to train with my uncle…"

"Do you achieve levels like with other skaptis?" Brodin asked.

"Sort of." We stopped outside the warden's office, and she shuddered. "We can…talk about this later." Her voice brightened. "You two ready? It's… There's no way to explain what we'll see inside her office, because it changes each time you come here."

My skin prickled with unease. "In what way?"

"Seeing is the only way to understand, but be careful."

A non-answer that did nothing to make me feel better about this.

Brodin nudged himself between us and the door. Nice that he felt protective, but we had no choice but to enter. "This is a formality, right? She'll give us approval."

"Of course," Jacey said. She eased around him and knocked, and a foot-wide spider dropped from the ceiling, dangling from a sturdy strand of webbing.

While Brodin and I stumbled backward, Jacey held herself steady.

"Business?" the spider said in a deep, gravelly voice.

"We have an appointment with the warden," Jacey said. "She's expecting us."

The spider leaped onto Jacey's face, and its legs wrapped around her head while its hairy belly compressed itself against her mouth, her nose, and her eyes.

I'd be flailing and doing everything I could to rip it off, yet Jacey's arms remained placidly at her sides.

The spider detached from Jacey and swung backward. "You don't lie."

What a scary way to verify someone was telling the truth.

"You may enter," the spider said. Grasping onto the web, it ratcheted itself back up toward the ceiling, where it scurried through a hole in the corner.

The door split down the middle and vaporized like fire wicking across paper, but the opening remained dense, making it impossible to see into the room.

I blinked and tossed Brodin a worried glance. His eyes met mine, lending assurance.

Jacey pushed her way through the gelatinous mass blocking the opening and disappeared from view. With a shared shrug, Brodin and I followed.

Through the doorway, I found myself standing inside a completely round room made up of milky glass. The dome overhead was equally impenetrable, as if we stood inside a large, white ball with a level floor.

Warden Bixby stood in the center with nothing around her except Duvoe. He, naturally, smirked.

This was her office?

"Sit," Bixby said. She pivoted on her heel and strode away from us, though she couldn't go far since the room only appeared about fifteen feet across. It expanded like someone blowing bubble gum, accommodating her as she moved.

A flick of her hand and a chair appeared beside her, a big, plush, teddy bear-styled piece of furniture. The total opposite of anything I'd ever picture her sitting in. Somehow, I'd thought she'd have a desk and a captain's chair with wooden arms and a leather cushion for the seat.

While Duvoe strode around to the back and braced his hands on the high chair back, Bixby dropped onto the cushion and propped her knee up on one fuzzy arm. Her spiked heel shifted back and forth, back and forth. "I said sit!"

My heartbeat accelerated as spiders like the one outside dropped from the ceiling, suspended on webs.

I flung myself away from them and smacked my hip against a chair that hadn't been there moments ago. Gulping, I dropped onto the surface and contemplated the solid wooden arms. The spider that had lowered itself near me snickered and clambered back up to the ceiling, where it melded into the gooey surface of the upper part of the dome.

"So, you wish to form another triad, do you, Jacelyn?" Warden Bixby said. She studied her nails and frowned.

"After what happened last time, I'm surprised anyone would dare take a chance on bonding with you."

"You know I didn't do anything to them," Jacey said, jolting forward in her chair. I half-rose, ready to jump into the attack alongside her, but snakes exploded from the back of her chair and snapped forward, latching onto her. They hauled her back against the wooden frame and encircled her waist, chest, and neck. She flinched but maintained eye contact with the warden.

Duvoe leaned forward, enjoying the show.

Bixby's hand dropped onto her thigh, and she sighed. "Do remain seated from now on. You wouldn't want to stir them up again."

A solitary tear trickled down Jacey's face, and her cheeks flushed, but she held still. The snakes released her and slithered inside the back of the chair.

Gulping, I pressed myself against my chair, determined not to stir the snakes into action.

Her fingers tightening on her armrests and her foot dropping onto the floor, Bixby leaned forward, all humor erased from her face. "This is a fool's errand."

"We're going to form a triad," Brodin said. "With or without your approval."

"Actually," the warden smirked at me, though her humor dimmed when it fell on Brodin. "Jacey. Perhaps you should explain for your potential triadmates exactly what happened to Rohnan and Kylie." Her index finger flicked forward, and beetles erupted from the floor. They scampered up Jacey's legs to her belly, then onto her chest. Wings fluttering, they perched on her shoulders, head, and thighs.

Jacey gasped and held steady, but another tear trickled down her face, meeting with a beetle on the way by.

"If you think you're going to surprise us or scare us

away, think again," I said. Fuck the snakes and beetles. I leaped from my chair and stalked toward the warden. "She already told us. Something *did* happen in the catacombs, and I bet you're to blame, not Jacey."

"Silence." Bixby waved her hand and snakes snapped out from my chair, wrapping around my throat and chest. They cut off my air. While I clawed and flailed, they tightened around my neck and dragged me backward. Darkness closed in, shutting down my mind.

"Stop, Tria," Jacey said, her urgent voice breaking through the gloom. "Relax. Don't fight them. They'll loosen. I promise."

"*I* don't promise," the warden said dryly.

Brodin growled. I assumed his fangs had appeared. Would the warden call him out for shifting in front of her? But since I'd stopped struggling, the bands around my neck relaxed. I sucked in air and couldn't contain my shivers.

A fluffy toy poodle appeared at Bixby's side. Its fur ruffled, and a low, deep huff resounded in its chest.

None of us moved. Not because we were afraid of the poodle. It was probably fifteen pounds, max. We remained still because of the snakes and the beetles, which still crawled all over Jacey.

The bands dropped from my neck and wrapped around my upper arms. They hauled me back until I tumbled down onto my chair. While the snakes released me, they draped at my collar like a thick, writhing necklace. Move again and the next time, they wouldn't loosen.

Ignoring us, Bixby stroked the dog's head. It leaned into her hand and whimpered before settling on the floor beside her feet. "Jacelyn was just explaining how she murdered her roommate and…" Her mouth tightened. "The court advisor."

Huh?

Jacey's feverish gaze met mine. No mistaking the pleading there.

"I didn't murder them," she grated out. "You know that."

"Explain, then," the warden said. "Why you're here and they're not."

Her chin lifted and her voice grated with complete confidence. "They made it through to the Reformatory."

"You know it's impossible to complete the challenges without a full triad," the warden drawled. "Which means—"

"I didn't kill them!"

Duvoe slunk around from behind the chair, stopping beside Bixby. His arms linked on his chest.

She stood. "It's time for you three to leave."

"But we haven't gained your permission to form the triad yet," I said.

"Your answer is no."

Duvoe cackled. Evil creep.

"You." Bixby pointed at Brodin. "No one..." Her smirk fell my way, and she stared at the floor. Duvoe leaned closer to her and whispered. Rallying, Bixby's steely gaze fell on us again. "No one cares about you, Brodin."

That wasn't completely true. The Master Seeker was very interested in Brodin. I didn't know why, but would someday find out.

"But you and you?" She waved to me and Jacey. "Especially you, missy..." As she strode forward, the little dog skipped at her heels. She smacked Jacey's shoulder hard enough my roommate flinched. "The king wants you to remain here at the prison."

Where they could more easily eliminate her.

"And you!" The Warden's gaze sunk into me like a

spear. "It seems many are interested in your actions. One wizard, in particular, keeps enquiring."

The Master Seeker.

"Strangely enough, another wizard also seems equally excited about your fate." Bixby's attention wandered down my front as if seeking my worth. Her snort told me she'd found none. "Someone at the Reformatory told me not to let you enter the Challenge."

My father must know I was here, that I'd—

"Go!" Warden Bixby made a shooing gesture. "I won't discuss this further. Get out of here and don't come back."

The snakes retracted, and we rose and left her office.

"What are we going to do?" I asked as we strode down the hall. We took the stairs to the first floor then joined the crowds mingling outside the cafeteria, slinking into a corner, where we could hide.

"I need to stop by our room," Jacey said softly, watching the other inmates. "I need one tiny item."

"And then what?" Brodin asked. He peered up at the ceiling, and I followed his gaze but saw nothing. No spylings hovering nearby, and no tick-tick-tick, either, which should be reassuring, but wasn't.

"We're going to form the triad." Satisfaction came through in Jacey's voice. "She won't stop us."

"We can do it on our own?" I asked, though I savored the idea of going behind Bixby's back.

"We..." Jacey frowned.

"What aren't you telling us?" Brodin asked, linking his arms on his chest. His foot tapped on the floor.

"I know the mechanics, but when we formed one last time, the warden gave us the boost of power we needed to solidify the bond."

"How will we get around that?" I asked.

"I have an idea." Racing through the building, we

stopped while Jacey went into our room then went on to the entrance we'd used after escaping Titan.

"We're going outside?" I asked. "Isn't the arboretum on the inside of the circle of buildings?"

"It is, but we need more magic."

"Akimi," I breathed.

All three of us shared a grin.

"If she'll help us, we'll be able to form our triad," Jacey said. "Then," she held up a slender piece of metal, "we'll use this key to force our way into the Challenge."

Chapter 28

"Psst. Akimi," Jacey whispered, peering into the branches spread in a leafy canopy above us. We hovered close to the tree where she'd pulled us up to keep Titan from ripping us to shreds.

Pitch black outside, only a slice of a moonlit the area. Shadows drifted across the ground, creeping me out because the stillness was punctuated by something grunting and stomping through the woods behind us.

"Akimi?" Jacey called again. Her hands fisted and frustration dug deep lines into her face. Her shoulders slumped, and I hated that she must think this was it. She'd have to give up on the dream she'd clung to since her boyfriend and roommate had been lost in the catacombs.

If only there was something I could do. I'd suggest humming, but the last thing we needed was to draw the attention of the creature nearby.

Brodin watched me as if he expected me to come up with some sort of solution. Funny since he was the one trying to save us all the time. If only I could access my Seeker skill.

My tennas flickered, reminding me—again—that my skapti magic was useless here. But… I closed my eyes and pulled in sketar mist, not quite sure what I'd do with it this time, but following a hunch. It built inside me, much like thread magic did in my stone, but making me the conduit instead.

I pushed it out.

Akimi. We need you.

I opened my eyes to find her emerging from the tree beside us.

"Yes. Finally. You've come to form the triad," she said, dipping a slight bow at each of us.

"How did you know?" Jacey asked.

"It's part of your secret as well as mine. 'Tis time." Her hand swept out, toward the forest, and she drifted in that direction, her multiple, rooted feet skimming across the ground.

As Jacey took off after Akimi, Brodin indicated I should go ahead of him.

I rushed to catch up with my roommate with Brodin hot on my heels.

When we hit the edge of the overgrown lawn, Akimi sunk into the cool darkness, sweeping around trees and brush, with us following behind. I tripped over a root and snagged my sleeve on raspberry bushes, but kept going. Without a trail, let alone much light, it was nearly impossible to see.

"Quickly," Akimi said over her shoulder. "If we don't hurry…" She peered toward the right, where something hiding in the dense brush growled low and deep. Swirls of red and orange spiraled upward from where the sound had come from, and the particles drifted toward us, a plague-ridden mist.

Goosebumps erupted across my skin, and I hugged my arms around my waist as I backed away.

Brodin grabbed a stick off the ground and shouldered past Jacey and me, putting himself between us and the ether, but Akimi knocked the branch from his hand.

"Any challenge will be accepted," she said.

"But if we act passive…?" Brodin said, brushing the bark off his hands.

"You live."

He blanched. "Got it."

While her attention was trained on the brush, orange flickered in Akimi's eyes before the color faded to her usual, muted blue. A creature howled in defeat and thuds moved away from us, its smoky magic tugged along behind as if on a string.

"Come," she said, rushing left. Her branch limbs brushed trees that swayed away from her, parting to leave a clear path for us to follow.

We came to a small hill with a circle of suckling trees surrounding the base, their leafless branches stabbing toward the sky. Akimi glided up to the top of the hill, and we followed, finding three large square rocks that had been sunk into the ground, forming the points of a triangle in the center of the mound.

"Hurry," she said, staring toward the forest. "Each of you stand on one."

Crashes and roars erupted nearby, and the sounds grew louder. A pack of monsters moved this way.

"What can we expect here?" Brodin asked, stepping onto one of the stones while Jacey and I took the others. His muscles bunched as he prepared to attack whatever came near.

"Even I don't know," Jacey said, her face pinched. "When I was part of the other triad, we climbed into pods in the arboretum and our minds merged to solve the riddle. It was simple. I…didn't know this triad location existed."

"Close your eyes." Akimi darted into the center of the circle and lowered herself onto the grass. Her roots sank into the soil, and she huffed in relief. "If we're quick, we'll get this done and depart, thus avoiding the drom."

"Drom?" I peered into the vegetation but saw nothing rushing toward us yet. The erratic thud of my heart echoed in my ears like thunder.

Akimi's gaze lifted to the trees. "It hunts and it is hungry."

Nice.

"Please," she said. "Remain motionless, no matter what comes next."

Because…?

My body was ejected up into the sky. I soared into the night and it sucked me into its shadowy embrace. I bit back my yell, refusing to draw anything to us. Hunters existed everywhere, even in the sky. The three of us jumbled together, grunting when our limbs collided.

The world winked out and I dropped, coming to a stop with my butt planted on solid ground. My eyes opening, I rose and I brushed the sand off my clothing while taking in the wildly-colored wasteland surrounding me. A deep purple sky arced above me, peppered with foreign constellations, and highlighting three glowing orange moons. Rolling hills of deep blue sand continued for as far as I could see.

"Jacey," I said in a low voice, not eager to give away my location. Who knew where I was or what else might be here with me? "Brodin?"

The ground shifted beneath me. Tossed sideways, I extended my arms to maintain my balance but the sand slid out from underneath my sneakers, and I tumbled forward. Rolling, I rose onto a crouch and peered around. "Brodin? Jacey?" We had to get out of here. No, we had to figure out how to solve this riddle and *that* would get us out of here.

My friends didn't reply.

I was rising to my feet again when the world started shaking. Thrown forward, I smacked on my chest and the wind was knocked from my lungs. While I gasped and tried to suck in air, something erupted from the sand by my feet.

Looming over me, a ten-legged creature about the size of a horse, with a gray-plated, scaly hide tipped back its head and shrieked.

I scrambled backward, gouging my palms on rocks in my desperation to get away.

The beast bellowed and came after me, its legs churning through the sand. Each foot ended in a single claw that dug into the soil. Another creature sprung from the sand, and its milky-white eyes trained on me. Grunting, with saliva dripping from its chin, it joined the chase.

Leaping to my feet, I bolted, not caring in which direction I ran. I needed to find Jacey and Brodin, and then hide.

I raced around a hill, hoping I'd find sanctuary somewhere below, but only more sand awaited me. Panting, I scaled another hill. At the top, I'd be able to see.

The creatures kept pace with me, their claws spearing the ground, their spit flying, and their keening cries echoing around me.

My mouth drier than cotton, I hit the peak of the hill and paused to feverishly peer in every direction. Only an endless sea of sand awaited me. No way out.

By the fae, I wouldn't give up.

Spying a stick on the ground nearby, I brandished it at the beasts clawing their way up the hillside. Yeah, I shouldn't challenge them but they were already attacking. They'd be on me in seconds. Stabbing me. Pulverizing me into the ground. I could fight them off or let them take me.

As my stick whistled through the air and collided with the beady head of the lead beast, the ground dropped out from beneath me.

I plunged down, into the darkness.

Chapter 29

I dropped feet-first into the water, sinking down, down, until my feet touched a rocky bottom. Kicking, I swam to the surface. My head burst above the surface, and I gasped, drawing in air choked with sand, dust, and crud. It filled my lungs, as eager to drown me as the water raging around me.

Spying the shore some distance away, I made for it, swimming as fast as possible, eager to get out of the water and whatever might be lurking beneath the waves.

I dragged myself out of the water and up onto the shore of what had appeared to be an island, though it was unlike any I'd seen before. In addition to dark blue sand and purple trees, this world had a pale green sky overhead. No sun or moon, but the sky's glow spilled enough light I could pick my way through the boulders scattered on the shore.

As I approached the densely wooded inner part of the island, trees parted, creating a path I was confident I should follow. My sneakers squished water and my prison clothing rubbed in all the wrong places as I moved, but I was soon walking through a dense tropical landscape. The low hum of billions of insects was punctuated by sharp bird calls. I came to a fork a four-way intersection and paused. Which way?

Choose. The low voice hummed around me.

Three paths, I'd understand, but why four?

With a shrug, I went right, weaving through denser woods until the trail ended at a door mounted in a craggy stone cliff. A click rang out and the massive wooden panel creaked open.

Inside, I was met with complete darkness. I stopped and listened but was greeted by only my coarse breathing and the steady drip-drip-drip of water dropping off me and onto the hard surface below my feet.

A light bloomed ahead, flickering across the steel-plated walls of a small room and outlining a stone basilique statue standing on a pillar.

I walked toward it.

The surface of the statue melted then reformed as the basilique came to life, stretching out its wings and tipping back its head. Its striped segments rippled across the surface of its scaly skin.

The basilique settled on the ground and dipped its head toward me. "Greetings."

"Umm…" What did a person say in a situation like this? "Greetings, yourself."

"You've come to solve the puzzle."

"Yes, but I thought I'd be working with my friends, that we needed to do this together to form the triad."

"Each of you is granted the same options. How *you* choose determines your final outcome."

"What do I need to do?"

Four tall columns descended from the ceiling, their footers thudding on the metal floor in a line in front of me.

The front of each pillar opened to reveal two strands of glistening silver ribbon suspended inside.

A gleaming silver half-sword appeared at my feet.

"You must cut one ribbon for each of three pillars."

"But there are four."

"If all possible paths in life were clear, we'd find no joy in living."

"So, I need to pick three pillars, leaving the fourth alone, and cut one of each of the two strands inside those three pillars?"

The creature dipped its head in agreement. "Choose wisely."

I studied them but couldn't see any difference, and each ribbon looked exactly like the others. "I don't understand."

"Take one step onto each path. But then, you will need to decide."

Frowning, I moved forward, approaching the column farthest on the left. I reached toward the left ribbon but stopped my fingers before touching. A glance at the basilique showed its mouth curled back to reveal jagged teeth. Its tongue flicked out as if it tasted the air around us.

"Okay," I whispered. "Let's do it." My fingertip connected with the left strand.

Arms wrapped around my waist from behind, and Brodin kissed my neck. Delicious shivers chased down my spine, and I tipped my head back and savored the thrill of his touch. Being held by him felt good and right and... Okay, so I did kind of like, like him.

I turned in his embrace and cupped his shoulders. Fire gleamed in his eyes, a flame lit for me alone.

We sunk into each other, kissing. Heat swirled through me, sparking something inside me I'd never felt for anyone else before.

"You kids," someone said with a chuckle, and we burst apart.

My face overheated, but Brodin just laughed. The sound sunk through me, bringing me infinite joy. Unable to keep the grin off my face, I turned to find Professor Trarion striding across a flower-filled meadow to join us.

When she reached us, she laughed again and nudged Brodin's shoulder. "Aren't you glad you agreed to take that internship with me at the Academy this summer?" Her twinkling gaze fell on me. "Tria." Only warmth and affection filled her voice.

Here, she lived.

Here, I was happy with Brodin. I wasn't branded a murderer.

Brodin's fingers trailed down my arm to my hand, and he clasped my fingers. Squeezed them. The crooked smile he sent me made my heart beat faster. "Yeah, Mom. I'm glad."

Professor Trarion dropped a picnic basket on the grass and, pulling a cloth from inside, spread it out on the ground. "Sit," she said with a wave. "I brought lunch. I also snitched a bottle of verdeen from the kitchen, plus three glasses. Let's drink a bit and get silly. We can lie back on the blanket and point out the shape of creatures in the clouds."

"Sounds great, Mom," Brodin said, releasing my hand. He strode forward and helped her take things from the basket while I stood beyond the edge of the cloth, watching.

There had to be a trick here. This wasn't real. It could never be real, even though, in many ways, I wished it was…

"Tria?" Brodin said with a teasing smile. He dropped to the ground and patted the space between his outstretched legs. "Join us, sweetheart."

I used to hate it when he used the nickname, because it had been used as a taunt. Now…I loved it.

"Yes," Professor Trarion said. "Join us." She winked and for one solitary moment, her face shifted, and she became someone else…

I had to be mistaken. This was the same Professor Trarion I'd known for a year, no one else.

"I brought you a surprise," Brodin said with a mischievous smile. Leaning sideways, he picked a yellow flower and held it out to me.

"Brought it to me, now did you?" I said with a grin, taking it from him.

He tugged me down to sit with him.

"Let's have a toast," the Professor said, handing Brodin a glass of verdeen. The fiery liquor was universally blue, yet this verdeen gleamed blood red through the etched glass. "To you and Tria. May you both find whatever you deserve."

What did that mean? Frowning, I turned toward her.

She tipped her head back, and coarse laughter erupted from her throat.

I reeled away from her, bumping into Brodin. Her face changed. …into that of the Master Seeker.

This wasn't Professor Trarion, and Brodin didn't know it.

"Drink it all," the Master Seeker growled, nudging Brodin's glass toward his lips.

Before I could knock the glass from his hand, he upended it and drained the liquid. The cup dropped, clunking on the blanket. His face flushed scarlet, and his wide eyes met mine. Choking and gasping, he slumped to—

I yanked my hand away from the strand.

"That's…" I sputtered, unable to voice what I'd seen. "Horrible!"

Poison.

"Next?" said the basilique. "No need to sever the first strand without taking the opportunity to savor the other."

The second must be for Brodin, too. Four pillars with two choices each. One must contain ribbons for our combined group.

I didn't like this. It felt wrong. But what choice did I have? I could move forward or remain locked in the untenable present.

Growling, I reached for the second strand.

Brodin smacked his shoulder against the front door of the Seekers' Headquarters. "Damn you, let me in! I know you did it, and you're going to pay!" Backing away, he rushed forward and slammed into the door again. A third time and it collapsed beneath him, falling inward and rattling on the foyer floor.

The Master Seeker waited for him inside. "You," he growled.

"You knew I'd come," Brodin said.

Ah, so Brodin knew Ramseff. He must if the Seeker wanted Brodin dead.

Brodin leaped sideways and grabbed a fillinette lying on a polished table near the entrance.

A fillinette was used to amplify power to a lethal level. How could Brodin, an Influencer, harm the Master Seeker with the device?

He raced toward Ramseff, aiming the weapon. "This is for my mother."

On this path, he knew I hadn't murdered Professor Trarion.

Lightning arced off the tip of the fillinette and slammed into the Master Seeker, who stumbled backward, clutching his chest.

How had Brodin done that? An Influencer couldn't throw fire.

Ramseff's neck arched back, and he roared. A flick of his hand and Brodin was lifted and thrown into a wall. He crashed against it and slid down the surface, landing on the gleaming floorboards. Groaning, he climbed to his feet, where he wavered before his fingers tightened on the fillinette. He pointed it at Ramseff again.

I silently cheered, do it!

Ramseff stalked forward and grabbed Brodin's arm. With a twist, he wrenched it sideways, dislocating the limb at the shoulder. Brodin bellowed in pain and struggled to break free. His hand flexed, and the fillinette slipped from his fingers. It clattered on the tenet floor.

The Master Seeker grabbed and lifting it. He aimed it at Brodin.

Brodin lifted his chin. "Do it. Murder me like you did my mother. Always knew you were worthless, Dad."

Ramseff was Brodin's father? I'd never guessed anything like this.

A twist of his body, and Brodin drove his knee toward his father's belly.

Lightning burst from the end of the fillinette. Close contact meant the Master Seeker—no, Brodin's father—couldn't miss.

Gasping, Brodin slapped his palm over the gaping wound in his neck. He sank to his knees. With a gurgling cry, he keeled onto his side. Blood spurted from the widening hole in his neck.

His gaze left the Seeker and found me. With his final gasp, he whispered, "Tria".

I jolted backward, wrenching my hand from the ribbon.

"No," I said, my heart on fire. I couldn't bear it. Brodin! "I won't pick either of these choices." The words were wrenched from me as if dragged from my very core.

"Yet you must select one," the basilique said, his snake-like expression calm. But his eyes focused on my every movement, and his severed tongue flicked through the air. "One choice for each. There is no other option."

Fury churning through me, I stepped sideways, stopping in front of the next column. I thrust my hand inside and latched onto the ribbon on the left.

Jacey, a sword in her hand, battled with a man whose back faced me. Tall, broad shoulders, dark hair.

I had no idea who he was.

"You killed my uncle," she shouted as their blades banged together. "Die, you asshole!"

This must be the fae king. I leaned forward, raptly watching the fight. Eager to see his face when she killed him.

Her blade darted forward, aiming for his chest, but he deflected it aside with his own. Their feet scrambled on the ground as she drove him backward, into a wall. He tumbled forward, rolled, and then rose to his feet in a crouch.

Though I strained forward, shadows continued to obscure his face.

Swinging wide, she lobbed her sword toward his head, but he wheeled away and rolled, coming to his feet again.

Rushing toward him, she struck, but he parried her blow.

His leg swung out, tripping her.

She stumbled to the side and her anguished cry split the darkness, but she regained her footing and rushed at him, her sword a blur of vengeful, flashing metal.

He tripped and fell to the ground, onto his back.

Following him down, she used the weight of her motion to drive the blade into his chest.

His hands rose to grasp the hilt, and he gaped up at her. Blood seeped around the gleaming blade.

The clouds parted and moonlight shone down, outlining him lying beneath her. She'd done it, fulfilled her need for revenge. He was dead and—

His face morphed from one to another.

"No." Tipping her head back, Jacey shrieked in shock and pain. "No. Rohnan!"

I yanked my hand away from the ribbon. "That's…" I gulped back bile as horror sunk through me. The king must've bespelled Rohnan. He looked like the king, and I assumed he'd been forced to fight her. I couldn't imagine the pain she must've felt when she realized she'd dealt him a lethal blow.

"Again," shouted the basilique. "Time continues to unwind."

My fingers fell on the second path for Jacey.

Late at night, Jacey crept through the halls inside Darkwater Prison. She'd approached a staircase I hadn't seen before and climbed, her breathing ragged. When she reached the top, she turned and clutched the railing, looking down at the large room beneath her.

Warden Bixby loomed up behind Jacey.

No, wait… Not Warden Bixby. Her image wavered, replaced with the oozing mass of a gorelon.

Were they one and the same? Terror burst through me, and I snarled my fingers through my hair. No. Run, Jacey!

"You didn't think I'd let you leave here alive, did you?" the warden-gorelon said. Her hand flicked forward, and a fiery spear of magic hit Jacey in the chest. Arms wheeling, she tumbled backward. As she lost her balance and fell down the stairs, her scream echoed around her.

Like a doll that was soon broken, she flipped down the staircase, not stopping until she smacked onto the wooden floor at the base.

She lay unmoving, her head tipped sideways in an unnatural position.

Her wide, terrified gaze stared forward…

Tears trickled down my face, and I wrenched my fingers off the ribbon and cupped my cheeks with my palms. "These aren't choices. They're nightmares!"

"Life deals many paths," the basilique intoned. "You have been given the gift of choosing an outcome for your friends." His wing uncurled and pointed forward, toward the remaining columns. "Dawn grows near and…" Pausing, his head tilted, and his gaze trained on the wall behind me.

I peered over my shoulder but saw nothing. "What's going on?"

"Nothing for you to know." His tail curled and his wings fluttered before settling on his back again. "Hurry."

"But I—"

His feral snarl ripped through the room. "One more column waits, and then you must slice through ribbons."

Outside, something howled. Claws scraped on the door.

"There's no way out other than severing a ribbon?" I asked, hoping—no, praying—the basilique would say this was all a joke and that no decision needed to be made.

"Choose a third column," he intoned.

I passed the third in the row and stopped in front of the fourth. Taking a deep breath, I reached for the ribbon on the left.

I'd expected two paths for me or two for the three of us. Instead, I found Akimi.

As she moved above the path leading toward the prison, she tossed a feverish glance over her shoulder. Stark fear was etched into her face. Picking up speed, she floated across the forest floor, her roots scraping grooves into the ground and her branch limbs smacking against trees. She winced but kept going.

Reaching the edge of the woods, she stopped and peered around. Dawn peeked on the horizon, heralding a new day. One filled with promise or shattered dreams?

She poked one root foot forward, onto the grass, testing before she moved forward. Slowly. Carefully. She was afraid, but of what?

I recognized the exact location. "You're almost there," I wanted to shout. "A few more steps and you'll reach your tree.

Thunder boomed overhead, and Akimi jumped. Lightning followed, outlining a raptor crouched near the base of Akimi's tree. Titan.

As if she didn't see him waiting, poised to pounce, Akimi inched forward. When her branches strained forward to touch her tree, he leaped, landing on her and knocking her to the ground.

While she struggled and bucked, his claws dug deeply. Leaves and branches flew in every direction as he ripped her apart. She flailed, her branches striking out, but his claws and teeth sunk through her bark.

When she finally lay still beneath him, he tipped his head back, and his triumphant roar pierced the sky.

My body shook as sorrow swept over me. "No," I whispered. "Please, no."

"Not that path?" the basilique asked.

Rage consumed me, and I glared. "You fiend."

"You are a member of this challenge, not me." His tail whipped back and forth. "You have one final ribbon."

I reached out, and my fingers curled around the strand.

Akimi stood on the stone steps leading to the prison, her roots straining to reach the grass.

Warden Bixby lifted her arms while Duvoe tipped back his head and cackled. I'd come to hate that sound. Like when I'd arrived, he leaned against the outer prison wall, his arms crossed, watching the show his sister put on.

Did she do this for his pleasure?

"For your part in this escape attempt," Bixby said. "I sentence you to no movement and no true one."

Duvoe's slick smile rose, adding credence to my suspicion.

"You'll take my fated mate from me?" Akimi's voice quivered. "You cannot. My mate belongs to me!"

Bixby's fingers twitched, as did Duvoe's. "It is done."

"No." Akimi's leafed hands cupped her face and she stumbled backward, toward the grass.

"No movement. No movement," Bixby chanted. "It begins…" Her gaze shifted to Duvoe before her shoulders tightened. "Now."

Akimi crumpled forward, but her body had reached the ground. Straightening, her arms elongated, reaching toward a sky she'd never touch. Her roots sunk into the soft soil, where they'd stretch forever and never reach what she needed most.

Her face stilled, though her mouth parted and one final gasp escaped. "True one," she whispered in a voice overcome with sorrow.

"Choose," the basilique said as my hand snapped away

from the ribbon. "Lift the sword and slice through one path for each, leaving the other for them to follow."

"I can't." My voice cracked, and my knees wobbled. How could I do this to Jacey, Brodin, and Akimi?

"You must."

My spine tightened. "No."

"Then they will relive both fates forever, one after the other, for the rest of their days."

"I won't let you do this." I strode over to the sword and lifted it. Facing the columns, I stared forward blindly. Shivers took over my frame.

"Choose!" the basilique said.

Left ribbon or right.

Neither was a true option.

"Now," the basilique shouted. His teeth glistened, and his body bunched as he prepared to spring.

I backed away from him with resolve filling me up to overflowing.

My shakes ceased.

I dropped to my knees and drove the sword into my chest.

Chapter 30

"Wisely done," the basilique said.

I lay on a hard, stone slab. Feverish, my hands rose to cup my chest, but I found only smooth skin. No wound.

"I didn't choose," I said.

"Oh, but you did."

Kai jumped onto the slab beside me. *Ready?* he asked in my mind, speaking to me for the first time since I'd met him.

We can talk in our minds?

He blinked at me blankly, making me doubt I'd heard him at all, but I nodded, since I believed he'd asked me a question.

In a blink, I returned to the meadow. While Kai leaned into my leg, I gaped around, unable to believe it was over.

Jacey grinned and rushed over to me. She wrapped her arms around me, then picked me up and spun me around. "Thank you. Thank you!"

Akimi bowed to me, her bark face stretching in a beautiful smile.

"But I couldn't do it," I said, laughing as Jacey set me back down. "I didn't choose."

One of Akimi's branches stroked my arm. "I thank you as well."

Jacey held out her left hand. "Look." A symbol gleamed on her palm, bright green with yellow streaks.

"It's not a triangle," I said. "It has four sides."

Jacey grinned at Akimi. "We each chose her pillar, which means we formed a quad. I saw my paths, Akimi's, and our group's. Akimi saw the same."

"Neither of you saw Brodin's?"

They shook their heads.

My eyes sought him out where he stood, some distance away, at the crest of the hill. Not looking this way, he stared down at his exposed palm.

Lifting my hand, I admired the gleaming proof that we'd bonded together. But what had Brodin seen?

"There were two equally terrifying paths for each of us and then two for the group," Jacey said. "But like the rest of us, you refused to let us follow those paths, and that was the point of the exercise."

"I couldn't do that to you or Akimi." For that matter, I couldn't do it to Brodin.

And there it was. While my blood bond might haunt me for the rest of my days, there was no way I could see it through. I could never kill Brodin.

Jacey's grin widened and she danced in place, compressing the grass. "I couldn't do that to you, either."

Had Brodin seen our kiss and the scene with the Master Seeker? I ached to shout out the question. Did he finally see I hadn't killed his mother?

Coming closer, he stopped when he reached the flat stone he'd taken when the trial began. Speculation gleamed in his eyes, plus a hint of the fire I'd felt in his first path, right after he'd kissed me. He held out his hand and, for a moment, I thought he wanted me to take it, that he'd tug me close and wrap his arms around me like he had in the dream—the alternate reality that now might never come true.

Stupid, but I wanted part of it, the parts only he and I had shared. Rubbing my chest, I tried to put the memory aside, but it persisted, sinking through my limbs. As if we'd stepped into a future full of possibilities, the barriers I'd erected around my heart fell.

"Bonded," he said, showing me the matching symbol on his hand.

My chest tightened, and though my lips trembled, I nodded. "Who would've thought we'd form a quad, huh?"

"Yeah." But he still watched me…

"We must go," Akimi said. "While those paths may not remain, others wait for us to start down them."

In the distance, a raptor roared. Titan.

My skin peppered over with goosebumps.

"Run toward the prison," Jacey said. "Bixby must know what we've done, and she sent Titan after us."

"Will you allow me to help?" Akimi said with a soft smile, holding out a leafy arm to each of us. Her symbol gleamed on the tip of her limb. "I would like to be the first to do something for our quadrad."

We each grabbed a branch, and she closed her eyes.

A bolt of lightning shot from the sky and struck the ground nearby.

In a wink, we stood in the inner courtyard of the prison, the arboretum.

Titan's hunting grounds.

Kai rubbed against me and meowed, then nudged me toward a trail winding through the thick vegetation. Urgency gleamed in his eyes.

"This way." Jacey pointed to the path. She reached into her pocket and pulled the slender key. "There's a secret way into the Challenge."

"Go," Brodin said, peering past us. He hefted the shared half-sword from our dreams and brandished it in the air. "We've got company."

The roar of a raptor shifter echoed around us as we raced through the arboretum, followed by the lizard's shriek and the larbeera's whoop-whoop cry—the last stretching across the sky. Titan's feet slammed the ground. As he shouldered his way through the forest, trees toppled. If we didn't reach the entrance soon, Titan and his friends would rip us to shreds.

Lars soared above us, his menacing, fifteen-foot wing-span blocking the moons. Diving low, he tried to snatch me up off the ground with his razor-sharp claws, but I ducked as he passed over me. His hot breath blasted across my neck. Kai leaped into the air and dragged his claws across the larbeera's scaly belly. They cut deep and blood dripped onto the path.

My pulse pounded in my ears, and my lungs raged. The third in Titan's group, the croc-sized lizard shifter, thundered across the ground to our right in an attempt to flank us.

"We're close," Jacey called out from ahead.

Akimi coasted above the ground at my side, her rooted feet snagging on dried leaves. They scraped the forest floor like loose sacks of brittle bones. She tossed back spells to slow the shifters' progress but they kept coming. Titan and his quad—now a triad—ruled the arboretum and, while we were stupid to come here at night, it was our only chance to steal our way into the Challenge.

"Go!" Brodin shouted, rushing up to join me and Akimi. He'd taken the rear, in protective mode as always.

He and I… Well, we held a shaky truce that would continue for now.

He smiled, and his tap on my back urged me to go faster. "Keep lagging, sweetheart, and you'll be left behind."

I sensed no sneer, only teasing in his words. It lightened my heart and made it possible to keep running. I couldn't stop thinking about that kiss…

Akimi dropped back to take his spot, and her spells lit up the night, arcing toward the shifters.

I caught up to Brodin and he grabbed my hand. His squeeze sent reassurance.

And a hint at a path we'd never taken…

We emerged from the bushes and slammed into a solid stone wall.

Crap. Dead end.

Jacey jumped and hauled on vines drooping across the surface, revealing an oval wooden door hewn into the cliff face. Without Jacey, I wouldn't have known the door was here.

Brodin leaned close to me. "One of these days, we're gonna have to talk."

"At the Reformatory?"

He growled. "I won't wait until then."

My heart shouldn't be singing. He still hated me.

Or did he?

"There won't be time during the Challenge," I said.

"We can make it."

"Tell me," I ground out.

His gaze fell to my arm. "When I ran into you…" He shook his head and his hair flopped forward. "Not *you*, someone else. She wore short sleeves and had a scar on her arm." Lifting my hand, he tugged my right sleeve up to my shoulder then ran his fingertip across my smooth skin. "I wasn't sure what I'd seen until—"

"The bird grabbed me in the yard," I finished for him.

"Then I knew. We haven't had time to talk since."

But now, we'd make the time. I couldn't wait to hear whatever he had to say.

"Hurry," Akimi hissed from behind us. She sent another bolt of deep green magic through the narrow opening in the tall shrubs, and someone bellowed in pain. When she pressed up close to me, her rough bark skin dug into my spine. "I cannot hold them for long."

Fingers fumbling, Jacey dropped the key. She snatched it up off the pine-needle strewn ground and inserted it into a small metal circle in the middle of the door. Blue sparks spurted from the hole and drifted down like falling stars.

The world shuddered, and the door creaked inward. Steps descended downward, proving the catacombs must network beneath the prison. For all I knew, they snaked underneath the entire island.

"Are you prepared for whatever might come next?" Akimi asked in a soft, light voice reminiscent of leaves whispering in the wind. "Now 'tis the moment to back away. Once inside, we can only go forward." Her gaze flicked toward the thunder of approaching raptor feet.

"Yes," I said with a stiff spine. "You?"

"More than ready. I think…"

"What?"

"I want to find out where this takes me. Takes us."

I cocked my head. "*Us?*"

He chuckled and flicked his hand forward. "You first, Seeker. See what you can find." Only deep satisfaction came through in his words. "I'm right by your side."

While the path might be rocky ahead, the future held a lot of promise.

Kai hissed. Latching onto my fingers with his teeth, he dragged me toward the entrance.

I stepped inside after Jacey and was swallowed by darkness. I could barely see the stairs dropping downward in front of me. Brodin cupped my shoulder, adding his strength to mine. It felt…good. Welcome, like I'd finally come home.

As the door boomed closed behind us, we crept down the stairs without saying a word. At the bottom, the passage widened. Tiny lights winked on. They coated the walls, and their iridescence surrounded us.

A cave-like chamber waited, and our only exit appeared to be an arched entrance to a dark, gloomy tunnel on the opposite side of the bone-strewn room.

Jacey took in the bones and keened. Had Rohnan, her boyfriend, only made it this far? As she dropped to her knees and feverishly sorted through the endless piles, Kai leaned against my leg and whimpered.

A gust of wind filled with the sharp tang of pain swirled past us, continuing down the corridor behind us.

The world shuddered, and a bang rang out at the top of the stairs.

Titan's roar sought us out in the cave-like chamber, and the dull thud of his feet rushed this way. As my friends and I ran toward the tunnel ahead, my gaze was drawn to the ceiling.

Horror spilled through me, a slick taint I'd never be able to shake.

An opaque creature oozed across the top of the cave.

Tick-tick-tick.

My eyes flicked from Jacey to Akimi, then to Brodin, and the panic bolting inside me was reflected in their eyes.

Palms sweaty, I ran faster.

The main entrance door slammed shut again, trapping us inside the Challenge.

Look for *Wicked Challenge*,
Book Two in the Darkwater Reformatory Series,
coming soon to Amazon.

Turn the page to read the first chapter....

About the Author

Marty writes young adult fiction and infuses it with suspense, romance, and a touch of humor. When she's not dreaming up ways to mess with her character's lives, she works as an RN. She lives in New England with her husband, three children, three geriatric cats, and a spunky Yorkie pup who keeps her on her toes.

Want to hear what Marty's working on next, win ARCs of her books, & chat? Sign up for her Bookish Things: FB Reader Group or her newsletter. You can also find her on her website.

Other books by Marty Mayberry

Crystal Wing Academy

Outling

Dragonsworn

Unraveler

Darkwater Reformatory

Call Me Wicked

(A prequel in the anthology, *Magic is the New Black*)

Wicked Betrayal

Wicked Challenge

Wicked Rebellion

Dead Girls Don't Lie

Romance & romantic suspense

as Marlie May

Some Like it Scot

Simply Irresistible

Twist of Fate

Fearless

Ruthless

Reckless

Wicked Challenge

DARKWATER REFORMATORY, BOOK TWO

***Shadowspell Academy* meets
*The Hunger Games***

To reach freedom at Darkwater Reformatory, Tria and her friends must complete the Reformatory Challenge, a series of dangerous trials that take place in the magical, ever-changing catacombs below Darkwater Prison.

Along with her are Brodin, a hot guy with secrets, who's determined to kill her. Or is he? And her roommate, Jacey, a fierce friend whose loyalty will be tested. And finally, Akimi, a tree nymph with her own agenda.

If only working together to complete each test was the only difficulty Tria faced.

They're also being hunted...

Chapter 1

A cave-like chamber waited, and our only exit appeared to be an arched entrance to a dark, gloomy tunnel on the opposite side of the bone-strewn room.

Jacey took in the bones and keened. Had Rohnan, her boyfriend, only made it this far? As she dropped to her knees and feverishly sorted through the endless piles, Kai leaned against my leg and whimpered.

A gust of wind filled with the sharp tang of pain swirled past us, continuing down the corridor behind us.

The world shuddered, and a bang rang out at the top of the stairs.

Titan's roar sought us out in the cave-like chamber, and the dull thud of his feet rushed this way. As my friends and I ran toward the tunnel ahead, my gaze was drawn to the ceiling.

Horror spilled through me, a slick taint I'd never be able to shake.

An opaque creature oozed across the top of the cave.

Tick-tick-tick.

My eyes flicked from Jacey to Akimi, then to Brodin, and the panic bolting inside me was reflected in their eyes.

Palms sweaty, I ran faster.

The main entrance door slammed shut again, trapping us inside the Challenge.

"Go!" Brodin yelled as the multiple stomps of three shifters echoed down the corridor. Veins stood out on his neck. Fangs bared, a feral gleam in his eyes shouted beware. His ghostly Eerie form had burst through. Would he fully shift? He should only be able to transform into an Eerie in dreams, yet here we were.

As Akimi and Jacey disappeared into the dark tunnel ahead, and Brodin urged me on with a hand on the back of my waist, I peered over my shoulder. Kai leaned against me, his lips peeled back and a growl rumbling in his throat.

The gorelon remained near the cave entrance. Its glowing eyes tracked my every movement, but it didn't give chase. Why?

During the trial, I'd discovered the gorelon and Warden Bixby were one and the same. Did she shift, or did she direct the gorelon from afar? No surprise she thrived on murder, but why? Someday, I'd find out why the death rate was so high at the prison. Yes, the guards and wardens enjoyed evil pranks, but the thrill of hunting someone couldn't be the only reason.

Titan poked his head into the cave, and fear rippled across my skin. I ducked into the shadows while he arched his neck back and bellowed. Teeth snapping, he raked the cave floor with his claws, sending bones and rocks slamming into the walls. He spied me watching, and shifted back into his six-seven wizard form. I expected him to yell out a taunt, but he remained silent while the two remaining members of his quadrad, Lars and Micah, shifted into wizard form as well. They glanced up at the gorelon, and their evil grins joined Titan's. As he stalked toward us with fists clenched at his sides and rage blazing on his face, the gorelon oozed in this direction above him. The confirmation they were working together made my knees shake. How could they without the fourth in their quad?

I ducked into the tunnel, eager to get away before they reached me. Though they'd find it a challenge to stand upright in the narrow, low-ceilinged channel, they could partly shift, long enough to rip into us with their claws and chomp off our heads.

With Kai snapping and snarling at my heels, I moved forward. The walls closed in on me, a trap of jagged rocks and sticks. I hoped they were sticks. Catching up to the others, I followed as the channel grew narrower, the rocky sides scraping my arms and legs. I had to hunch forward and inch along. Akimi's branches scraped across the ceiling, creating a spine-jarring shriek. Bits of leaves and sticks fell beneath her, and she whimpered whenever a big piece was torn from her head.

Jacey dropped down and started crawling, and we did the same.

A cold wind whipped through the narrow passage, nipping at my cheeks and making goosebumps flash across my skin.

"It's..." Jacey's voice echoed from ahead of us. "Hurry, guys. I've found our first challenge."

I crawled out of the hole after the others and while shuffles and swears told me Titan and the guys weren't far behind, I was more afraid of what lay ahead.

A vast cavern stretched for what looked half a mile, the dark, open area interspersed with circular, floating landmasses no wider than a foot. The mini-islands swayed and spun and shifted positions. All the sides, smooth walls cupped the cavern like the inside of a steel bowl, rising to an oval ceiling.

The ledge we stood on, about three feet wide, continued to our left and right a short distance before melting into the walls.

Tiptoeing forward, I peered over the edge but, if there was a bottom, it was too far below to see.

"Okay," I said. "Looks like we need to cross to the other side." A gut-wrenching distance I couldn't imagine crossing.

"We'll use the tiny islands," Brodin added, joining me on the tip of the ledge. He studied the moving bits of land. "There must be a pattern."

"We'll find it," Jacey said from the entrance. Brodin moved over to discuss options with her, while I internally plotted a course. The small chunk of stone and grass to my right and half a leap out from the wall might make a good starting point. And then I could…

The ground beneath me jolted, and the three-foot-wide space jerked backward, disappearing into the wall. It tipped up forward slightly, and I was knocked in that direction. Arms spiraling, I yelped and scrambled to find something to latch onto. Adrenaline shot through my system and sweat burst from my forehead. I fell toward the endless, gaping expanse.

One of Akimi's branches slapped down onto my shoulder and dug in, not deep enough to break the skin, but enough she could haul me in her direction. I was dragged up against Brodin, who stood between us, and his arms went around my waist. A stupid time, but my mind returned to the meadow scene, when his lips captured mine. Clutching his forearms, I stared up at him. His eyes warmed, something I'd never seen outside of fantasy.

"No," I said, pulling away and stepping to the side. "We…"

The floor underneath us moved again, stealing more of the space beneath us.

Gasping, I plastered my back against the wall but peered into the corridor to gauge how much time we had before Titan's crew arrived. "We've got to…"

A set of glowing eyes bit through the darkness as the gorelon slid across the upper surface. Relentless, it wouldn't stop until I was dead. While I didn't see Titan, he'd be close behind the creature, his friends with him.

"Time to go," I yelled. My heart on fire, I jumped away from the opening. "Every third spot flips on a regular basis, while the others remain stationary. Be careful. Some jump up a foot or so suddenly, while others drop down. But we can cross this."

Brodin faced the corridor, brandishing his sword. "Every test in the challenge has a way out."

If we were lucky. I was banking on it.

"I'm on it," Jacey said with an excited gleam in her eyes. She hopped off the ledge and onto the mini-island I'd marked in my mind.

"Quickly," Brodin said, his gaze shooting downward. "We're about to lose the ledge."

Akimi stepped out, and her roots sunk into the mini landmass Jacey had just vacated.

When Jacey stepped onto another, it dropped. She swore, and her foot slid off the edge. Smacking onto the flat surface on her belly, she clung to the sides.

Akimi didn't wait for Jacey to get to rise, she jumped forward, onto a different island.

"Go ahead of me," Brodin said, waving to the spot Akimi had left.

Jacey swayed on her feet, then sprung from one island to the next with Akimi—roots trailing—right behind.

Peering into the narrow tunnel and still seeing only shadows, I nudged his side. "You go. I've got…a plan."

"I—"

I tapped his side. "I won't be long."

He studied my face before nodding. Nice that he trusted me, because I wasn't sure I trusted myself.

While he stepped out onto the first small surface, tossing a heavy—*get to it*—glance my way, I pulled in sketar mist, grateful it still worked in the catacombs. Our tennas remained on our wrists, which meant our regular magic remained blocked. If we found down-time, we'd have to explore the magic granted to us by our new quad. What power would we get from Akimi?

The mist flowed into me, seamless and soothing, like I'd draped a favorite blanket around my shoulders. It didn't always respond to my call, but if there was a time for it to cooperate, it was now. I nipped it off before it overwhelmed me, then sent it out at the tunnel with a command.

Collapse.

The ground shook, and the walls of the passage— where Titan and his friends, plus the gorelon stalked our way—compressed and wobbled. As it gave way, rocks tumbled down the wall from above me.

Coughing and clinging to the wall, I waved at the dust and dirt clouding around me. When the air cleared, I released a huff. A mound of rubble had sealed off the entrance. Deep, deep inside, beyond the blockage, Titan released a furious bellow.

A satisfied smile on my face, I turned to take on the first challenge. Mini islands awaited me.

"Watch out," Brodin shouted over his shoulder, his gaze trained at my feet.

The last of the ledge jerked into the wall behind me.

WICKED CHALLENGE IS book two in the Darkwater Reformatory Series. You can find it here, on Amazon.

If you'd like to know what I'm working on next, sign up for my newsletter and join my Facebook reader group, Bookish Things.